INTO THE DARKNESS

by
Mia Scaletta

DORRANCE PUBLISHING CO
EST. 1920
PITTSBURGH, PENNSYLVANIA 15238

Dorrance Publishing Co
585 Alpha Drive
Pittsburgh, PA 15238
Visit our website at *www.dorrancebookstore.com*

ISBN: 978-1-6495-7180-9
EISBN: 978-1-6495-7689-7

PROLOGUE

The sounds of gunshots and the hoots and hollers of children could be heard from outside Coleman's basement door. It was cold, way too cold than it should have been in March. The wind was howling, howling so loud that it kept Bill Coleman tossing and turning in his light green, checkered sheets. It was not the laughter of his brother's friends or the stereotypical shooting video game sounds. No, it was the eerie wind that sounded in Bill's ears was getting louder and louder by the second.

Bill was about ready to run into his parents' room and spend the night with them. Safe in a bed with adults, because adults aren't scared of a thing or that's what Bill thought. He didn't want Noah to know. It's not like he thought Noah would tease him about; Bill knew for a fact that he definitely wouldn't. He also knew that teenagers didn't run into Mommy's and Daddy's room because they were scared of some stupid wind.

The wind continued on howling, and Bill had absolutely enough. He curled the fresh pillow over his ears and turns victoriously around his bed which causes the bed to creak. He calmed himself down and stopped his movements with the pillow still squished firmly over his ears. He removed the pillow off his ears and pushed the warm covers off his body. The cold air made Bill's arms pop up with goosebumps. He ran his small hands up and down his arms, feeling the small bumps all over them. Bill swung his feet off the old wooden bed and placed them on the cold wooden floorboards.

They creaked and squeaked with every step he took to the bathroom. Bill opened the dirty cream door, trying his hardest not to be loud knowing his sister is right across the hall and is most likely asleep. The dirty white and blood-red walls made the bathroom look like a lousy attempt at being fancy. With the marble countertops and dark wood, his mother almost succeeded. If it was not for the mold by the shower and the cheap towel holder that breaks almost once a month. He placed his palms down on the countertops and stared at himself in the dirty mirror. He was barely tall enough to reach the mirror, but he could still see his chestnut-colored hair and his dark brown eyes that had purple and greenish splotches under them from his lack of sleep. No regular ten year old should have those. His eyes darted over to the shower curtain, thinking that he heard something. A monster? A demon? Maybe even a ghost?

He knew whatever he thought he heard could not be anything good. The sound of his footsteps was the only thing that could be heard through the silence. His bare feet stuck lightly to the bare, tiled floor. He pulled the curtain to the left. The metal hook glided against the rusty white rod. His hand began to shake as he continued to pull. Bill dreaded what he might find behind that curtain.

He pulled it all the way and saw...nothing. Nothing at all. Just the plain dirty bathtub that his dad was meant to clean last week. Bill sighed in relief and turned on his heels and walked back to his room. He didn't pay attention to the floorboards that were just cracking a few minutes before. He walked into his room shutting the door as quietly as possible. The wind was nonexistent outside. Barely heard in his ears. Bill laid on his bed facing the window and just stared. Stared at the blank sky that has no stars to be seen. Then out of the darkness, he saw a quick flash of red. Bright almost glowing red. He bolted upright and rushed to his window sill. It was like a bolt of energy shocked through the young ten-year-old's body. He climbed out his window, turning off the child lock lever, and pulled down the broken screen. The dark red shingles on the roof caused Bill's feet to tingle. He was sure that he could make the jump off the roof. It was just like his jump from the diving board in his town pool. Easy as cake.

Bill crawled his way to the edge of the roof, the scratchy top of the shingles rubbed against the skin of his hands causing it to redden. He didn't acknowledge that he couldn't stop seeing that glowing red. That terrifying glowing red that was stuck in his mind. He reached the old rusty gutter and got off his knees, getting ready to jump. Bill knew it wasn't going to be that bad so he took in a breath and just jumped. *Crack.* Bill winced as his ankle twisted, which caused a quiet crack to occur in the quiet night. He fell to the ground, and let a cry come out of his lips.

His eyes opened up to meet a pair of eyes, the same red eyes he couldn't stop seeing. Bill got ready to scream, a scream so loud that would wake his mother up from her sleep and save him from that stranger. That attacker. He screamed with all the air in his lungs, but nothing came out, it was silent. It felt like a hand was gripping his throat preventing him from screaming. A dark figure emerged from the shadows, he tried his hardest to crawl away, but with his ankle and the feeling of the hand on him, he barely went five inches. The mystery figure got closer and closer, then everything in his vision went black in Bill's brown eyes as he screamed an ear-deafening scream.

CHAPTER ONE

"You suck, Noah." Lilac laughs when Evan eliminates him from the violent video game. The March air is cold even in midday. The wind is freezing on the hottest of days and on the worst ones it snows, sometimes blizzards. Large chunks of white fluffy powder fall from the sky with no sign of stopping. So there the group of six sit, huddled up by the Coleman's medium flatscreen TV wrapped in scratchy thin blankets. Where the cold air still manages to come through and shivers and goosebumps still exist. The old heater is terrible down there, doing little to nothing to stop the frigid cold. Being used almost every winter for the past sixteen years, had done it's number on the poor tan metal. Noah slams the controller down on the little wooden end table that's in front of the stained couch. The stains had grown over the years, from apple juice to spaghetti sauce, the couch has seen it all. The slam causes the table to shake slightly. He turns his head to look at Lilac who's sitting by Evan at the end of the couch. They all have unofficial assigned seats. Lilac on one end of the couch, Evan beside him, Noah on the other end, Mya and Jordan on the floor, and Alex on the small chair next to the couch.

It is a normal ritual for his group of friends. The group of friends that has been set since kindergarten, aside from Mya who came in later in first grade. The group of friends that deemed Noah their leader. Not that he doesn't like the title, sometimes it just gets a little tiring. They always get together, all six of them, almost every day and just act like stupid middle schoolers that they are. Although sometimes, it will be five of them depending on how late in the day it was or if Alex is allowed to come over or if he physically could. Noah's mom doesn't really like the idea of girls being over at the house after dark, even though they were all strictly just best friends. Plus, Noah isn't the type to get a girlfriend, no girls are interested, or none that he knew of. And Noah is perfectly fine with that, even though it gets lonely sometimes. He has his friends and that's all that matters. Noah looks over at Lilac and sees his bright, icy blues shining in the dim window light, they're glued to the TV screen watching the remaining players in the game intently.

"Shut up, Lilac."

Evan shifts his head from the screen at the sound of Lilac's name. Even though everyone thinks Lilac's name is sort of weird and odd, especially for a boy, Evan quite likes it. It isn't a name you hear often. But he turns his head back to the screen without being noticed by the others.

"You're not even playing the goddamn game," Noah snaps.

"Video games rot your brain." Lilac retorts. "And why even play them if you know you suck, huh, Noah?"

Evan pushes up his big glasses that start to fall down his perfectly shaped nose. He laughs. "But he's not wrong, Noah my boy," Evan says, battling Mya and Jordan fiercely. "You suck ass."

"Language," Alex comments, without looking up from his book. Alex hates video games; the violence and fake blood were just too disgusting.

"Someone's in a mood today," Jordan mumbles, killing Evan, while Evan mutters curses under his breath. Alex slams his brand new hardback book shut and glares at him "I am *not* in a mood."

Even chuckles. "What?" he asks. "Brothers getting on your nerves?"

Noah glares at him. "Really, Evan?" He asks him in disbelief. It is a touchy subject, everyone in the room knew that. "Was that necessary?"

Mya doesn't pay any mind to the bickering boys behind her back, she wants to win and she just figured out a way to. She might not be some expert, but she has watched her brother enough to kind of know what she's doing. Mya shoots Jordan as he stands on top of an old run-down building causing him to fall all the way down to his death. "Dammit," Jordan says, throwing the controller down on the ground. Mya looks to the side and smirks at him, attempting to rub it in as much as possible. Alex's face flushes a deep dark shade of red. The vein on the side of his neck grows more prominent, and Lilac swears he can see his eyes darken. Lilac smacks Evan on the shoulder with the back of his hand. "

Stop, Ev," he whispers. His blue eyes bore into Evans' dark brown ones. Evan smiles, pushing up his glasses, "Ok, Little Li, I promise I'll stop" Evan says, ruffling his chestnut hair. Lilac smacks Evans's hand away "Don't even start you, dingus." Evan can't help himself from laughing again "Mya sure has rubbed off on you." The blonde girl turns her head at the mention of her name. She looks at Lilac, then looks over to Evan and raises her plucked brows. When she and Evan make eye contact he flirtatiously winks, which makes Mya roll her eyes and turn back away from him. Evan stands up from the dirty couch, his long legs almost hitting the light wood coffee table. He smooths the wrinkles on his old raggedy band shirt. He falls back onto Lilac dramatically; Lilac tries to push him off and he also tries to look mad. But he can't and he also can't help but burst out into laughter. But still, Evan is basically crushing him to death. Evan is nearly half his body weight, thanks to Lilac's short height.

"Oh my sweet tarts," Evan says in a fake overly sweet and innocent voice. "My poor little Li." He turns around so he's face to face with Lilac. He grabs his head, one of his palms on each one of his cheeks. Evan rotates his own face around and looks down at Jordan and Mya who are both struggling to hold in their laughs. "He's been corrupted!" He mockingly faints, rolling off of Lilac's body and onto the floor, where Mya and Jordan quickly move away from and falls to the carpeted ground with a *thud*. Shaking the floor under him. Noah almost yells at him for almost damaging the delicate floor but doesn't.

They all burst out into a fit of laughter, well most of them. Alex rolls his eyes but tries to hide a smile because of his friend's actions. The laughter abruptly stops when they hear soft footsteps coming down the creaking wooden stairs.

"Noah."

. Noah's head whips to the stairs, and sees his little brother, Bill, hesitantly coming down the old steps. Immediately after Bill is seen, Lilac runs up and sweeps him off his feet. He walks back to his spot on the couch, Bill still in his arms; he sits back down, and places Bill in his lap.

"Getting jealous over here." Evan comments, propping himself on his hands staring at Bill and Lilac. Lilac shoots him a quick glare but besides that he ignores him. He would rather not cuss Evan out in front of the child. Instead, he gives his attention back to Bill.

"How's school going, buddy?" he asks sweetly. He always had a soft spot for kids and especially Bill. Lilac has known Bill since he was a baby and was basically like a little brother to him; he's never had siblings, despite yearning for one all his life. Sister or brother he really didn't care, as long as he had one, it didn't matter. Now though he has come to terms that it is never going to happen.

"It's okay," Bill replies, turning his gaze to Noah, who sits there silently watching Bill and Lilac. "Mom told me to tell you," he points to Noah, "that Alex's brothers are here to pick him up." They all groan including Alex. It is well known in their small group that Alex's brothers are the absolute worst type of people in town, and not just to Alex, to the rest of them as well. Alex will never hate them, despite the list of reasons why he should, being longer than any novel that Alex has ever read.

Alex picks up his brand new looking light brown book bag, shoving his book in harder than necessary. "You wanna ride?" he asks Lilac. Lilac could go over to Alex's or the other way around. They have lived right next to each other all of their lives, and Lilac nods, taking Bill off his lap and setting him where Evan was once sitting. He doesn't have a book bag like Alex, who takes that thing everywhere and practically sanitizes it every day. Seriously, Lilac has no idea what he even carries in there, besides a ridiculous number of books. Lilac believes he's smoldering a pop up library in there. He did, however, have a coat that was thrown carelessly on the floor with everyone else's.

"Have fun riding in a car with those assholes," Evan says, still propped up on his hands.

"Language, around children. Someone cover this child's ears," Mya says, squeezing in between Noah and Bill.

"Oh shush, Mya, you swear all the time," Jordan pipes from his spot on the floor.

Mya rolls her dark blue eyes. "Yeah, but not around small children, I'm way too nice for that."

4

Bill makes a face. "I'm not small." He crosses his arms over his chest. Mya nearly snorts.

Jordan doesn't pay any attention to the ten year old. "I can recall you saying you cussed out your little cousin who and I quote 'was annoying'."

Mya puts her right hand on her chest and leans back. "Touché," she says.

"You ready to go?" Alex asks Lilac while he slips his long skinny arms into his jacket.

"Yeah," he replies, putting his own jacket on.

"May the force be with you little, Li," Evan calls at Lilac with a two finger salute.

Lilac rolls his eyes beginning to walk up the stairs before saying, "Stop fucking calling me that *Even*." He can hear Evan's annoying laughter as he opens the basement door and steps into the kitchen.

Jordan looks at Evan. "One day that kids going to beat your ass," Jordan says, slightly warning him.

Evan laughs. "Yeah right. I could literally step on him."

Alex wraps his book bag over his shoulders; he is about to walk up the steps until he feels a hand lightly grasp his arm. He jumps before he turns around and is face to face with Noah. "Are you going to be ok?" Alex looks at Noah's hand that's still on his upper arm. Noah is catching up to his height. He is always the second tallest (behind Evan who has giraffe legs) but it seems Noah is about to pass him. He nods at Noah's question and gives him the smallest of smiles. He is not in the mood to smile, but he doesn't want to make Noah worry about him. Even though he knows Noah will anyway. He always does, despite Alex's reassurance. "Just call me if you need anything," he adds.

Alex nods again. "Okay," he replies.

Noah lets go of his arm and Alex starts up the stairs. "Be careful!" Noah yells after him.

"I will!" Alex yells, closing the basement door behind him. His two brothers Austin and Allen stand in the kitchen talking respectfully to Mrs. Coleman. While Lilac stands on the other side of the small beige, looking like he wants to gouge his own eyes out with a spork.

"Oh. Alex sweetie. I was just telling your brothers about the sleepover next weekend. They say they didn't know anything about it."

Shit. Alex mentally wants to shake Mrs. Coleman. Make her realize what was going on. Of course, he isn't going to tell them. They will just have something rude to say about it or not let him go at all. He smiles tightly standing next to Lilac "Oh, um, I guess it just slipped my mind."

Austin turns to look at him with a hidden glare. "A lot of things seem to slip your mind lately," he says, with a secret rude undertone to it that only four out of the five people in the room will recognize. Austin is always the meaner one; Allen is just always an asshole to everyone, but Austin always seems to have an intense and deep hate for Alex. Lilac knows there has to be a reason, because no sane person would treat someone like that for the hell of it. "Anyways, we should probably get going," Austin says. His respectful tone makes Lilac want to vomit; he knows what Austin is doing: acting like a little angel when he's really the devil.

"Ok bye, boys," she says, smiling at Lilac and Alex.

"Bye, Mrs. Coleman," they reply in unison, walking out the front door. Austin's smile disappears once they exit the house.

"It took you long enough," Allen says to Alex, once they're fully away from the house. Lilac opens his mouth to say something, yells at Allen for being a dick. But the look he receives from Alex told him to let it go.

"Sorry" Alex whispers, knowing that they will hear him. They step inside Austin's freshly cleaned white car.

Once, he told Lilac that if he smudges the black leather seats he will die. Lilac retorted with a simple 'I'd like to see you try' and proceeded to lick his pointer finger and run it down his seats. The way Austin's face turned bright red like a tomato was priceless. Lilac couldn't bite his tongue that day, and they didn't do anything to him. No, they never do anything to him, but he wishes that they would. The next day they saw Alex with tear-stained cheeks and a nasty blue and purple bruise covering his eyes. Those were the only bruises they saw, but Lilac knew there were more.

That's what they did if someone in their little group mouthed off, they would beat someone else up. It was usually Alex and either Lilac or Evan were the ones that couldn't control their temper. Lilac remembers a time where Evan told Allen to 'suck it' and the next day

6

Alex's body was covered in colored marks. They were ten and that was the first time Lilac felt pure hatred run through his veins. The first time he realized the type of people Austin and Allen were.

"So why didn't dad pick me up?" Alex's soft voice breaks Lilac out of his thoughts.

"He was busy," Allen says, looking at his phone, bored with the silence. Austin positively refuses to turn on the radio. He likes driving in silence. Alex doesn't ask him to elaborate by the word 'busy' like Lilac would have done. He just looks out the window in the awkward air around them.

"So" Lilac says, clapping his hands together and breaking the silence. "Can I come over today?" he asks Alex.

Alex opens his mouth to reply before he's cut off by a sharp "No" from Austin. Lilac has the urge to slap him.

"Was I asking you?" Lilac snaps.

"Did I say you did?" Austin replies, his grip tightening on the steering wheel. "You wanna tell him why, Alex?" He looks at him in the rearview mirror. His eyes stare angrily in the reflection.

Alex looks down at his fingers, fiddling with them, Lilac pretends not to notice his anxiousness. "It's just a family thing" Alex mumbles.

Allen scoffs, eyes still looking down at his phone. "That's one way to put it." Austin cackles loudly. Lilac stares at Alex, waiting for an explanation about what the hell is happening. But Alex avoids his gaze and just stares out the window, trying to blink away the liquid that wells up in his eyes.

Lilac sighs, looking out the windows, which seems completely boring since it's all woods for the next four miles. He fiddles with the sleeve of his coat until he pulls it up revealing the dark brown crescent moon shaped birthmark. He rubs his thumb over it, it's undeniably weird, but his dad says when he adopted him, he had it and doctors say it's just a weirdly shaped birthmark. He's not sure, but it's just always been a part of him. The hopeful and optimistic side of him wants to believe that it means something. Something important. That he's important. But the realistic side knows that it doesn't mean a thing. He rubs a bit harder on the mark wishing that it would just go away. His stupid name, the stupid birthmark. So unordinary. He feels the hatred going back into his body and moving back through his veins.

CHAPTER TWO

That was the last day everything was normal. It has been a week since Bill's unexpected disappearance and Evan is just starting to notice the small changes in everyone's behavior. The streets are quieter, the eighth-grade teachers are giving them more and more free days in class, less homework, and everyone is constantly looking at him and his group of friends. The stares of pity and wonder, which definitely doesn't help his friends cope with the sudden loss. It is hard enough without Noah not being around. He is spending the past week at home and is ignoring the group's numerous phone calls and texts. Evan thinks it is obviously reasonable, but he can't help but be a bit upset that he hasn't even talked to anyone in the group. Especially Lilac, who is having a harder time dealing with the fact that Bill is missing and has no clue when he could be back, where he is , or most importantly if he is safe. He was always closest to Bill behind Noah. To be frank, Evan is really worrying about him. Lilac's dad even let him stay home Monday.

"Will you *please* stop staring?" Lilac says, his back turned to Evan as he shades in the lilac flowers he's drawing on the messy white desk. Colored pencils and crumpled up pieces of paper nearly overflowing from the simple structured desk. "It's getting kind of creepy."

Evan lets out a scoff. "How'd you know I was staring?" Lilac turns around in his torn up desk chair. The shiny black leather squeaking as he does so. Lilac raises his eyebrows at Evan, who's on his side with a perfect view of Lilac's bright white desk. His eyes scan the old. Movie-poster-covered walls. Half of them, he hasn't even heard of, but he can imagine that he'll have to watch them at some point. When he notices Lilac's eyes on him, he quickly flips onto his stomach and slams his face into Lilac's soft covered mattress. Lilac fondly rolls his eyes, getting up out of his chair and walking over to his bed. He sits on the edge, the edge of the mattress where Evans' feet lay. The bed dips when he puts his weight on it. Lilac's sock-covered feet hang off the edge of the white bed, which contrasts well with the baby blue walls and the clean white trim. He grabs the pillow that's lazily placed on the other side of his bed and throws it at the back of Evans head. His messy black hair is going all different directions. Evan breathes out a laugh, which causes his glasses to get covered with fog, blinding him temporarily.

"If you break your glasses here, it's gonna be my ass," he says. He hears another one of Evan's muffled chuckles.

He flips back on to his back and leans up to look at Lilac. "I mean, your dad finally let me in the house. So. Progress?" Lilac can't help but laugh at the hopeful look in Evan's eyes. James, his dad, has never liked Evan. Every single one of Lilac's friends have been in his house, with permission, except for Evan and it honestly did make him feel bad. James is crazy and strict, but he is the type of guy that you want to be liked by. He has a soft spot for Lilac though, considering he is his only child. Lilac is the only thing he had. Without him, he is just a sad lonely chief of police in their small town where nothing bad seems to happen. Well until Bill. Now the youngest child of one of the most respected families in town had just gone missing. And James has a feeling as to why, and it scares him, it scares him half to death.

"Um, Evan?" Lilac speaks through heavy breaths of laughter.

"What?" Evan asks, confused about why in hell Lilac is laughing so hard.

"You, um, snuck through the window" he breathes out.

Evan groans in frustration as ever. He goes back to his position. His face squishes in Lilacs peppermint smelling clean pillows. "He hates me" he muffles out.

Lilac stops laughing all together. "He does not hate you, Ev," he says stubbornly.

10

Evan sat up this time, his eyes piercing into Lilacs. He knows that he was lying. "Then why does he let every single person in this goddamn house but *me*? You know that sounds like hate to me," he rants. Lilac goes to say something but is interrupted. "Yeah. You know. When I *adore* someone, I totally don't let them in my house. Instead, I let all their friends in and tell them to get the hell off my lawn, cause you know I *love* them. Oh and I tell their son to stay away from the boy. And that he shouldn't trust him. Oh *and* that he's a bad influence. Yeah, cause that makes perfect sense Lilac," he finishes. Evan regrets it as soon as he was done saying it, but he knows he can't take that back. Lilac hates that take back shit. If you don't mean what you say, then don't say it in the first place.

"He doesn't hate you," Lilac protests.

Evan scoffs "Oh yeah, how?" he replies, crossing his bare arms. It is always super hot in the winter at the Smith household and also freezing cold in the summer. But Lilac always likes it that way.

"Because he loves me," Lilac says, Evan stares at him questioningly "And love makes you do stupid things." And does Evan know that all too well. They sit in silence, the air around them tense. The only sound being the TV that James is watching downstairs. Lilac shivers in his seat and gets up to grab a hoodie from his white closet.

"How are you cold? Evan asks, looking at him with crazy eyes.

"How are you not?" he replies, slipping the plain dark blue hoodie over his head disheveling his light brown hair. All of a sudden the TV stops playing and the pair hears footsteps that got louder and louder by the step. Lilac's gaze darts over to Evan, who looks like he just saw a ghost.

"What do I do?" he whisper yells at Lilac. The footsteps draw nearer.

"How the hell am I supposed to know?" he angrily replies. His blue eyes look around his room, they move quickly and stop at his still open closet. "Closet," he whispers.

Evan looks like he just came out of a haze "Huh?" he asks. "The closet!" he points rapidly at it.

"Oh," Evan says in realization. Evan shoves himself in it, his long limbs cramping in the small space. Lilac shuts the door as quietly as possible. He can tell that his dad is walking up the stairs by now. He hastily walks to his messy desk snatching the sketchbook that he was sketching in not too long ago. He sits back on his bed trying to sit on it as casually as possible. Lilac leans back on his blue and white pillows, moving the old and small light blue bear to the side. He can't help but stare at it for a split second. His big shiny black eyes, the once silver glitter bow around its neck that has been cast over by dirt, and the end of his ears flopping slanting to the side because of the time that had passed. He and his friends won it at the school's carnival in fourth grade. They blew most of their money on it and it took almost a million tries. Since Lilac contributed the most money he was the one that got to keep it. Keith is what they decided to name it. It was after the lead love interest in *Some Kind Of Wonderful,* which was and still one of Lilac's all-time favorite movies.

When Lilac finally gets comfortable in his bed, a soft knock is heard from the narrow hallway, full of picture frames. "Come in!" he yells in reply. James slowly opens the door, stepping into Lilac's warm bedroom. He looks at his son, who sits in his room all alone. Lilac has been doing that a lot. And James would be lying if he says that he isn't worried about him. "Did you need something?" Lilac questions, closing his sketchbook. James looks at him weirdly. He doesn't choose to say anything about it, just walks over to Lilac's bed and sits.

His back facing away from the closet. "So how are you holding up?" he asks.

Lilac shrugs his shoulders, looking at his dad who is wearing his sheriff uniform still. "Ok. I guess" he says, looking down at his cut fingernails. "Any updates?"

James sighs. "No not really. They think he might have run away."

Lilac can't help but roll his eyes, even though he knows how much his dad hates when he does so. "*Bill* wouldn't do that. And whoever thinks he would is a damn idiot" Lilac rages.

James gives him a pointed look. "They don't know Bill. And his parents said they agree."

Lilac stares at him with wide eyes. "They what?" he asks in disbelief. James rubs his eyes causing his reading glasses to go up to his forehead and to slide down his nose when he finally stops.

"They're just looking for a reason, Lilac," he says in frustration.

"Well, instead of looking for the easiest solution," Lilac says spitefully, "maybe they should be looking for the truth. But I guess that wouldn't make any sense would it, Dad."

James takes off his glasses, folding them onto his light brown colored button-down. He stands up, "You have no idea what they're going through, Lilac," he says, stepping towards him.

Lilac avoids his gaze. "You have no idea, either, and yet you still have an opinion." Evan wants to open the closet door and run out to sit by Lilac. He can imagine the look on his face, and it makes his stomach churn. Silence overtakes them and for some odd reason Lilac feels annoyed being around his dad in that moment. He just wants to be alone. Well, alone with Evan.

"Can you just go?" he whispers.

James frowns. "Yeah. Sure. Of course." And without another word James walks out of Lilac's bedroom, not forgetting to cunningly glance at Lilac's closet. Lilac goes over to his closet and opens the door. He doesn't wait for Evan to get out when he turns around and sits back on his bed, opening his sketchbook back up.

"Lilac-" Evan begins but is quickly cut off.

"Do you think they'll find him?" he asks, eyes watering from looking at the meniscal lilac tree that Bill drew him for his thirteenth birthday. Evan doesn't know how to answer. He and Lilac both made a promise never to lie to each other.

The whole system started in kindergarten when Lilac asked Evan if he thought his name was stupid. Evan asked him if he wanted the truth, Lilac replied with "I always want the truth." He told Lilac that he thought his name was awesome and he wished he had a name like his. Lilac at the time was kind of self-conscious about his name and every time Lilac did ask his dad about his name, his dad would say that's the name his parents wanted him to have and would try his best to change the topic as soon as possible.

"No," Evan says, Lilac looks at him, puzzled. "They won't; they're way too stupid," He pauses before he says, "But we will."

Lilac smiles, "Pinky promise?" he held out his small pinky finger. Evan connects Lilacs and his own, feeling the warmness of Lilac's hand.

He smiles back at Lilac as he says, "Pinky promise." Their fingers still intertwined.

CHAPTER THREE

Noah lays in his bed, looking up at his starry ceiling. He has been laying there and looking up a lot that week. The feeling of his dark blue, blues closing in on him is stronger than it ever was before. He's got up very few times to pee or grab something to eat, but only when absolutely necessary. Bill always says he liked stars and insists on having Noah put glow in the dark stars on his ceiling. For some odd reason that their mother never told them about, Bill is not allowed to have them in his room. Noah had his own opinions about the situation. Noah feels like he's the only one that even cares about Bill. His parents have been fighting constantly about whose fault it is instead of trying to fix the problem. His sister, Sam, found comfort in spending time with Mya's older brother Jon, instead of spending time with her own brother. It irritates Noah to put it gently. He hasn't talked to his friends either, even though he is worried about them and he knows they're worried about him too. Bill, in some way, is like everyone's little brother. Noah just didn't know what to say. Or how to even start the conversation.

His phone rings on his bed, causing him to turn sideways to see who's calling. *Evan* the name reads. Of course, it's him, he has already called him over twenty times in the past week. No doubt about something with Lilac and how he's doing. His finger hovers over the red decline button, but something in him screams at him to answer.

Answer the Call! the voice in the back of his mind screams so loudly that it's the only thing he can hear. Jesus, he really is losing it. *Answer!* And he does.

"Hello," his voice is gravelly from lack of talking the whole week.

"Noah, my boy!" Evans's cheerful voice says. His voice miles away from Noah's mood. "Meet us at the clubhouse, pronto."

Noah's face wrinkles together. He must have misheard him. "What?" he asks. He can practically hear the look on Evan's face. The 'you sound really dumb' look that Evan always has glued on to his face.

"The clubhouse, dude. Our clubhouse. You know the one we've been going to since the first grade. You know the one where-."

Noah cuts him off "Yeah. Yeah. I know what clubhouse. But why are we going there?" Noah remembers when Lilac brought up the idea for the clubhouse and truth be told, Noah thought he was bluffing. That was until two months later he knocked on Noah's front door with the rest of the group and told him that they had to show him something. They brought Noah to the woods near Lilac and Alex's house and told him to look. There Noah saw probably the nicest clubhouse he has ever come across. The wood looked brand new and neatly cut. It had a big red door with a plastic pine reef that started to break within a few months and even glass windows. The inside was even better, tan carpeting, a small couch, a pile of folded blankets in the corner, and a little end table. It wasn't really warm, but besides Noah's basement, it was one of their gang's main hangout spots.

He hears the sound of bike pedals in the background and Lilac's voice yelling at Evan loudly. "Top secret information that I can't tell you through the telephone. Someone could be listening" Evan says in a fake spy-like whisper. "Ok well see you there, Noah my boy, gotta split," he says normally. "Wait, but I didn't-" Noah begins, but Evan has already ended the call. Noah shakes his head and smiles a little at Evans' peculiar ways. He sits up getting out of his red striped covers that were designed exactly like Bill's. He steps out of bed. It feels good to finally have a purpose, the only time he was out and about is to go to the bathroom, shower, or get his remote that he flung across the room. His parents have been giving his meals to him in bed, it is most likely the nicest thing they've done for him since the whole mess had started. And they had the audacity to think that Bill would run away.

The very thought makes Noah's blood begin to boil. Noah walks over to his lightwood dresser and pries the drawers open with his fingertips, most of the silver handles had fallen off and Mrs. Coleman hasn't had the time to get him new ones. He lazily throws on a plain red old baseball team shirt and some black sweatpants he's thrown on the floor. It isn't much of a difference between his plaid pajama pants but it feels nice to be in something different. He walks out of his bedroom, avoiding looking at Bill's bedroom door. The house feels odd, the TV that is usually always on was turned off. His mom spends most of her time in the kitchen, baking cookies and cakes all week to get her mind off her son. She doesn't even notice Noah who puts on his coat and shoes and walks out the aged door. He grabs his dark blue rusty bike from the garage, which has a light layer of frost over the side and pedals quickly through the small town. Passes the high school which is the only high school in their small town. Passes the ice cream shop that's closed in the colder months. Passes the public library where Alex has dragged him to more than a hundred times in their friendship. They used to go every Sunday, but ever since seventh grade it stopped. Alex was suddenly insanely busy. The streets are quieter than usual even in the winter. There were always kids playing outside on skateboards or bikes, but that day it seems like he's the only one on the road. There aren't that many cars on the road. He rides through the woods. The frosted ground crinkles as his tires thread over them. When he gets to the clubhouse he sees five bikes outside, two parked nicely with the kickstand down and the other three thrown carelessly to the ground. He places his bike on the ground next to the others and stops in front of the big red door. He knocks on the door one time. "Password!" multiple voices yell. He rolls his eyes but knows that it was necessary for him to do the knock. People outside of the group always try to get in the clubhouse and Lilac's the only one with the key. So they all agreed on a knock to let the others know it was them coming in and not some intruder. One knock. Pause. Two knocks. Pause. Three knocks. Pause. One knock. Almost magically the door pops open right away.

"Took you long enough," Mya says while she closes the door behind Noah. Candles litter the carpeted ground making the room smell of vanilla, everyone seems to have their own soft blanket and are all sitting in a circle. The walls bare and wooden. It looks like they are some demonic child cult, like something in *Children of the Corn*.

"What the hell are you guys doing?" Noah asks.

"Sit down," Lilac ushers, patting the spot next to him. He sits down and wraps himself in the blanket that is waiting for him. "Alright," Mya says, clapping her hands together. "Everyone's here. So can someone please tell me what we're doing here." There are a few mumbles of agreement that swept over the room. Lilac looks nervously to his left, where Evan sits. He nods at Lilac, reassuringly. "I'm sure you guys heard the latest theories about Bill." Noah scoffs bitterly, "You mean the fact that those dumbasses are saying that my brother ran away. Yeah, trust me I heard." Everyone turns and looks at Noah, who is practically sizzling with rage, everyone except Alex, who finds the tan carpet particularly interesting. Noah can see the tiny bruises littering his face.

Evan coughs awkwardly, "Well, thanks Noah for clearing that up." Lilac tries to hide his smile. "In other news, I came up with the brilliant plan of taking matters into our own hands." Jordan raises his hand like a child in a classroom. The window light causes his brown skin to shine slightly. "And that means what exactly?" he asks. Evan, before, had some crazy ideas in the past. Most of them have had Jordan as a key player in them. This one however feels different, this one made Jordan's stomach hurt and red flags pop up in his head. "It means genius." Jordan rolls his eyes. "That *we're* going to find Bill." Silence. Not a sound can be heard, except for the sound of the outside world. Birds chirping, trees shaking in the bitter wind, the small flames from the candles blowing lightly.

"Have you lost your ever-loving mind!" Jordan yells.

Noah whips his head around him, his eyes transfect into a glare. "What's that supposed to mean?" he questions in defense mode. "We're thirteen for god sakes," Jordan says like it's the most obvious thing in the world. Lilac can't blame him for saying this though. "Um, rephrase. All of us are fourteen except you young grasshopper," Evan retorts. Jordan silently dismissed him. It is crazy. Probably one of the craziest things Evan has ever thought of. But right then, he won't exactly call himself sane. "We should just let the police handle it." Noah gives out a laugh that holds zero humor and runs a hand through his light brown hair, with frustration.

18

"You mean the police? Who think Bill ran away. No way am I gonna sit back and let those assholes handle it." He gives a quick look around the room. Mya's stares at him with pity swirling through dark eyes. Noah knows that Mya heard exactly what's going on with Jon and Sam, and he also knew how she feels about it. Evan looks at him with the same look as Mya. Lilac just stares at him, expressionless. Alex is still not looking at him, but Noah can't bring himself to care. And Noah doesn't even want to look at Jordan.

"I'm going to look for him. Tonight," he finishes. Evan stares at him, wide-eyed.

"Tonight!" he exclaims. "Look who lost their mind now." Noah stands up from his spot on the floor, going over to the door. "I'm not asking any of you to come with me, but I'm not saying I wouldn't want your help." He walks out the door, slamming it behind him. He goes over to his bike and starts to pick it up. Until Noah feels Evan put a hand on his shoulder. "It was my idea; you really think I'm not going to be a part of it?" he says. Noah looks around at everyone else, even Jordan nods in agreement. "We're in." Despite saying it, Jordan knows that they're screwed.

CHAPTER FOUR

"This is the worst idea Evan's ever had," Alex says, wrapping his grandma's knitted light green scarf around his neck.

"You'll live," Lilac replies, putting the maroon winter beanie on his head, making sure to cover his ears. It is beginning to snow and that definitely is not something Alex agreed on. He's already on thin ice with his dad, so if he finds out about this Alex will never see the light of day again.

"Down here!" a voice yells. Alex and Lilac huddle over to Alex's bedroom window. Mya, Jordan, Evan, and Noah stand below, their own winter gear on their bodies and their hands holding their bikes, shaking from the bitter cold. Flashlights in each one of their hands being the only source of light. Alex slides open his window. The cold air hits Lilac and him suddenly. It causes both of them to shiver.

"Can you be any louder?" he whispers.

"Yes! I can be louder!" Evan screams. Alex sighs dramatically, Evan knows how to get on his nerves like no other. "Turn on the TV," he says, turning towards Lilac. Lilac nods, grabbing the remote from Alex's clean white nightstand. He turns on the TV flipping it to a random paid program channel that will bore anyone to death if they actually watch, then throws the slick black remote carelessly on to the made bed. He looks over to the door when the lights turn off. Lilac glanced toward Alex who is barely able to be recognized if not for the bright TV light.

21

"Done this before?" he asks. Alex doesn't answer. Instead, he walks toward the window and pokes his head out. Looking down he sees the metal ladder that shines in the bright moonlight. He turns to Lilac again "You wanna go first?" Lilac nods, putting the wool gloves over his hands covering the crescent moon birthmark on his right wrist. He lets out a shaky breath, climbing out of the window, and putting his booted foot on one of the thin metal rungs. It rattles with every step which only increases his nerves. He reminds himself not to look down, that's what people always say about amusement park rides, is this any different? He doesn't necessarily have a fear of heights; he just doesn't like them all that much. When his feet touch the small amount of snow on the ground he instantly feels relief. Evan points his phone towards him, blinding him with his light.

"Took you long enough, Little Li," he says. "Thought someone would have to hold your hand to get you to come down."

Lilac picks up a handful of snow, and he launches it at Evans's face, hitting him straight in the glasses. "Shut it, dimwit."

Evan wipes off the snow with his gloved fingers before he says, "Why you little-" he goes to pick up a handful of snow before Jordan grabs his arm. "Will you two *please* stop acting like children for two seconds?" he says. Lilac decides not to answer and turns on the flashlight on his phone. He points it to the ladder where Alex is just getting off. "Can you go get our bikes?" Lilac asks Alex.

Alex rolls his hazel eyes, putting the hat over his light brown curls. "Both of them?"

Lilac frowns at him. "Please."

Alex rolls his eyes again and sighs loudly. "The things I do for you" He turns around and begins to walk to the old garage where their bikes lay.

"Love you!" Lilac calls after Alex.

"Hate you," he replies back, but he smiles to himself as he says it.

"It's cold as balls out here," Mya says. She is definitely not supposed to be out there. Mya knows her mom is going to find out, she finds out everything. She found out about the crop top she wore at school, she found out about her being in Lilac's room (which she got heavily grounded for because Lilac's a boy). So why wouldn't her mom find out about this? Her dad won't care as much, he will be mad at her for about a day or so then get over it. He was always more lenient. Her mom, on the other hand, is not. Sometimes it shocks Mya that they are actually married.

"That makes literally no sense" Jordan mumbles.

Mya narrows her eyes behind her glasses, which are covered in melted snowflakes. "You wish" she retorts. "Why would I wish," Jordan argues.

"Look who's acting like a child now" Evan teases, receiving a high five from Mya. Alex gives Lilac his dirt-stained bike, while his clean red one shines in everyone's flashlight.

"Ok, let's just get this over with," Alex says, sitting on the black leather bike seat and beginning to pedal. Everyone follows his actions.

"So where are we looking, Noah?" Jordan asks. Trying to keep up with Noah's fast pedaling through the snow.

"The woods," Noah replies simply. He's been quiet ever since Jordan and Evan met him at his house.

"The woods!" Evan exclaims. "At night!"

Lilac smirks pedaling up the now covered in snow, grassy hill. The woods at the top go on for about six miles. Alex remembers a time when he got lost in the woods. His family and close family friends were having a big picnic. He was five and saw a bunny run into the woods. He ran after it. He ran and ran and ran until he became out of breath by then he was about a half a mile into the woods and had no idea where he came from. He looked around, the trees looking like they were seventy-two feet tall to the younger version of himself. He was terrified and the only thing he could think to do was scream. He screamed so loud that it burned his throat and he wasn't able to speak for week after. His eyes watered and he choked out a sob as he screamed again. The tears and snot mix together which at five makes him feel so dirty. But all that he thought about is the bugs that were in the woods and the unknown monsters that could be lurking anywhere. He must have passed out because the next thing he remembers was waking up in his, at the time, dark red bedroom with his dad scolding him right when he opened his eyes. He has been afraid of the woods ever since, which was definitely not acceptable in his family.

"Scared, Ev?" Lilac teases when they get to the top of the hill. "Need someone to hold your hand?"

Before Evan can answer, Noah says "Let's go." And on they go. For miles and miles, they continue to walk on. The tread on their bike wheels made marks on the light snow. They dismount their bikes and push them on the ground, which causes an uncomfortable crunching sound. That sounds too much like teeth munching on bones to Lilac. The phone flashlight is their only source of light in the pitch black woods, which make for a creepy Blair Witch type of experience that is eerie, to say the least. But Noah insists on going on. He insists on finding Bill and that night is the night that he is going to do it. The thought that Bill might be dead doesn't dare cross his mind. No he won't let it. His brother isn't dead. He can't be. How could Noah go on in life without his little brother? He can't.

About an hour in the first complaint is finally voiced. "I can't feel my fucking feet," Evan groans. It is his fault, he was the one who made the decision to wear sneakers at the beginning of March. When it is the harsh middle of winter in Pennsylvania, especially in Jeffreyville.

"You'll survive," Mya says from the front of the line where they are all still walking their bikes.

"Shit, Shit, Shit, Shit." Lilac hears Evan say.

"What's going on?" Noah questions, from the front of their line. He stops abruptly in his tracks, resulting in him getting hit in the back of the leg by Mya's wheel. "Fucking footprints!" Evan yells. Noah doesn't even say a word, just shuffles over to where Evan stands and has his phone pointed to the ground. Everyone huddles over there, their bikes bumping on each other, and all their flashlights point downwards.

"Those footprints are too big to be Bill's," Noah cries.

"Yeah, but it's a start," Mya replies, she is trying to look at it in a positive light, but Noah is making that fairly difficult. She knows that he's on edge because his brothers missing, but God can't he be a little optimistic. "We should follow them," Lilac decides suddenly.

Alex goes to put his two cents in, but his phone ringing in his thick coat pocket stops him. Everyone turns to look in Alex's direction, whose hands are shaking as he looks at his dad's name on his phone. "Should I answer?" he asks, looking around at the group.

"I think it'll be better if you did," Lilac says.

"Maybe soften the blow." Jordan adds. Alex nods, fingers shaking vigorously as he slid the bright green answer button. "Hello-" he barely gets the word out as his dad's voice comes blaring in his ear. "Where the *hell* are you, Alexander!" he yells.

"Do you know how worried your mother is? How worried *I* am!" Alex flinches as he yells. He hates getting his dad mad but he always seems to. "I'm sorry I-." He is interrupted once again

"Get your ass home right now," his dad says.

Alex could tell he is seething with anger. "I can't," he whispers into the phone.

"What do you mean you fucking can't?" Alex closes his eyes and inhales and exhales a breath.

"I'm only going to ask one more time, Alex. Where the hell are you?"

Alex, if possible, holds the phone tighter to his right ear. "I gotta go, Dad," he whispers again, beginning to remove the phone that is practically glued on to his ear. "Don't you dare hang up on me. Alex! I swear to-" is the last thing Alex hears before he ends the call.

They all stand in silence, the only sound in the woods being the trees blowing in the cold wind and their own erratic breathing. "Ok. Lilac's right. We should follow them," Noah says, his blood starting to boil as he starts to walk in the direction of the medium-sized sneaker prints. Alex stays in the back hoping to be left alone, but Lilac has other plans.

"You okay?" Lilac asks, even though he knows the true answer. He wants to hear it from Alex.

"I'm a dead boy walking, Lilac," he says, irritated, "Do you expect a freaking dead boy walking to be ok, Lilac!"

Lilac flinches and Alex feels a sense of regret wash through his lanky body. "I guess I shouldn't have asked," Lilac says in a half-assed sorry tone.

"Sorry." Alex looks down at his handlebars "You don't need to apologize," Alex mumbles.

Lilac brings his left hand up from his handlebar and slams it back down in frustration. "Well, obviously I do," he says, "I don't know what you want me to say or do at this point. Why do you keep letting them do this to you! Treat you like that!" Alex looks back up at him but doesn't answer. No answer will have been the truth, so what is the point in answering.

"Holy shit!" Mya yells from up ahead. Alex and Lilac both rush up to the front. The scene that plays in front of them, takes every face muscle Lilac has to keep his jaw from dropping into the fiery pits of hell. A girl who looks about their age stands before them. Small, only slightly taller than Mya and only slightly smaller than Lilac. Her legs covered by a pair of dirt ridden blue jeans, and a long knee length dirty shirt that left her arms bare. Her shoulder-length brown hair also has mud staining the tips. Lilac and the mystery girl's eyes met. Blue and blue clash together, like two turquoise waves colliding.

"U–Um Lilac," Jordan stutters "Look at her wrist." He pointed his flashlight at the girl's right wrist. Plain tan skin is the only thing discovered, nothing unusual. But when he points the light at her left wrist, he has to stop himself from screaming. His blue eyes feel like they might pop out of his sockets. On her wrist is a dark brown colored birthmark in the shape of a crescent moon.

CHAPTER FIVE

The silence is the worst part for Lilac. She is just sitting there like a statue, on Noah's dirty brown couch. Staring at them, in her muddy clothes, and identical wide blue eyes. No one says a word, but Lilac wishes someone would. *Say something stupid, Evan!* He thinks. *Crack a joke. Make us all laugh. Say something that will make me want to yell at you and roll my eyes.* Still, no one says anything. Lilac makes a point to cover his wrist, but the mystery girl keeps looking at him almost knowingly. God, can she be any creepier. This is already scary enough without her looking at him like *that*. Like she knows something he doesn't. The mystery girl gets up out of her seat and walks over to Alex who's slowly backing away from her. She grabs both of his hands, turning them over and examining them like a doctor. He stays completely still, not moving an inch as she inspects him creepily. She moves on to Jordan when she grabs on to him, he jerks his hands back. The girl hisses at him viciously, and Jordan gives his hands back to her immediately. She skips Mya but side-eyes her as she passes.

"Ok, what the hell is this bitch doing?" Mya says, finally breaking the terrible silence. The girl turns her head and glares. She then looks at Lilac and grabs his right wrist. She gasps, rubbing hard on Lilac's birthmark, to make sure it was really there. That she really found him. She's rubbing so hard that it's almost painful, and Lilac knows the skin is going to shade a light red.

"Lilac?" the mystery girl whispers, still looking down at his tan skin. Lilac's eyes widen and he lets out a gasp. Who the hell is this girl and how the hell does she know his name? He jerks his arm away from her. He expects her to hiss at him as she did to Jordan, but she doesn't. She just continues to stare at him with a hazy look in her eyes.

"Who are you?" Lilac asks breathlessly. Evan subconsciously steps closer to Lilac. The girl doesn't answer, she digs into her now crusty with dried mud back jean pocket and pulls out a folded piece of paper. She puts it in Lilac's hand, not stepping away from him in the slightest. When he unfolds the paper he feels his stomach tie into knots. It's a picture. A picture of two twin toddlers, a boy and a girl, with light brown hair and blazing blue eyes and two crescent moon birthmarks on both of their wrists.

"Isn't that you?" Evan asks from over Lilac's shoulder. That comment makes everyone else huddle around the photo, pushing the girl out of the way. They all mumble 'oh my god's' and 'there's no way's'. Lilac pushes his way through them, his blood runs cold, as he looks at the girl. "It's not possible," he says, clenching his fist around the picture. "Mom and dad-."

"No!" he yells, a book falls from the wooden shelf that stands by Noah's staircase. The book is wrapped in blue glow, but when it hits the ground it breaks into nothing. No one notices, too focused on the scene in front of them. "It's not possible" he repeats through gritted teeth.

"They just told me yesterday. And I-I just had to find you" she says softly. Lilac shakes his head turning his back to her.

"Well, maybe you shouldn't have," he whispers spitefully. Evan's shocked. In ten years of knowing the being that is Lilac Smith, he's never seen him act that way.

Noah walks over to the girl, who looks rather confused. Lilac glares at the back of his head. "U-U-Um hi, I'm Noah," he holds his hand out awkwardly. Mya and Alex look at each other stifling their laughs.

The unknown girl looks down at it and then back up at him. Their eyes connect. "I'm Violet Montgomery," she says, grabbing Noah's wrist and shaking it violently.

Evan cracks a smirk. "Hey, Lilac and Violet. What, were you two picked from the same garden?" Lilac rolls his eyes and the rest expect Violet to follow. "Get it? Because you know, they have flower names and they're twins."

"We got it, Evan. It just wasn't funny" Mya says.

Evan pouts, "So wadda we gonna do with her," he says, gesturing to Violet, who's still violently shaking Noah's wrist.

"I mean it's not like we can leave her out in the streets," Mya says. "Especially wearing that." Violet scowls at her when they make eye contact, Mya avoids her gaze after that look.

"Debatable," Lilac says to himself, turning back to face his friends.

Mya yawns, putting her dark blue nail polished hand over her mouth. "Well, I should get going," she says, looking around Noah's roomy basement, but avoiding Violet's eyes. She stops at Jordan who has been oddly quiet. He's normally always shouting his opinion, even when nobody wants to hear it. "You wanna go with me?" she asks him.

He nods, still not talking. "Go out the basement door," Noah says. He finally has his wrist away from Violet and is looking over her shoulder at Mya and Jordan who are about to walk out.

"So my mom doesn't see you." Mya raises her brows. "What about her?" She gestures to Violet, who turns around, her big blue eyes widening. "I guess she'll stay down here," he says. "My parents don't come down here anyway." Mya shakes her head, turning around and walking out the door, Jordan follows her.

"What about Sam?" Lilac says, fully engaged with Mya and Noah's conversation. "Won't she think it's weird having some *stranger* in your house." Violet bows her head, tears welling up in her eyes. Nobody ever made her feel like such a freak. An outsider. Especially not someone who's supposed to be family. She's always felt like something was missing in her life. It is good no doubt, with her mom and dad and her outside family, but there was always something that didn't feel right.

"She's your sister, Lilac," Noah says, trying to keep his cool. He feels bad for the girl and maybe she knows something about Bill. She's his best shot at finding him.

"Bullshit," Lilac spits out.

"No, what's bullshit is the way you're acting," Noah spits, just as bitterly.

"Enough!" Evan yells. It shocks the boys in the room. Evan is rarely serious so when he is you know it's a big deal.

Lilac's phone vibrates in his coat pocket. He turns it over and sees that it's his dad.

"Hello," he says, annoyed. "Get your ass outside," James says.

Lilac hears a voice in the background, "Who are you with? And how did you find me?" he asks.

He can practically see his dad roll his eyes. God, did he hate when he did that. "Alex's dad, tell him to come out with you." He turns to Alex, who is looking at Lilac curiously. "Ok. Fine, we'll be out in a minute." Lilac ends the call not even bothering to wonder why his dad didn't just answer the second question he asked. He looks over at Alex, who stands there quiet like usual. He's always quiet, but after the phone call he had with his dad he has been ridiculously quiet.

Lilac couldn't blame him, though. "We have to go," he says, avoiding looking at Noah and Violet. Honestly he's had enough of both of them for the night.

"Wait, we?" Alex asks, a look of terror crosses his tan face. "Is my dad here?"

Lilac decides not to answer. Whatever response he could muster up in his mind would not calm Alex's nerves. He knows that almost for a fact. He grabs Alex's wrist dragging him out the basement door, without looking back or saying a word to any of the remaining people inside. Evan can't help but feel the slightest bit of hurt wash through him.

They walk outside, the headlights from James's police cruiser blind them as they walk. "What do we do with our bikes?" Lilac calls out to his dad.

"Leave them" answers Alex's dad, Andrew. "You won't be needing them anyway." Alex visibly flinches at his dad's voice. He doesn't want to get in that car. He'd rather walk through the woods to get home. "I don't think I was asking you, but whatever," Lilac says. Alex and he walk painfully slow to James's dirty light brown Sheriff's car. Alex goes to the left, behind his dad who sits seething in the passenger seat. He shuts his door softly, trying to make sure he doesn't make the slightest sound. Lilac, on the other hand, slams his door so hard that it echoes in the quiet night. Alex's dad starts ripping on Alex. Screaming in the car, Lilac wants him to shut up. He digs his nails so hard into his palms that he feels the skin start to break, causing a warm crimson liquid to drip down. He looks over at Alex, who's looking out the window, trying not to be seen. Lilac sees through the reflection in the window, Alex has tears rolling down his cheeks, not bothering to wipe them away, knowing that there's no point and he'll only create more. Alex doesn't say a word though, he just takes it. That's what makes Lilac's skin crawl. Right when he's about to say something to the devil himself, the car comes to a halt. He didn't even realize they were close, he was too focused on not jumping out of the vehicle and grabbing Alex with him. Andrew stops yelling for a split second and thanks James for the ride. Before he harshly grabs Alex's arm, causing a colored pattern to show up days later. Lilac knows the outcome, he's witnessed it too many times before. He would give anything to get Alex out of that house if only for tonight.

"Let's get inside," James says to Lilac, his voice steady and calm. Too calm for Lilac, especially because of the events that happened earlier in the night. They walk into the house, Lilac in front of James walking normally. But as soon as that door shuts everything goes to shit.

"Have you lost your *mind!*" James yells, throwing his keys on the table after locking the front door back up. "With everything that's going on, you thought it would be a good idea to go dilly-dallying in the woods."

Lilac just finished taking off his shoes when he fires back with "Oh, don't even start with me" he snaps.

"What so you weren't going to tell me? Were you just gonna keep it from me for the rest of my life and hope to god that I don't find out!" by the end, he's full-on yelling. All the rage inside of him is boiling up just waiting for the explosion.

"What are you talking about?" James asks. He's the one who's supposed to be mad, Lilac is the one who just left without a trace and had James running around like a chicken with its head cut off. "Violet. You know my 'twin' sister."

James stands there a flash of fear crosses his face, but he quickly replaces it with a stone-cold look. "I have no idea what you're talking about," he says with little to no emotion.

Lilac laughs sourly. "Oh I think you know exactly what I'm talking about dad," he says, slamming the picture of him on the dark wood dining table. He storms out of the kitchen and runs up the steps, trying to get to his room. Lilac slams his door, the sound bouncing off the walls of his quiet bedroom. Lilac and his dad have never fought like this, but ever since Bill has gone missing Lilac feels their relationship straining.

31

He takes his winter gear off his body leaving him in a pair of stained gray sweatpants and a matching (stained as well) gray sweatshirt. He climbs into bed getting into the warm heavy covers. He wishes he could stay like this forever. The only problem is that after an hour of laying in the dark he can't fall asleep. It isn't his own intrusive thoughts that keep him wide awake. No. It is the screams and sobs coming from next door. He closes his eyes wishing that he could hear nothing. That silence will just consume him.

CHAPTER SIX

"You think he likes me?" Mya asks Lilac and Alex, who are silently dying at the question they get asked every time they sit in literature nine. They all sit at a three-person table in the back corner of Mrs. Scott's bright yellow classroom. Generic English posters and homemade rule lists cover almost every inch of the small classroom. Mrs. Scott is an older woman with skin that wrinkles every time she smiles and bleach-blonde greasy hair. She is also by far Mya's favorite English and Literature teachers ever. Her obvious love for words is very refreshing from the past English/literature she had. Mrs. Scott also lets the three of them sit at the back table so that's a plus.

"We've been over this," replies Lilac. Alex silently agrees. He hasn't talked much today, just one word answers. With both Noah and Jordan not being here, it makes it even worse that Alex's practically refusing to talk. When he came into the first period which he had with Lilac and Mya. Mya immediately asks what the cut lip and the red, blue, and purple designs that covered his neck and arms. Lilac knows that those aren't the only markings he had, but he doesn't bring it up, knowing that it would upset Alex. And that's something he never wants to do. Alex already has enough of that.

"He stares at you like every five seconds, he fucking flirts with you constantly, and basically stalks you. Shawn likes you, Mya," Lilac says dully . She blushes at the sound of his name, maybe he was her dream boy, with his dark brown hair and gorgeous brown eyes, and his tall form.

Jon, her brother, says he's goofy looking which Mya replies with, "You should not be talking."

"Shawn Linch is a douchebag" Alex says, "Also a player. He'll only break your heart."

Mya rolls her eyes. "And how would you know, you barely even know him" Mya defends, pulling out her phone. Today Mrs. Scott let them have free time, which Alex is grateful for. Alex is about to correct her before he stops himself. "I know him a lot better than you do," he says instead, flipping open the cheesy young adult book that makes him think he's losing brain cells with every word he reads.

"Trust me, you don't know him as well as you think, Mya."

Mya closes her phone, slamming it on the navy table. "Really because you're the one who-"

"Mya, stop!" Lilac yells he's sick of hearing them argue about this. It has been back and forth between them since November when Mya says that she likes Shawn. Everyone in the group was a bit skeptical because everyone knows the type of crowd he runs around with. The stupid football players who date every single girl that they deem hot. Lilac always thought Mya isn't the type of girl to fall for one of those boys, hell, he can't even imagine her getting a boyfriend. Sure she is pretty to him and she definitely isn't mindless, but he and her both have a tendency to be rude to the people that they like. It is their greatest weakness in the realm of crushes. The bell that signals that seventh period is finally over rings and Alex quickly leaves the classroom without another word.

"I don't know what his deal is," Mya sighs, picking up her stuff from the dirty school floor. Lilac shrugs, acting as if he doesn't know. He wonders how Mya hasn't connected the dots already, she knows how rude Alex's family is to him. Actually rude is an understatement to how they treat Alex.

"Is he coming over to Noah's today?" she asks, walking across the hallway to their last period of the day, Math. Possibly, the worst part of his day. Lilac has Mya *and* Evan in the class, but Mya sits all the way across the room next to Shawn and Evan sits by Lilac even though he's really not supposed to.

"No. He has some family thing" Lilac replies, avoiding their math teacher, Mr. Ryan's eyes. Mr. Ryan says that Lilac's a 'distraction' for Evan, but assigned seats have never and would never stop Evan. They walk in, Mr. Ryan is always standing out in the hallway, staring at students, waiting to write them up for whatever reason possible. Mya holds her breath as she walks into the light yellow math room. The walls are bare (comparable to Mr. Ryan's personality), only having a big line chart on the big black bulletin board. Her mind wonders if Shawn is going to talk to her or completely ignore her like the day prior. It's like a game. A game that she absolutely hates and resents but a game she plays never the less. She doesn't feel like a player in the game; she feels like a game piece and he's the game master, pulling her by a string.

He looks at her when she fully walks into the door. His dark mysterious brown eyes staring into hers. "Wow, Mya, you're actually catching up to Lilac," Shawn says, commenting about both Mya and Lilac's short forms. His classic smirk planted on his lips. Mya forces herself to roll her eyes. Maybe it is an act. Her family all say it is. The bitchy attitude, the snide and crude remarks, the roll of her eyes. Maybe it is but she would never admit that out loud.

"Suck a dick, Shawn" she says rudely.

"Simmer down, Mya," he says in the same tone as her. Lilac gives Mya a knowing look before he walks to his seat. He looks down and fiddles with his pencil bouncing it on the pencil marked desk with various profanities.

"Wassup fuckers." He doesn't even have to look up to know that it's Evan.

"Oh look, Lilac" he hears his name over the ruckus of other children, which causes him to look up from the gray desk.

"Your boyfriend's finally here" Shawn says. "Maybe you'll be in a better mood now." Lilac simply looks back down at his desk, trying to hide his flushed face, and shows him his favorite finger. He won't give Shawn a reaction, he'd rather not waste his breath.

"Trust me, Linch. If I could get a hot piece of ass like Lilac," Evan says, looking over at Lilac. The comment irritates Lilac beyond belief. He knows that it's supposed to be a joke but it is particularly unfunny to him. Lilac picks his head, looking straight at Evan and glares.

"I would," Evan finishes. He stalks over to his seat, which is right in front of Lilac's. He goes to turn around to talk to him, but the look he receives from Lilac stops him dead in his tracks.

"Noah wants us to meet him after school," Lilac says. Evan goes to turn around. "That doesn't mean you get to turn around, *Even*."

Evan stops his movements again and asks, "Why?" Lilac sighs running a hand through his disheveled hair, which is usually styled to perfection. "I don't know, but I'm guessing it has something to do with *her*," he says the word like it physically hurts him. Evan wants to say something about it. That she's Lilac's sister and he should be a little bit nicer. But instead he looks straight ahead, as the bell for eighth-period rings. The rest of the kids still don't stop talking and they continue to run around the classroom like three-year-olds. Even when Mr. Ryan walks in and begins his lecture, the kids still talk and Lilac thinks that this day couldn't get any worse.

⸻

The whole math class consisted of Mya and Shawn bickering like a married couple and staring at each other constantly. The whole thing makes Lilac want to vomit. They are staring at each other so much that Lilac is surprised they got any math work done at all. Lilac walks down the hallway both Evan and Mya are at his side. They plan on walking to Noah's since it's only about four blocks away from the school. They go down the back stairwell, where the exit is right by where all the buses are and the parking lot where parents pick up their children. Lilac spots Alex, walking through the parking lot looking around lost. He spots Austin standing outside his white car, arms crossed and with an irritated expression. When Austin sees Alex he begins to yell, even from across the parking lot he can hear it so clearly. Alex just opens the door in the back and sits there and stares out the window as Austin drives away.

"He's hiding something," Mya says.

"He always was," Evan replies. Lilac turns away from them and starts walking the other direction. Mya and Evan have to run to keep up with his fast walking.

"We need to find out what it is, it's gone on long enough," Lilac says, continuing his fast pace. "Tonight."

Evan grabs his arm loosely, turning Lilac around.

"What do you mean tonight?" Mya asks. Evan still has his hand wrapped loosely around Lilac's arm, they both make no attempt to separate.

"I mean, they're having a weird family thing, I say we crash it," Lilac says. He knows Evan will agree, he agrees to practically everything Lilac says. He just sometimes needs a little convincing.

Mya stares at Lilac incredulously. "Crash it!" she whisper yells. "What if they're like a murder cult or something."

Lilac rolls his eyes. "You've been watching way to may slasher movies" Mya glares. "They're not a murder cult. It's Alex we're talking about. Alex who won't even drink the school milk because he's afraid it'll have some disease."

Lilac gets Mya there, but she still thinks it isn't a good idea. The pain in her stomach is a clear sign. Mya crosses her jacketed arms. "Noah's not going to like it," she says.

"Then we won't tell him," Evan says, still having his hand on Lilac's arm.

"You guys are going to kill me one of these days," Mya says walking in the direction of Noah's house.

"You'll survive," Evan says, withdrawing his hand from Lilac's arm. Lilac and Evan walk side by side, not speaking but they both know what's going on in the other's head. When they get to Noah's, Lilac immediately spots his bike that's thrown lazily to the ground right by the rusted metal door. Evan knocks on the front door. Mrs. Coleman answers, her light brown hair askew, her cheeks tear-stained, and thick purple dark circles under her eyes.

"Hey, Mrs. Coleman," Mya says sweetly. Even in times like this Lilac wants to roll his eyes at her tone of voice. "Is Noah by any chance home?"

Mrs. Coleman rubs her tired eyes. "Basement," she says in a monotone voice. She then quickly scurries off into the kitchen. They walk to the basement, where they can hear the TV blaring loudly through the door. Mya opens the door, they walk down the rickety steps that creak with every step. Violet sits on the couch, still in the muddy clothes that are starting to stink. She's looking at the TV, with a puzzled look on her face. Noah just watches her, like he's studying her, trying to figure her out. When he turns around and sees the trio he breathes a sigh of relief. "Oh thank god you guys are here. You won't believe this," he says, an excited look on his face.

"Believe what?" Lilac asks, bored. Honestly, he's annoyed with the freaky girl's presence. Like come on, she's covered in dirt for Christ's sake. He wouldn't trust the stranger with a ball of yarn. "Her!" Noah points at the girl dramatically. The girl turns away from the TV, immediately spotting Lilac.

"Her?" Evan asks, raising a brow questionably.

"Yes, her" Noah states. He walks over to Violet grabbing her wrist, in a faint grip and standing her up next to him. "So I was throwing that ball around." He points to a red medium-sized foam ball that's sat on his coffee table. "And then I thought 'hmm why not throw it at her,' she just kept looking at me. So I threw it at her. And she fucking caught it!" he exclaims, an excited smile on his face. The three gave him an odd look.

"Isn't that what you're supposed to do with balls? You know like catch them?" Mya asks.

Evan snorts. "No, you don't understand. Without her *hands*." Evan and Mya stop, stop everything, even breathing for a second. Lilac laughs "What?" he asks in disbelief.

Lilac's definitely not taking him seriously not in the slightest. "Watch," Noah says. He lets go of Violet's wrist and whispers to her to step away from him. She does so, taking three long steps back. He throws the ball under hand in the air in Violet's direction. Lilac expects Violet not to catch it, she's proved that she's not the brightest bulb and probably grew up in the middle of nowhere in some worn down garden shed. But she doesn't nor does she catch it either. The red foam ball stands still in midair not moving with a bright blue hue wrapped around it like plastic wrap. The blue that looks identical to both Violet and Lilacs eyes glows. Glows so bright that it's almost blinding. Her eyes in a strange way are difficult to look at but even more difficult to look away from. Violet stands there her left hand up in a stop gesture, which shows off her dark brown birthmark, that shines in the window light. She flicks her hand to the right, in Lilac's direction, causing the ball to fly quickly in that direction. The blue slowly disappears as Lilac's reflexes kick in right before the ball hits him, he catches it in mid-air stopping its movement. Violet looks at Lilac and smirks at his shocked expression.

Nobody speaks, Noah stands there with a smug smile on his face, knowing that he was right, and the satisfaction is so very sweet. Lilac's face looks pale white, reminding him as a ghost. He can't believe what he just saw, he can't seem to swallow it. Mya looks as if she's about to scream and she probably would have if she didn't know that Mrs. Coleman was upstairs. While Evan with his dark brown eyes wide, only has two words to say. "Holy shit."

CHAPTER SEVEN

Lilac sits in the bushes right outside the woods with Evan and Mya on each of his sides. The events of earlier in the day replaying in his mind. He looks straight ahead, the tiny green leaves in his vision but he can still see the large fire in the middle of the bare field behind Alex's large house. The fire blazing wildly in the soft wind. Cracking every second and echoing in the silence. The cold air surrounds them and the faraway fire does absolutely nothing to sooth the bitter cold. He's surrounded by green and feels the leaves brush his shoulders as the wind blows softly. Lilac has no idea how long they've been waiting there. Maybe a few hours? He isn't sure, and he stopped checking his phone a while ago. Lilac isn't thinking of that though. Nor was he thinking about the fact that he can't feel his feet in the light sneakers. He keeps thinking about Violet and the way she made that ball float without laying as much as a finger on it. Or how the blue hue around it, which looked identical to his and her eyes. Only hers were glowing. If he wasn't creeped out before he is sure as hell creeped out after seeing that. His heart begins to race rapidly every time he thinks about it for too long.

"I can't feel my ass," Mya says; she regrets agreeing to this. It's stupid they're probably not going to find out anything anyways. It's boring bookworm Alex, there spying on.

"What ass?" Evan replies cheekily. Mya plucks him on the back of his neck which makes him wince.

"Shh!" Lilac quietly yells. "Listen!" Footsteps approach rapidly, getting louder and louder by the second. Lilac immediately spots Austin and Allen in the front of the crowd of people. The group doesn't look that old, teenagers, very few young adults, Lilac even spots some people he's seen around middle school. Then, he sees Shawn among the people, he turns to the left to spot Mya's reaction. In the dim firelight, he can see her blonde eyebrows are furrowed and she has a confused expression on her face. For a second, Mya thinks her eyes are playing tricks on her, then she gets the urge to vomit. Alex is near the end, his head down and arms crossed over each other. The only reason Lilac knows it is Alex is because of the light brown curls that cause him to stand out in a crowd. They all stand around the fire, everyone's deadly quiet. Alex near the front, still not daring to look up.

"I'm telling you — a cult," Mya whispers.

"Shut up!" Lilac groans in reply. Austin stands in the middle, right by the fire that crackles and pops.

"I will be leading the meeting tonight," he says loudly and formally. It makes Lilac's body shiver.

"When are you not?" someone murmurs sharply.

Austin turns quickly in that direction "Shut the hell up, Jason!" he growls lowly in his throat. Lilac jumps at the harshness of his voice Austin clears his throat, glaring once more in that direction. He runs a hand through his perfect hair. "Anyways," he says. "We have a few things that Alpha wants us to discuss."

"*Alpha?*" Evan whispers in confusion, looking to Mya and Lilac. Mya looks back at him, while Lilac continues to look through the bushes. "I read about that somewhere," she whispers back to him. "It's like some animal leader or something."

Lilac shakes his head, without looking away from the complicated scene in front of him. "There's no way," he whispers more to himself then Mya or Evan. "It's impossible." He can't believe himself however, after what happened today, he has no idea what's possible and what isn't anymore. And the trees around him feel as if they are consuming him, with every second that ticks by. "Rouges are coming, from down south. Alpha wants us to vote on whether we let it go or take care of the problem."

Lilac feels like a total idiot, he feels so lost so confused. What the hell is going on? "And let me remind you that most rogues are loose cannons and would more than likely be dangerous to the pack. So all in favor of taking care of it," Austin says in the same formal and powerful tone that makes Lilac's skin itch. The majority of people lift up their hands, Shawn and Allen included. Alex doesn't, however, just continue to stare at the frosted grass. Austin glares at him, clearly annoyed by the fact that Alex didn't lift his hand. "All opposed?" Very few lift their hands, Alex included but he still does not lift his head. "May I ask why?" Austin says, looking in Alex's direction. He wants a reaction out of Alex and Lilac knows it.

"Because I don't think we should solve the pack's problems with violence" A girl in the front answers and Alex can't agree more. "Well sometimes violence is the only solution," Austin says. He looks straight in Alex's direction. "And if people are too weak to admit that. Then they should just leave." It's an obvious dig to Alex, they seem to always be. Some people around him snicker at the comment. Most of them are a part of Austin and Allen's stupid little group. Where they follow them like lost puppies.

"What the hell is happening?" Evan says a little too loudly. Alex whips his head back in their direction, a terrified look in his light brown eyes. He can just barely pick up the sound of Evan's voice. *Please God don't let them be here,* Alex thinks. *Please don't let them find out like this.*

"Alexander!" Austin yells. Alex turns his head back to the front, he looks back down. "Can you tell me what I just said?" he asks. Alex shakes his head. Austin quickly walks over to Alex and pulls his head up by his brown curls. Lilac nearly runs through the bush. "I can't understand you when you don't talk. Use your words, Alexander. You know how much dad hates that shit," he says, Alex shudders. Lilac wants to kill him at this moment.

"No," Alex says in defeat. "I don't know what you said." Austin gives once last tug to Alex's hair, before letting it go completely, letting Alex's head fall back down. He walks back to his previous spot.

"Well Alex, we were just discussing your boyfriend's little brother," he laughs. "Care to comment?" he asks mockingly. He earns a few laughs from the crowd. Alex lifts his head up, startled by hearing anything about Noah or Bill. Austin hates when Alex brings him up, so Alex rarely does.

"He's not my boyfriend." *He's just a way better brother figure then you or Allen will ever be* Alex says through his teeth. "Ohh. Is that attitude I hear?" he asks mockingly. "Because it sounds like I'm being threatened by a Chihuahua."

Alex clenches his fist. "Piss off," he mutters. Something dangerous flashes in Austin's eyes, Lilac can still see it in the fire light.

"What the fuck did you just say to me?" he asks, his handsome face beginning to turn the lightest shade of red. "N-Nothing" he stammers. *Of course he had to hear,* Alex think to himself.

"No because it sounded like you said, 'piss off.' Or am I just hearing you wrong?" he starts to walk closer to Alex, Allen starts walking closer to Alex as well. Lilac's ready to pounce.

"I didn't s-say it" Alex lies. "I-I promise." When Austin gets to Alex he draws his hand back, "You're a fucking liar." Alex flinches, ready for the impact when he hears a voice scream.

"Stop! You son of a bitch!" Lilac yells, standing up. Evan and Mya follow his movements. But Mya just wants to pull Lilacs arm down and pretend that this never happened. Everyone turns back to them. Alex shakes his head, feeling tears well up in his eyes. "No," he chokes out, shaking his head violently. Shawn stares at Mya in shock. She avoids his eyes as if her life depends on it. Instead, she focuses on Alex. Seeing them treat Alex like that makes anger boil up inside of her. It makes her hate them. All of them, including Shawn. Bones cracking turns people gazes away from the trio. Allen stands there, his eyes bright gold, fangs coming out of his mouth, claws replacing his usually cut nails. "Lilac we need to go," Evan says, pulling on Lilac's arm. The changes slowly get bigger and bigger, thick dark brown fur starts popping up around his arms and his bones start cracking more and more. Besides Mya, Evan, and Lilac nobody else looks shocked, not even startled. Austin's holding Alex back, who is struggling to get out of his brother's grip. He has seen what Allen's done to deer he's hunted before, he can't imagine what he will do if he gets a hold of his friends. Allen shifts into a dark brown wolf with blinding gold eyes. Shards of clothes cover his surroundings, and the crowd backs away from the large wolf. Mya lets out an ear-deafening scream as the wolf charges at them. Mya takes off into the woods shortly followed by Lilac and Evan who is the last one to start running. The woods are cold and dark, with no trace of light. The sound of the beast panting and their pants are the only things to be heard.

"I'm in fucking *Twilight*," Mya says, continuing to sprint blindly through the dark woods. Her dark red jacket flailing behind her.

"Were literally about to fucking die and all you can say is something about stupid *Twilight*?" Evan asks, his breathing ragged.

"It's appropriate!" she defends, not slowing down her pace. The wolf's catching up to them, and the three of them are starting to slow down. Their legs feel numb and jelly like and their sides are cramping and throbbing. Evan slips on a wet log, falling to the ground with a loud *thud*. Lilac turns around and bends down to grab Evan's arm trying to pull him up, while Mya screams for them to hurry, the urge to throw up becomes apparent in her stomach. The wolf growls as he stands only about a foot away from them and is getting ready to pounce. Evan attempts to scurry backwards, but he isn't fast enough compared to the monster that stares in front of him. He jumps up in the air coming towards them, it's teeth bared in a menacing sneer. Lilac feels like he's being controlled, the feeling of being on autopilot possesses his body. He flicks his left hand to the right, blue coming out of his fingertips, and wrapping around the wolf's body, and slamming it into a nearby tree. The wolf's bones crack on impact and it whimpers as it lays there, still. The tree cracks, slowly breaking into two and falling to the ground. Lilac looks down at his hands, that burn like liquid fire. His eyes are wide, and he starts to breathe heavily. *Burning.* They feel on fire. The stupid birth mark, his head, his hands, everything's burning. Lilac's chest rises and falls, his eyes become heavy and lidded. The last thing he sees before everything goes black is his father's calming brown eyes in the darkness. Guiding him into a restless sleep.

CHAPTER EIGHT

Darkness. Darkness is the only thing to be seen in Lilac's clouded vision. It is cold, ice cold. The coldest he has ever been. His hands burn and so did the birthmark on his right wrist. The little light flashes so fast that Lilac nearly misses it. The flash of the glowing blue. "Traitor," a harsh voice whispers right next to his ear. The voice is so close. So close that Lilac can feel the hotness of their breath. "Traitor." The word rings through Lilac's mind. How is he a traitor? He puts his hands over his ears but quickly removes them when he feels them start to burn. "Traitor!" The voice whispers again, louder and harsher than the time before. "Traitor." The word repeats in his mind. It's agonizing that particular word is the only thing he can hear, the only thing he can think about.

"Stop!" he screams helplessly, he can't stand that word. "Please," he cries.

A dark and bone-chilling chuckle is his only response. "Why should I?" the cold voice asks. A pair of blue eyes glow, this time not disappearing after a few seconds. They remain permanently in the darkness.

"Because I'm not a traitor," Lilac says firmly. The voice chuckles

47

again. Lilac flinches at it. It's just as loud as the voice, if not louder. He puts his hands over his ears, this time they actually burn. He quickly removes them, and he feels his skin start to blister. He cries out in utter pain. The voice continues to laugh, enjoying the boy's cries.

"Oh don't lie," the voice draws. The pain is just too much for Lilac. He hears a distant cry from farther away, a girl's cry. Lilac falls to his knees sobbing uncontrollably, feeling the worst type of pain ripple through his body. "You can't lie to me," the voice says, their blue eyes continuing to glow. "You can't lie to yourself."

Lilac bolts upright in a cold sweat, his breathing erratic. He sits up, his hand on his chest, he tries to calm himself down, but is instantly taken aback by seeing himself in Alex's bed. "Let me see him, assholes," a voice yells from downstairs. Lilac swings his feet off of Alex's bed. His bare feet rub against the soft carpet and clean feeling carpet. If Lilac is in his own room he would have to dodge the clothes and colored pencils that litter his floor. He walks through the hallway that leads to the stairs.

"Calm down, Evan!" he hears Alex yell. He instantly stops in his tracks, recalling what happened earlier. He feels anger and hurt rush inside of him.

"Don't you dare tell me to calm down, you fucking liar!" Evan yells back. "Don't talk to him like that!" Lilac looks through the tiny rails that hold up the stairs railing. Evan's walking over to Austin who stands there with his arms crossed and looks into Evan's eyes almost challengingly.

"Just because *your* bitch fainted" Something frightening flashes in Evan's eyes, Some people might not have seen it but Lilac did. "Doesn't mean that–"

"That's it." Evan practically runs at Austin, whose arm is grabbed by Alex. James grabs both of Evan's arms in a tight grip, making sure that he can't slip out even if he struggles. He still continues to try and get to Austin, mumbling curses under his breath. Lilac walks down the steps, making everyone in the room heads snap to his direction. James lets go of Evan when Lilac goes to stand in front of him, even though he wants to drag Evan as far away from Lilac as possible.

"What the hell are you on, Ev?" Lilac asks, crossing his arms. He doesn't even spare a glance at Alex, and definitely doesn't plan on doing so. It just hurts too much to even look at him.

"Nothing. I'm sorry. That asshole just" he pauses with a frustrated sigh. "Gets on my nerves" Evan says running a hand through his out-of-control curls. "I honestly couldn't care less what that dimwit says."

Austin scowls, "I'm right here you know."

Lilac ignores him and looks around the room. "Where's Mya?" he asks Evan. Evan opens his mouth to answer but is beaten to it.

"She's in the bathroom," Alex says.

Lilac doesn't bother to turn around. "She got sick. My, um, dad already called her mom. She's on her way now." He thinks about ignoring him, but he doesn't have the stomach to. But he also still doesn't want to look at him either.

"I wasn't asking you. But you know whatever" he says coldly.

Alex looks back down at the ground, twiddling his fingers turning to the steps and beginning to walk. "Ok, sorry" he says softly, Alex runs up the stairs and into his room. Austin looks at him as he goes, feeling the hurt radiate from his body. Alex slams and locks the door. Lilac signs running his fingers through his hair.

"We should check on her," Lilac says, referring to Mya. Evan nods his head in agreement, subtly grabbing Lilacs wrist and pulling Lilac along to the downstairs bathroom. James cringes. The sounds of gagging and coughing are heard through the hallway which leads to the bathroom. The hallway is filled with pictures of Alex's family, looking picture perfect. Lilac frowns. It couldn't be farther from the truth. When the pair reach the door, they stand there looking nervously at it and then back to each other.

"Should we knock?" Evan whispers, looking at the door. They continue to hear Mya gagging and a soft whisper.

"I'm guessing" Lilac replies in the same quiet tone. He taps the door softly with his small knuckles.

"Come in," they hear, but it's not Mya's voice. Evan opens the door, Lilac rushes to Mya's side, who's bent over the clean toilet, with

49

her hair being held by Avery, Alex's mom. Her light brown hair tied up in a bun messy, and her pajamas on her slender body. She was beautiful despite her age, but Lilac can't help but resent her. How can he like someone who is okay with what her husband and sons do to Alex? There is also no way she wouldn't have known about it. Because from what Lilac hears, the abuse is constant. Mya throws up again, and Avery rubs her back comfortably. The bitter acid burns her throat as she does so, and her choked cough only makes it feel worse.

"It's going to be okay, sweetheart," she says softly like she's talking to a small child. Lilac wonders if she ever talked to Alex that way.

"What happened to her, Mrs. Miller?" Evan asks, standing next to Lilac who's kneeling on the clean tiled bathroom floor. Avery sighs, continuing to rub up and down Mya's clothed back.

"I'm guessing stress. It can be quite unsettling to find out what we are," she says. Evan and Lilac don't say anything, just continue to stare at Mya worriedly.

"Is Alex ok?" Avery asks after about five minutes of awkward silence.

Lilac snaps his eyes at her. "Why would you care?" he asks rudely. She looks at him, hurt spinning through her green eyes.

"He's my son, Lilac," she says, her gaze burning through Lilac's body.

"A mother's supposed to protect their child. No matter what," Lilac barks back, his gaze is just as sharp as hers.

"You don't know as much as you think you do," she says breaking the stare off between the two.

"And what the hell does that mean?" he says, with all the attitude in his voice. Avery sighs again looking back down at Mya who is wincing at how sore her throat is.

"If Cynthia was here to listen to this. She would be *so* disappointed at the lack of respect" she mutters. "What-" but Lilac is interrupted by a heavy knock on the front door.

"Austin, honey. Will you get that?"

Evan scoffs loudly, "*Austin honey*" he mocks in Lilac's ear. Lilac snickers quietly.

"Yeah, Mom." He walks over to his front door, going over what he's going to say to Mrs. Copper in his mind. That woman hates him, for a reason that's unknown to him. Austin unlocks the door and twists the shiny gold knob to the right. He pulls and immediately scowls when he sees Jon standing in the doorway. A hood over his head and his dirty blond hair poking out of the front. Making him look like a goddamn pineapple. He hates him with a burning passion and not for any particular reason. Maybe it was the smartass attitude, or how he made every little thing a joke. It could be because of his some might say good looks, that make the girls swoon over him. But he could make anyone like him, with a simple word or phrase. Or for god sake even a singular look. And everything thinks he's *so* funny. But Austin sees right through that bullshit.

"Oh, it's you," he says, bored. Jon just laughs at him. "You seem *thrilled* to see me" he replies pushing past him to get in his house. "Where's Mya?" he asks looking around at the nice kitchen.

"Right here" Mya says, her blond hair a total mess and her pale face even paler.

"You ok?" Jon asks her.

"Yeah, I just puked my guts out, but I'm totally fine, J," she says, rolling her eyes and walking out the front door. Not forgetting to glare at Austin as she passes. He can't complain though because he does the exact same thing to Jon when he passes.

"He really hates you," Mya says to Jon as they walk to their mom's car.

"Like I give a shit" he says. He looks down at his sister, continuing to walk.

"Why do you hate him so much anyways?" Mya goes over to the backseat. Knowing the rule about the oldest getting to ride shotgun. "Classified information," she says, opening the door and stepping into the car. Evan and Lilac walk out of the bathroom not saying another word to Avery.

"Do you need a ride?" Lilac asks Evan, looking up at him. He knows Evan's mom works late nights at the hospital, she does what she has to do supporting Evan and herself. And secretly Lilac admires her for it.

"No. It's fine" Evan replies. Maybe he does need a ride but he doubts Mr. Smith will give him one.

"But it's dark outside and, and you don't have your bike," Lilac argues. Evan sighs, going to ruffle Lilac's hair but his pale hand is quickly slapped away.

"I'll be fine, little Li" he reassures. Lilac doesn't say anything about the nickname.

"Please, Ev," Lilac pleads.

"Fine" Evan sighs. Lilac smiles and runs down to the living room, where his dad stands talking to Mr. Miller.

"Dad," Lilac calls.

James turns around, "What? Are you ok" he asks, eyes softening.

"Yeah, I'm fine. Can you give Evan a ride home?" His dad gives him a look, so he quickly adds a quick, "please."

James sighs and rubs his eyes. "I guess, Lilac," he says, annoyance laced in his voice. Lilac gives him a small smile before running down the hallway, to Evan. James sighs again to himself "dammit" he mutters. Andrew laughs from behind him.

"You really hate that kid," Andrew says. James walks over to the wooden clean coffee table, grabbing his keys off of it.

"Yeah, well you hate all of Alex's friends, so I don't want to hear it," he replies, turning back around to Andrew.

Andrew narrows his eyes. "That's not the same thing" he argues. "I don't understand why *you* don't like him. I mean he literally acts just like-"

"Yeah I know who he acts like!" James yells. "That's why I don't want him near Lilac." Andrews taken aback by James's outburst. Yeah, he expected a reaction but not a reaction at that level.

"Uh, Dad?" Lilac asks from behind the two. James turns around. "We're ready to go," he says, with Evan standing behind him.

James throws him the keys, which Lilac catches. "Go wait in the car," he says. "I'll be out there in a minute." Lilac nods his head, walking away to the car with Evan trailing behind him. James runs a hand through his graying auburn hair, before walking over to the Millers dark brown couch where his navy blue coat lays. He slips the jacket on his arms.

"Look, I wouldn't be so hard on the kid," Andrew says. James scoffs "Yeah like you're one to talk," he mutters, walking over to the front door and heading to his car. Evan and Lilac are silent inside, the air around them tense. They stay like that for the whole ride and James is definitely not complaining. When the car stops James doesn't bother to turn back at the sound of two seatbelts unlocking and two doors opening.

"Do you have your key?" Lilac asks, walking over to the passenger side. He rests his hand on the handle of his dad's brown cruiser.

"Yeah, I'm not that dumb, little Li," Evan says. Lilac fondly rolls his eyes "That's debatable." Evan lets out a small chuckle before turning around and walking towards his small house. "And don't fucking call me that!" Lilac calls out before opening the passenger door and stepping inside. "Language," his dad mutters when Lilac is fully seated and buckled into the car.

"Sorry," he replies. "So you're a werewolf, right?" he asks, looking over at his dad.

James looks straight ahead when he answers with a simple "yes."

Lilac runs a hand through his hair. "What am I then?" he asks, hoping for a logical answer of what happened in the woods. He wonders if there's even a logical answer, but he'll settle for the truth. "You're not a werewolf if that's what you're asking," James says, eyes still placed on the road.

"That's not what I was asking," Lilac says, feeling a slight pinch of irritation.

"A mutant," James mumbles.

"Excuse me?" Lilac must have heard him wrong. There was no way, no possible way. It just didn't make sense. Okay never mind, it did actually make some sense.

"A mutant, Lilac!" he yells out.

"B-But How?" That answer isn't logical, not one bit.

"Your parents were mutants and two powerful ones at that." He pauses looking over at Lilac for a split second, whose eyes are wide. "They had you and Violet. Yes, I knew about Violet before you told me. They thought that you were going to be a girl because twin girls runs in your family, your mother was a twin and-"

"Was?" Lilac interruptus. He sees his dad's face harden.

"Her sister died a few years before you and your sister were born." Lilac doesn't go to correct him about the sister comment.

"Is that what the birthmark on my wrist means? A sign that I'm a mutant?" Lilac presses.

"You know what stop with the questions. I think I had enough for the day." James sighs.

Lilac rolls his eyes and huffs. "Whatever, Dad. Or should I even call you that?" he mumbles. James slams on the brakes, which causes Lilac to fly forward.

"What the hell!" Lilac yells.

"Don't ever say that again. You're my son. I raised you; he didn't!" James yells back, looking in his son's blue eyes.

"Okay" Lilac whispers, James feels regret wash over him. "I'm sorry." James says nothing as he starts the car and begins to drive. " Were you and him close?"

James doesn't need clarification to know who Lilacs is talking about. "The closest you could ever be," he says, his eyes still on the road.

CHAPTER NINE

Alex looks at himself through the dirty school bathroom mirror, his eyes filled with stinging tears. His palms resting on the stained and old white sink, he should be thinking about how many germs are on the sink and how many people have put their grimy hands on it, but he doesn't. He just stares at himself in the mirror blankly with tears running down his plain face. His bruises are all healed but his cheeks are tear stained and face pale. He's seen better days. But he's seen worse as well. Alex should be at lunch right now sitting with his friends laughing and talking about nonsense but here he is standing in the bathroom, alone, and too much of a wuss to face his friends. Noah and Jordan are back and he's willing to bet by the looks they were giving him, the looks full of pity, that they know who he is. *What* he is. The real question is if they know what Lilac is. When he saw the birthmark on Violet's wrist he knew that Lilac was a mutant. Before that he had no clue. His dad hates mutants but Alex always thought that they were quite fascinating. He can recall horror stories his dad used to tell him. Stories of war, blood, and betrayal. They were terrifying then and now. But it's crazy to think that Lilac's one of them. Do Noah and Jordan know about him? Lilac won't tell them but Lilac can surprise him sometimes. The bathroom door swings open, he quickly wipes his face with the tips of his fingers and places his palms back on the sink.

"Well, well, well. Alex Miller without his little posse, never thought I'd live to see the day." Alex knows that voice and it makes him cringe.

"What do you want, Shawn?" Alex sighs. Shawn stalks closer to Alex, which makes Alex's cringe increase.

"So where's Mya today?" Shawn asks. Alex can't help but laugh at him. A laugh that holds no humor.

"You really think I'm going to tell you. You're stupider than I thought" he says. Alex can practically see the rage building up in Shawn and he's known him long enough to know that he's at his breaking point. Alex takes his palms off the sink and looks at Shawn who has his arms crossed over his chest. He begins to walk out the door and right before he fully passes Shawn, his lanky body is thrown up against the blue and yellow tiled bathroom wall. Alex winces at the impact. Since when was Shawn this strong? Shawn has his arm holding Alex's body down on the wall.

"Where the *hell* is she?" Shawn asks through clenched teeth. Alex makes a move to get up but is held down. His whole body begins to clam up, but he reminds himself it's only Shawn. Young, stupid, Shawn. No one else.

"She's sick okay!?" He successfully takes Shawn off of him, by sliding his arm off his chest, and pushing him away. "And why do you care anyways? She doesn't go for douches, you know," Alex lies.

Shawn laughs obnoxiously, "Anyone would go for me, Alex" he smirks. Alex clenches his fists at his sides. "I wouldn't be so arrogant," he replies, turning around to walk out the bathroom door. "You're not *that* amazing."

Shawn laughs. "I don't think anyone who lets their own brothers hit them should be-." Alex turns around and his fist collides with the side of Shawn's face.

"Fuck," Shawn mumbles holding onto his mouth that began to bleed. Alex looks down at his knuckles that begin to turn a light shade of red and begin to shake. He has never punched someone before, doesn't even think he's been that angry before. "You-You *bitch!*" Shawn yells. "You wouldn't do that to your brothers, you pussy," he says and laughs again, but bitterly. Alex looks at him, the blood from the cut on his lip starts to drip down and land on the dirty tiled floor.

"You're not either of my brothers, as much as you want to be you are not." he turns around and starts to walk. "It doesn't make you cool, Shawn." Alex stops right in front of the door, his hand grabbing the dirty silver handle. He turns around to get one last look at Shawn before he walks out the door. "It makes you pathetic."

Alex stands in front of the entrance of Jeffreyville middle school, waiting for his brothers to get here. School ended just fifteen minutes ago and Austin is usually obnoxiously early. Allen couldn't care less however The high school is just across the street, so Alex can't fathom why they are late. So he just stands there looking at his phone every few minutes checking the time. He avoided everyone for the day. Noah tried to talk to him in the hallway, but Alex couldn't bring himself to respond.

"Alex," he hears a voice say. He looks up from his phone meeting Noah's eyes. Alex looks back down at his phone, not able to meet Noah's eyes again. "Alex!" he says again.

"What do you want, Noah?" Alex asks, looking up from his phone and turning to face him.

"Why didn't you tell me?" Noah questions.

"Would you really believe me if I did!" Alex snaps "Honestly!"

Noah sighs, tugging on his hair. "I mean it might have taken me a minute but I- ".

"It's a yes or no question, Noah!" Alex interrupts. "No, Alex! I wouldn't have; is that what you wanna hear?"

Alex nods his head to himself more than Noah. "Yeah." Noah can practically hear Alex's heart breaking. "It actually is," Alex whispers.

Noah tugs harder on his hair. "Come on, A. You have to admit, it's hard to believe," he defends. Alex scoffs to himself, slamming his phone into his front coat pocket.

"That's exactly why I didn't want to tell you guys. Seriously, it's not that hard to comprehend," Alex retorts.

Noah can't help but roll his eyes, which makes Alex roll his own. "I'm supposed to be your best friend. Hell, we all are. It really hurt Alex" Noah says.

Alex looks at the sidewalk. "You don't think this is eating me up?" Alex lifts his head.

A car pulls up right beside them causing them both to turn their necks in that direction. The passenger window slowly rolls down. "So very sorry to break up this *lovely* conversation but, Alex has to be going now," Allen says, looking at the pair with judgement in his eyes. Alex turns away from Noah's gaze looking over at Austin's car.

"Wait just a second-."

Alex snaps his head in Noah's direction. "Just let it go," he says to him. He goes over to the back door and makes a move towards the handle but Noah's hand stops him.

"Meet us at the clubhouse. Emergency meeting," Noah whispers. Austin beeps his horn which makes Alex jump. Alex doesn't provide a verbal answer, just nods his head and gets in his brother's car. He watches Noah stand there as they drive away, until his body slowly fades away.

"What did he want?" Allen asks turning around to look at Alex. Alex lowers his eyes, not meeting Allen's, he runs his hands lightly over the leather seats.

"Nothing," Alex says. He hears Allen laugh.

"Don't lie, Alex. Lying's a sin" he mocks.

Alex sneakily rolls his eyes, hoping that Allen didn't see. "I'm not lying," Alex defends.

Allen laughs again turning back around in his seat and looking at Austin who sighs. "We heard him. Alex. Don't try to be slick" Austin says, his evil eyes never faltering from the road.

"What, I can't talk to my friends now?" Alex asks, his voice not wavering in the slightest.

"Does he know?" Austin asks. Wanting a reaction out of Alex. He always wants a reaction. Alex believes he thrives on it. "Or is it only those three sneaky bitches."

Alex snaps his eyes up. "Don't talk about them like that!" Alex yells.

"Oh really?" Austin asks, his tone of voice menacing causing shivers to run up Alex's spin. "And who's gonna stop me, Alex?" Allen and he cackle loudly. "You can't even kill a deer let alone fight me." He looks at Alex through the rearview mirror, a smirk planted on his face. Alex fists clench up. "I don't give a shit, who you punched today." His smirk widens as he looks at Alex's face.

"H-How?" Alex cries softly.

"You can't hide anything from us, Alex." Austin replies.

"And here I thought you were supposed to be the smart one" Allen adds, pulling out his phone.

"Why?" Alex cries again.

"Why what?" Austin spits.

"Why do you do this to me? Is it my friends? Is it me? What did I do?" Tears run down his face freely. They are not tears of sadness; those are much worse and experienced way too often. They are tears of frustration. Why? A question he asks himself all the time. Why does his brothers and dad do this kind of stuff to him all the time, and why does his mom just let it happen? Why?

"Both," Austin says. "You act differently now. You don't treat anyone with respect. I blame your friends, you always were a follower." He pauses, looking at Alex throwing the rear view again.

"I don't want to be in the pack anyways" Alex whispers, Austin or Allen didn't seem to hear and if they did they chose to ignore him.

"Especially that Noah kid." Alex has tears clouding his vision. "Maybe I just need to have a talk with him 'cause you know dad doesn't like him either. So he wouldn't complain."

"He didn't do anything wrong!" Alex screams. "Let me out!" He tugs on the door handle, pushing and pulling, Austin continues to lock it every time Alex unlocks it. "Let me out!" He screams again. Pulling harder.

"Maybe we should just drive to that clubhouse of yours," Austin pushes. Tears are running down Alex's face freely as he continues to pull. He tries to block out his words. But there the only thing he can hear, the only thing that's on his mind. The handle starts to crack. Alex's eyes darken, burning red unlike when his dad or brothers begin to shift. Austin continues to talk but Alex can't hear a word, now. With one last pull, the handle flies off, causing the door to pop open. The movement of the car opens the unhinged white door.

"Austin!" Allen yells. Austin slams on the breaks, which causes all of them to fly forward. Austin hits his chest on the steering wheel, Allen's head nearly hits the dashboard, Alex just sits there clenching and unclenching his hand and staring down at them with wide eyes. Austin turns back in sync with Allen. He looks at the silver handle that was once attached to his car. The handle is dug in, like a hand gripped it so tight that it left an indent on it.

Austin stares at Alex in shock. "You fucking mutt!" he yells. He goes to unbuckle the seatbelt and Alex begins to panic. He pushes the door open, steps out of the car and runs into the woods. Before Austin even had a chance to exit the car, Alex is already gone.

CHAPTER TEN

In times like this, Noah realizes how much of an idiot he actually is. Here he is walking down the pothole filled street, with Violet by his side. She no longer had dirt in her hair but did have the same filthy clothes on her body but had Noah's big puffy blue jacket on.

"Where are we going?" she asks, looking up at Noah with innocence in her eyes.

"To my friends' clubhouse. You know what a clubhouse is, right?" Noah hopes he didn't sound rude. However, she probably can't tell the difference even if he did. Violet nods her head.

"Is Lilac going to be there?" she asks again, hoping to see him again. Noah sighs running a hand through his hair.

"Um, yeah, of course," he replies, looking down at Violet. She was quite beautiful, Noah decided after about three days of knowing her. She has this curious nature about her that Noah has come to enjoy. The only thing fairly creepy was that she did look like Lilac a little too much for Noah to handle. But the way they acted was a million miles apart.

"He hates me," Violet whispers, looking down at her dirty tennis shoes.

"He takes time getting used to new people. It's normal for him," Noah recalls a time where he didn't like Mya. It was first grade when Mya changed schools. She was from some prep school in the next town over, which was Jeffreyville's rival. Even then, Lilac had walls built up and it took a lot for him to tear them down. Once he finally did, everything changed for the group. Noah feels a soft hand grasp his as they cross the gravel filled road that leads them to the woods. He can't help but look at her weirdly as his face flushes a shade of red.

"Dad says you should always hold someone's hand when you cross a road,"Violet says in the same innocent voice.

"Y-Yeah right," he stutters out. He grasps her hand and squeezes it gently.

"Where exactly did you live? You know before you ended up here?" Noah asks.

Violet's been avoiding talking about this, not sure what the correct answer would be. "In a cabin. In the woods with mom and dad." She pauses and inhales a breath, feeling tears well up in her eyes, but she blinks them away quickly. "Finn, Aunt Maven, and Uncle Jax would visit often however." Noah's eyebrows furrow together.

"Is Finn your cousin?" he asks her.

She nods quickly like a bobble head. "Finn's my best friend too. I like to call him Finny sometimes, but he gets really angry. He says some girl at school calls him that too, though I don't understand why" she rambles, with a soft smile planted on her thin lips. Noah's lost.

"So Lilac's your twin right?" Noah wonders aloud.

Violet frowns. "I guess," she whispers back. "I've always wanted a sibling. It can get lonely when mom and dad go to work. Finn and his siblings are usually at school too. I've never met any of his siblings," she says, letting go of Noah's hand as they step into the woods.

"Don't you go to school?" he presses. This all is just so confusing, it just makes no logical sense as Jordan would say.

Her frown deepens. "I want to, but Mom and Dad say it's not safe. They say when I'm more mature, they'll let me go" she replies.

"Why's it not safe?" She doesn't answer, and Noah's painfully reminded of Alex. "Violet, does it have something to do with your dream?"

Violet looks down. "I don't wanna talk about it" she mutters, putting her thumb to her mouth and subconsciously chewing on the nail. The pair don't say anything for the rest of the walk to the clubhouse. Noah did spare a few glances at her just to see that she was all right but he just found her with her head still down. Footsteps are heard rapidly coming at them. Violet turns around, her hand raised, ready for an attack.

"Wait!" Noah screams, seeing a familiar head of brown curls, coming out from the trees. "Alex?" He asks as Alex comes towards him, panting and gasping for air.

"Oh my god–I'm out of shape," he pants out.

"How far did you run?" Noah asks with concern in his voice.

Alex quickly evens out his breathing. "From the road, I basically jumped out of the car; I can't deal with them anymore, Noah. I seriously just can't," he says. Noah sighs, running a hand through his hair. He wants to help him of course but he doesn't know how, he never knows how. "I'm sorry, Noah," Alex adds. Noah stares at him, not looking at him in his eyes. Every time he and Alex get into a fight, Alex always apologizes first, even when Noah is in the wrong.

"We should get going," he says, after a while. "Everyone's waiting."

Alex nods his head, watching as Violet walks side by side, a feeling of disappointment running through him. The only sounds for the rest of the walk are the sounds of the birds chirping obnoxiously, the cold bitter wind, and their own heavy footsteps against the cold ground. Violet and Alex both look down at their shoes and fiddle anxiously with their fingers or the end of their coats, both dreading facing the same person.

"No! This is crazy! Absolutely Insane! I will *NOT* agree to this! No. No. No. *No!*" They hear Jordan yell. Violet looks at the door, her face in a puzzled expression. "Calm down Jordan!" a girl's voice yells back in reply.

"We're not asking you to do this with us!" Jordan snorts.

"Yeah, like you weren't asking me to follow you psychos in the woods, right?" Violet looks up at Noah with the same expression. "Why are they screaming?" she asks.

Noah tries not to make eye contact with her, reminding himself that he'll only get lost in her big blue innocent eyes. And god were they so different from Lilacs.

"When are they not?" Noah hears Alex mutter. He sighs doing the secret knock that's permanently memorized in his head. One knock. Pause. Two knocks. Pause. Three knocks. Pause. One knock. "Enter," he hears. He turns the door knob, pushing the heavy wooden door open. The busy room goes silent as the three walk in. Lilac looks away when Alex and his eyes meet. He doesn't want to say a word to him but he can't help wanting to know what he's doing and if he's alright. But his own stubbornness stops him from saying any of that.

"Okay, everyone out" Mya says.

Noah looks at her questionably. "Wait, why?" he asks.

Mya holds up a purple drawstring bag that's half full. "You don't expect her," she points at Violet, "to wear those clothes all the time, do you, Noah?"

Violet frowns. "What's wrong with my clothes?" She asks, looking up at know.

Noah smiles slightly. "Nothing. I love your clothes. You have, um, great taste in, uh, clothes." Alex can't help but roll his eyes, when he turns around and walks out the door. The rest follow, Noah being the last one to go before reassuringly smiling at Violet.

Mya stares at Noah and Violet, a fond smile planted on her lips. She pulls open the drawstring bag, spilling the contents on the wooden floor. Violet looks at the clothes but doesn't move a muscle. "You can put them on you know." Violet nods to herself, walking over to the pile and begins stripping off Noah's jacket. "Woah! Woah! Give a girl a chance to turn around!" Mya yells. Mya turns around, her back towards Violet as she fully takes off Noah's coat. "*So,*" Mya over exaggerates.

"Do you love Noah?" Violet asks, pulling off the disgusting shirt and neatly folding it before setting it gently on the ground.

Mya's tempted to turn around but decides against it. "Um" she coughs. "Y-yeah? Like a brother you know?" Violet can't help herself but smile, as she slips the light purple pullover over her head and pulls it down to cover her chest. "Why?" Mya asks. "Do you like him?"

Violet can't understand why her face begins to feel hot, like it all of a sudden raised a few degrees in the wooden clubhouse. Was she getting sick? "What do you mean like?" she asks.

Mya sighs looking up at the ceiling, wishing that she didn't say a word. She hates talking about stuff like this. Especially with random people she and her friends picked up in the woods. "Like when you well um *like* someone. Like you enjoy talking to them, you find them attractive, you um also get well nervous around them." The nervous feeling Mya feels deep in her bones every time she's around Shawn. Stupid Shawn. Asshole, dickwad, jerkface, Shawn. A guy she shouldn't want but wants so bad that it's almost pathetic.

"Oh," Violet whispers, smoothing over the creases in the slightly big black leggings.

"Can I turn around now?" Mya asks her.

"Yeah" Violet replies.

Mya turns around looking over Violet making sure that she put the pants and pullover on correctly. Thankfully, she did. She walks over to Violet and picks up the blue rounded hairbrush from the floor. She turns Violet around so the back of her head is the only thing Mya can see. "So do you like him?" Mya wonders aloud, as she attempts to get the big knots in Violet's light brown frizzy hair.

Violet winces with every tug of the brush. "He's very handsome." *Yeah, if that's what you want to call him.* Mya thinks. "And I enjoy talking to him," Violet says.

The knots feel like they're multiplying when Mya gets one out it seems like another one just seems to appear. "Have you ever brushed your hair before?" she says more like a statement than a question.

"Mom does before I sleep," Violet says. Mya stops brushing her hair for a minute and spaces out on the back of Violet's head. But she snaps herself out of it and brushes Violet's hair in silence. "Do you like anybody?" Violet asks, breaking the silence. Mya runs the brush through Violet's now smooth hair. Mya doesn't comment as she removes the brush away from Violet's hair and places it in the drawstring bag. Violet turns to her and lifts her left hand, to place it on Mya's right temple. Mya feels a shock of energy going through her body and pain erupts in her right temple. A pain worse than any migraine she's ever had (and she's had many migraines in her lifetime). Flashes and memories of Shawn cloud her vision. And his voice echoed in her ears. His obnoxious laugh, that rings in her ears. Flashbacks of them throwing paper balls at each other in math class. Them flirting during math class. The meaningless conversations vs. the meaningful ones that Mya's learned to hold dear. A younger version of themselves teasing each other is the last thing she sees before her mind is blank and she's looking back into Violet's eyes.

"Shawn," Violet says clear as day. Mya's breaths ragged as she stares at Violet. Her eyes wide as she watches the blood slowly drip from Violet's birthmark.

"H-H" for once Mya's words are lost. She grabs Violet's other wrist and pulls her out of the clubhouse door, leaving her discarded clothes just lying there. The other five stand outside looking at Lilac who looks to be at his breaking point.

"Mya?" Jordan asks.

"Her-Her she-she," Mya stutters. "

S-S-S-She what?" Lilac mocks, with his arms crossed.

"Show him," Mya urges Violet with a light shove in his direction.

"It won't work on him," Violet says, like it's obvious.

"Well, why not?" Mya retorts.

"Because he's a blue." Mya falls silent.

"I'm a what now?" Lilac asks, as he uncrosses his arms.

"A blue," she says again motioning to Lilac's right wrist.

"She looked inside my mind, guys" Mya says.

"That's-. No way That's impossible," Jordan argues. Alex nods in agreement.

"Maybe it's not," Noah argues back. Violet's face turns into a small smile as she and Noah look at each other. Mya eyes the two knowingly.

"Teach me then," Lilac says, not breaking eye contact with Violet. Jordan scoffs,

"You can't be serious" he laughs in disbelief.

Lilac ignores him. "Can you please teach me?" he asks.

Violet swipes the blood off her wrist. "Ok" she says. She walks up to him and grabs Lilac's right wrist. "You need another person," she says. Lilac walks over to Alex. "Now lift these two fingers." Violet holds up her pointer and middle finger. "And rest it on his left temple." Lilac does as told.

"Like this?" he asks Violet, shifting his eyes from Alex to Violet for a split second. She nods and Lilac puts his eyes back on Alex. Alex doesn't say a word, he watches with curious eyes.

"Concentrate on what you want to see. Clear your mind." He breathes in, feeling the power rush through his veins. He focuses on Austin and the events that he didn't see earlier in the day. Lilac's head feels as if it's being stabbed by a million needles as his head feels with memories through someone else's eyes. His eyes begin to water as he sees everything. The temperate feeling blood drips down when he retreats his hand back. Alex's eyes are filled with tears as he looks at Lilac.

Evan walks over to Lilac and goes to put his hand on his shoulder. "No!" he screams. Evan puts his hand back at his side. "This has to stop." Lilacs blue eyes are wild and blazing as he runs farther into the woods and in the direction of the Miller household.

CHAPTER ELEVEN

Austin can't help but smirk to himself as he smells the familiar scent of a certain Lilac Smith. He pulls up on the metal pull-up bar in his gym like basement, his sweat glistening off his defined abs. The basement is hot and stuffed tightly together with all the work out equipment. The concrete walls make the large room feel like an oversized prison. Lilac's scent stands more promptly in the crowd of werewolves which is rare. Usually he has another counterpart on him, like his dad or that goofy looking Evan kid. But today Lilac's scent stands on its own and the scent is strong. Coming towards his house like a train moving quickly down a railroad track. Honestly, he can't decide if he hates Lilac or just finds him annoying. It's kind of the same thing in his mind. Where the line between hate and like is blurred. Austin jumps off the bar, his expensive tennis shoe covered feet banging off the hard ground. He walks a few steps over to the metal butterfly machine. He sniffs the air again as he sits down on the red leather. Lilac's scent is rapidly getting closer, as if Lilac is rushing towards him. Austin can't feel any less threatened. Austin holds on to the handle, the weight already sitting at 230 pounds. He struggles to push it in then out but quickly begins to adjust to the heavy weight. The timber basement door slams open, slamming on the wall right next to the door. Lilac storms in, eyes blazing with fury. He stops in his tracks when he sees Austin.

"We need to talk," Lilac says with anything but intimidation in his voice. Austin wants to die laughing. If he wasn't the alpha's son he would get eaten alive in seconds. Maybe by him or one of his friends, depends on who would get to him first. Him and that mouth of his. Austin ignores him and continues to pull out and then back in. Lilac's jaw clenches, his teeth grinding together behind his lips. When Austin pushes halfway out, an outside force stops the machine. Austin pushes with all the strength in his body, but the machine doesn't budge. He looks up at Lilac whose thumb and pointer fingers are curved, blue hue coming out of his fingertips and wrapping around the machine halting it. Austin attempts to push harder. Lilac and Austin are staring at each other, challenging one another with their eyes. Austin if possible pushes harder, but Lilacs makes sure it doesn't move. Not even an inch.

"Damn," Austin whispers, looking Lilac up and down with judgement in his eyes. But there's something else in them that Lilac catches.

"What the hell are you doing here?" he says, his voice far from his previous whisper. "Like I said before we need to talk." He drops his hand, causing the handles on the machine to crash together, which makes a loud pounding sound to echo in the quiet room. Austin winces a little at the strong impact. Lilac's gaze lands on the discarded shirt on the floor. He picks it up. It's dampness with what is assumed to be sweat, makes him wrinkle his nose.

"And put a shirt on. Nobody's impressed by your abs," Lilac insults, tossing the shirt in Austin's direction. Austin catches it on reflex, he rolls his eyes at Lilacs previous comment.

"You must be as blind as your boyfriend, Smith," he gestures to his chest and abs, "if you're not impressed by this." Lilac's face flushes a shade of pink and he averts his eyes away from Austin. Austin smirks again. "So what's the issue?" he asks.

Lilac knows he's standing right in front of him. He feels his stomach start to hurt and his palms begin to sweat at his sides. *Jesus Christ Lilac pull yourself together, it's just stupid ass Austin.* He looks back up and into Austin's eyes. "You're really that dense," he fake laughs. "You know exactly what the issue is." Lilac crosses his arms over his chest.

"I don't actually," Austin replies. "Please enlighten me," he mocks.

Lilac rolls his eyes in his head. "You need to stop what you're doing to Alex. It's gone. It's gone way too far." Austin snorts. "And If you stop your little lap dog will."

Austin laughs, genuinely laughs. Lilac feels his blood in his veins heat up. "That's what this is about?" he asks in between his own laughter. Lilac just stands there with his arms still crossed. "What poor little Alex can't take care of himself. How sad!" Austin mocks again throwing, what feels like a degrading, fake pout into the mix.

"Watch your mouth," Lilac says through gritted teeth. His eyes narrowing dangerously.

"Or what?" Austin asks, his eyes glaring down intensely on Lilac. "What exactly are you going to do?" Lilac looks up at Austin, their eyes connecting but Austin breaks the stare off.

"Don't push me, Austin," he says, still not looking Austin in the eye. "You have no idea what I'm capable of." *And neither do I.*

Austin laughs at him again. "Oh how *threatening,*" he mocks. "I'm practically shaking in my boots." Lilac raises his eyes for a split second, then drops then when Austin notices, his palms begin to sweat excessively. "You can't even control your own power." Lilacs eyes snap up, immediately. "Judging by how you suddenly *threw* my brother. You fainted for god's sakes. " He laughs again. His cruel laugh, that makes Lilac's bones shake inside his body. "Could you imagine. A mutant who doesn't even get their powers till fourteen. How pathetic. "

Lilac clenches his fists. "You need to stop right now."

"Oh, come on, Lilac, throw me across the room. Or better yet snap my neck. You hate me enough. Come on *Little Li* do it." Austin taunts. Lilac tries, he really does. He focuses on Austin's body and tries to push him to the wall on the opposite side of the basement. But the power inside him feels as if it evaporated. It disappears like it was never there to begin with. "Aw, how depressing," Austin says with a fake pout. "You're as stupid as you are weak." His face inches from Lilacs. Lilac builds up salvia in his mouth and lunches it at Austin's face, where it lands and begins to drip downwards. Austin wipes it off with his shirt and fists clench at his sides, but Lilacs face stays neutral. "You weak little bitch," he says, his teeth clenched together, eyes darkening fearfully. "You're *so* lucky, you're Alpha James' son." Austin walks away and over to the hundred pound weights that are set near a running machine.

71

"I may be weak but at least I'm not a coward." Austin drops the weights which slam on the ground.

"What the hell did you call me?" Austin asks, stalking over to Lilac.

Lilac looks at him, his smirk gone and it almost makes him back off. Makes him think it's just an act. A facade to show off to other people. To show that Auston's all big and bad, when he's not. Then he remembers Alex and the bruises on his body. The tear stained cheeks and the words he's heard Austin speak. And his anger over powers any feelings of pity. Any and all feelings of understanding for the things he's done. "I think you heard me," he says his eyes on Austin.

"You do realize that you're just making everything worse for Alex, right?" Austin says. Lilac scoffs.

"You're even more of a coward then I thought," Lilac laughs. "Taking everything out on him then me that's what's truly pathetic." Lilac pauses. "Come on Austin. Snap my neck, or better yet just punch me. Or for Christ's sakes do something; you hate me enough, don't you?" Austin doesn't respond, just turns around, the rage coursing through his bloodstream. "What, no comment?" Lilac mocks, his palms have stopped sweating and the pain in his stomach is practically nonexistent.

"Just get the fuck out," Austin says, anger coming off of him in waves. "Whatever, Austin. Continue being a coward." And with that Lilac walks out of the basement, slamming the door behind him and feeling Austin's eyes as he walks away. Austin stands there for a few seconds, millions of thoughts running through his mind.

CHAPTER TWELVE

When Lilac sees his friends, he takes his time to study their actions. Evans pacing back and forth, Jordan's yelling at him to stop pacing, Mya's yelling at Jordan and telling him to shut his face, Alex is standing there looking over his shoulder every few seconds anxiously, while Noah and Violet sit on the ground. Noah looks a bit pale and has his eyebrows furrowed, Violet has the same and repetitive puzzled look on her face.

Evan looks into the woods and makes eye contact with Lilac. "Oh, thank fuck," he says before running towards Lilac. Evan tackles him to the ground roughly, nearly knocking his glasses off in the process. Lilac squirms, as his face begins to flush. "Get off of me, you big oaf!" Lilac squeaks, his face burning red. "God, Li, if you didn't want me to worry you shouldn't have run off like a fucking *psycho*. Like for God's sakes, little Li. " Evan ignores the breathless "Don't call me that," from Lilac. "Like seriously, you had me worried. And when I say worried I mean *worried*. You know I was seriously about to-"

"Evan!" Mya yells from behind the two. "One. You're literally crushing the poor little child." Evan gets off of Lilac and gives a hand to help him up. Lilac graciously takes it. "And two, you are *literally* rambling." Lilac lets go of Evan's hand when he notices the sweat building up on his palm.

"What the heck was that about Lilac!" Alex yells, running up beside Mya. Lilac takes a step forward.

"You can't let them keep doing this to you," Lilac says. He could scream at him. Tell him how stupid he is for caring about people that hurt him over and over again. But it won't make a difference. It's something he has done before. But he can't stop trying.

"You don't know what you're talking about," Alex says harshly.

"I don't. Really, Alex?" Lilac responds, just as harsh. "I've known you my whole life. We've been best friends for as long as I can remember." Alex sighs running a hand and throws his light brown hair.

"I know that, Li," he says.

"We tell each other *everything*. Why couldn't you just tell me?" Lilac cries in response.

"I thought you were gonna hate me," Alex says, water building up in his eyes, he blinks them away.

Tears build up in Lilac's. "I couldn't hate you, you idiot." They look at each other for a moment. No words are exchanged, they both know what the other is thinking. Noah coughs awkwardly behind them. Alex and Mya crane their necks.

"Um, can we talk about why we're all here. Now. Please?" Mya sighs, tilting her head backwards. "Why are we even here?" She repeats, fixing her head back to where it once was.

"Bill," Noah says simply. A silence passes through the group.

Lilac looks down at his dirty white high top converse. "And she's the key to helping us find him." Lilac can't help the snort that comes out of his mouth.

Noah's head snaps roughly in Lilac's direction. "What was that for?" He asks, crossing his arms.

"You don't even know this girl. And what you're going to let her *try* to find Bill, that's pretty stupid, don't you think?" Lilac says as he points to Violet who stands right at Bill's side.

"You're being ridiculous." Noah says. "But that's not unusual for you. Now is it?" he adds quietly.

"What did you just say?" Lilac says making a Jurassic move towards Noah. Evan grabs his arm, successfully stopping him from going at Noah.

"Can we all just calm down, guys? For literally two seconds, so we can listen to what Noah has to say," Mya says. Everyone quiets down. "Thank you," Mya adds in relief.

"Ok fine," Lilac sighs; he looks at Violet holding eye contact with her intensity. "Can you find him? Bill, that is."

Violet shivers at all their gazes at her. "W–Well, I know a way," she whispers. But loud enough for all of them to hear. "Um, it's actually how I found you. But I do need some things," she says.

"What? Anything?" Noah says urgently. "I need another mutant and something that belongs to the person you want to find," Violet replies, staring at Lilac just as intensely.

"Wait!" Alex pipes up. "I have a book Bill gave me a few years ago. It's in my room right now. Would that work?" he asks. Violet breaks eye contact with Lilac and nods. "Ok, well, then let's go" Noah rushes out. They all take a step in the direction of Alex's house, but soon stop dead in their tracks.

"Hold on a second!" Jordan yells from behind the group. "Are we completely *positive* that this is the correct move?" he draws. The group groans in reply, and they proceed to walk in the direction of Alex's. "It's a *completely* valid question because seriously this is–"

"Jordan!" Mya yells in frustration, as she stops and turns around to look at Jordan. "Enough already! Either come with us or walk your happy ass back home!" Mya turns back around, and quickly paces after the rest of the group. Jordan reluctantly follows.

"So how *did* you find me?" Lilac asks Violet who walks on his right side. Evan, Alex, and Noah walk in front having their own little conversation about some stupid book Alex's reading. While Jordan and Mya walk behind them silently. "Finn helped me," she says quietly. Lilac can almost feel the nervousness and tension between them, and he doesn't want to feel guilty, but he does.

"Is Finn your boyfriend?" Lilac wonders aloud.

Violet lets a little giggle slip. "Oh no. Finn's my cousin. Not by blood, of course, but he's father's dad's best friend," Violet says in between her breathy giggles.

"O–Oh um sorry" Lilac laughs awkwardly. "You said you need something. Like an object to find the person you want to find. Right?" Violet nods in agreement. "Then how did you find me?" Lilac asks. He can't help the skeptical tone in his own voice.

"Your baby blanket," she says, turning her head to look at Lilac.

He squints. "My what now?"

She says, "Your baby blanket. I have one, too. Only mine is purple; yours is blue." A smile is on her face, eyes wide and joyful. But suddenly her lips turn into a frown and her eyes squint. "The night before I found you, I wandered out of bed and when I walked past Mom and Dad's room, I saw dad holding on to your blanket; he was crying, and mom was rubbing his back. But she had tears in her eyes."

Lilac looks away from Violet. Her frown deepens. And Lilac remains silent for the rest of the walk to Alex's. "Fuck. Fuck. Shit. Shit!" Mya yells, looking down at her phone. "What happened?" Lilac asks as he turns around to face Mya. The rest of them follow his actions. Mya groans as her phone begins to ping rapidly, she puts her hands on her blonde head. "My mom just got home from work, and she found out that I snuck out. She's telling me to" Mya looks down at her phone, "'Get my ass home, right now.' In all caps." She puts her phone in her back pocket of acid-washed jeans.

"You should go. We'll tell you what happens tomorrow." Noah resounds, knowing that she'll probably be grounded.

"Ok, good luck, guys," Mya says as she runs off. "And be careful," she adds when she's a few meters away from them. They are a few steps away from Alex's house. They even have a clear view inside their windows. Alex sees his parents entering the dark blue car that Alex's grown to hate. He sighs as he watches them drive away.

"Let's just get this over with," Alex says, reluctantly while walking towards his house. He turns the knob of the big white front door. Feeling the doors unlocked. He gestures his friends inside as he holds the door open. His friends hurry inside and go straight to Alex's room. Alex is on their trail and is the last one to enter his own room. He forgets to close his door behind him. The warm winter sunlight comes in through the large shiny window. His gray walls which are partially covered by wooden message boards, that hold the black and white polaroid photos and white bookshelves with perfectly organized multi colored books filling the shelves.

"So where's the book?" Noah asks looking around the clean and familiar room.

"Calm down, Noah; just give me a second," Alex says, crouching down in front of his bed and putting his hands under it. He leans forward until his shoulders are basically touching the bottom side.

He pulls out a long, light wooden box that has a layer of dust on top of it. He swipes it off with the palm of his hand and drops it down in the middle of his bed. He unlatches the painted gold handles, while his friends huddle around him and the box, waiting eagerly to find out what's inside. Alex lifts the top of the box open revealing the contents inside. What lays in there is a children's chapter book with a big red dragon on the cover from bill, a selective pile of more polaroid photos of his friends, a pile of stupid old journal entries, an empty silver flask, a white lighter, and a full pack of Newport's.

"Holy shit, Alex," Evan says, eyeing the Newport's.

"What?" Jordan stands there next to Evan with wide eyes. "What is that stuff?" he asks.

"Oh, um." Alex laughs slightly. "It's stuff I don't want my brothers to find. They always like going raiding my room and stuff so I had to hide all of it," he says as he gestures at the content inside the large box. Alex leaves out the part of them burning things that they find. Countless things have been burned in front of his face.

"Didn't know you smoked," Evan says more to himself than to Alex.

"I don't," Alex responds. They give Alex a look. "Well, I don't do it often, that is."

Evan rolls his eyes. "Mhm sure." He picks up the Newport box. "Out of all the cigarettes never thought you would be the type to smoke Newport's," Evan says, as he opens the box and puts a cigarette in between his teeth.

Alex makes an offensive sound. "Listen it's not like I could afford anything else. I can't just go up to my dad and just ask for money. Don't be stupid, Evan," Alex retorts. Taking his own cigarette from the pack and putting it in between his middle and pointer finger. He picks up the small white Bic lighter. He swipes his thumb quickly down the wheel causing a flame to ignite. Alex connects the flame and the white cotton then puts it to his lips and takes a few puffs to help the cigarette ignite itself. He then inhales the bitter smoke and keeps it in his mouth for a few seconds before releasing it.

Jordan coughs. "Do you have to do that here?" he says, waving his hand up and down. "My parents would kill me if they smell smoke on me. Like Jesus, someone open a window."

Alex ignores him.

"Toss it here," Evan says, pointing to the lighter. Alex does so and Evan repeats Alex's previous actions. The room begins to smell painfully of cigarettes. Alex walks towards the large window that goes without curtains and opens it half way. "Ok," he says, picking up the children's book and tossing it to Noah. "Let her and Lilac do their thing." Noah nods and gives the book to Violet who then sits down on Alex's vacuumed carpeted floor and sets the book directly in front of her.

"Sit down, Lilac" she softly defends pointing to the side across. Lilac does so as his hands begin to shake. "Now set your hand with your birthmark on the book." Lilac and Violet both do at the same time. Their fingertips lightly touching. "Now think of the person you want to find. Focus Lilac. *Focus.*"

The word rings in his mind as he feels himself enter outside his body. He looks around and sees dirty walls in a spacious place with dirt and junk spread all around. A big staircase is set in the middle. The stench of mold and death fill his nostrils. Lilac feels a presence move beside him; his heart begins to beat faster than normal, which makes him turn around hastily.

He sees Violet and is instantly flooded with relief. "Where are you guys?" Noah's voice echoes throughout the assumed house.

"I don't know. A house I think," Lilac yells in reply. His birthmarks tingling which makes him wince. He sees Violet copy his actions. Booming laughter comes from upstairs. Lilac snaps his head in that direction instantly running towards it.

"Lilac what's going on?" He hears Evan yell. Lilac ignores him, focused on who the hell was laughing. Violet appears behind him. The hallways are covered with closed doors. But as the two walk further and further down the laughter gets even louder, but cries also come out of that laughter.

"You're so weak" a girl's voice says. "Can't even interrogate a simple human six year old." They hear a slap and then a grunt.

"I'm actually ten," a child's voice says in the distance.

"Bill!" Lilac yells, he makes a move to open the door, but Violet grabs his arm.

"Don't" she says sternly and with a look of terror in her face, which makes Lilac feel uneasy.

"But it's Bill, this is why we came here, Violet," Lilac says, trying to get his arm out of Violet's tight grip.

But Violet only holds on tighter. "No, Lilac, they'll kill you. Even if they can't see you right now, they'll know you're here and they *will* find you." She says even more sternly than before.

"Please" they hear a teenage boy's voice cry. "I d-didn't do anything," he sobs.

"Oh well, cry me a river," the girl mocks. "A whittle red crying because they're innocent, bullshit." The boy continues to cry. "Get out," the girl says. Sniffles get louder and louder as Violet pulls Lilac arm down the creaking steps. A teenage boy walks out the door, his cheeks red and tear stained. He can't be much older than them and by the looks of it and can't be older than Austin either.

"We need to get out of here," Violet says, closing her eyes and touching Lilac's birthmark. Lilac retreats his hand away from her.

"No!" he yells a little too loudly. "Bill is upstairs. We can get him," he finishes.

"Oh my God," the two of them hear from behind them. They turn around and their eyes meet with a pair of glowing red eyes. His dark black hair falls just over his eyes and his left hand touches the temple of his forehead.

"Taylor, get out here!" he screams, happy tears building up in his eyes. Lilac looks down at the man's wrist, a small star shaped birthmark placed in the center and the other wrist which has the same crescent moon birthmark only with a perfect circle around it and is bloody and scabbed. And looks to be carved into his skin. Lilac wants to vomit.

"Come on, Lilac, we need to get out of here," Violet says again, grabbing Lilac's wrist and this time Lilac let's Violet hold his wrist. He gasps as he's transferred back to Alex's room, blood running down his wrist. Blood trips from his and Violet's birthmark. Noah's hugging Violet from behind, while Evan walks over to Lilac. He goes to put his hand on Lilac's back, but Lilac slaps his hand away. His lips sit in a line.

"I'm fine," he says to no one in particular.

"We saw him," Violet whispers as she takes Noah's hands off her body.

Noah places his hands on her shoulders instead. "Was he alright? Where was he? Do you know who took him?" Noah questions rapidly.

"Hold on a second, Noah," Evan says, breathing in the nicotine from his cigarette. "Let them catch their breaths for a second."

Lilac breathes in and out and rubs the drying blood off his wrist with the end of his t-shirt. "No, I'm good" he breathes in, while running a hand through his damp with sweat hair. "From what we heard Bill's ok. For now that is." Noah sighs as he looks over at Lilac.

"Do you know where he is?" he asks, his hands still gripping on to Violet's shoulders.

"No that's the problem. The house or whatever it was, was really big, almost like a mansion, but it was really abandoned," Lilac says.

"Do you think it was in Jeffreyville?" Noah asks.

"I'm guessing," is Lilacs reply.

"What about the house on Luna drive?" Jordan asks thoughtfully. Everyone turns to him, including Violet.

"What house on Luna drive?" Alex asks.

"That old abandoned big red house. My sister was telling me about it. She and her friends snuck in there a few years ago, when they were freshman, says it was really creepy. Run down too." Evan looks at Lilac. "You think that could be where he is?" Evan asks.

Lilac shrugs. "I don't know, but it can't hurt to look."

Jordan makes a sound of protest. "Woah, Woah, Woah. That doesn't mean I'm gonna go in there 'cause that would just be stupid." He says. They ignore him.

"We'll go Saturday. When Mya's hopefully ungrounded." Noah says.

Alex giggles. "You think she's going to be grounded?" he asks halfheartedly.

"Hundred percent," Noah says. Footsteps rapidly come up the stairs, and deep laughter mixed with it.

"Crap," Alex says, lunging for Bill's book. Violet picks up her hand, shrugging Noah's hands off her shoulder. She levitates the book and makes a pushing motion towards the dresser where the book slides. Allen strolls into Alex's room, as if it's his own, three of his friends behind him, one of them being Erik who Alex probably hates the most. His light brown hair, light brown skin, and cold gray eyes show that you can never judge a book by its cover.

"What do we have here?" Lilac rolls his eyes, but fear is hammering through his body. "Never thought you would be a smoker,

Alexander." Allen's lackeys laugh at the so-called joke. Allen's gaze falls on the children's book.

"Aw, is this your brother's book, Noah? How sad that he's gone missing," Allen mocks. Noah's fist clench.

"What are you going to do about your little brother smoking?" Erik tauntingly asks.

"I don't know; what should I do, Erik the wise?" Allen taunts in the same tone. Erik whispers something into Allen which causes a smirk to come on to Allen's face. A smirk identical to Austin's. Alex can't help the shudder that passes through his body, he just hopes Allen didn't notice it. Allen walks towards Alex and takes the cigarette from Alex's fingers, Alex doesn't protest until he walks over to the dresser.

"Allen, don't!" he screams.

"Shut up, Alex!" Erik yells back. Noah stands up as Allen holds the cigarette by the butt and crushes the white cotton against the book, damaging the cover. The rooms silent for a second until Noah lunges at Allen.

"You asshole," he says. Going at him, Violet stands up and grabs his arm.

"Oh really?" Allen laughs, swiping the book off the dresser causing the pieces of the cigarette to fly all over Alex's carpet. "Don't you dare call me an asshole. Paying attention to some girl when your brother's missing, how fucking sad," he says through gritted teeth. Noah lunged toward him again. But Violet holds him in place.

"You hit your own brother and let the other boss you around like a bitch. So I wouldn't be talking." Allen could have hit him right there, as the vein in his neck comes out and his face turns as red as a fire truck.

"Get the hell out of my house."

Noah turns to Alex. "You're gonna let him kick me out?" Alex looks down. "Just go, guys" Alex whispers.

Allen snorts. "Yeah 'just go' Noah," he laughs.

Noah looks at Alex, Alex sees the disappointment in his eyes. "Whatever. See you at school," he says as he walks out. The rest follow, Lilac being the last to leave.

He bumps shoulders with Erik. "Watch where you're going, kid," Erik says.

Lilac rolls his eyes. "Screw you," Lilac replies, walking down the hallway. Alex frowns at Allen before turning around and sneakily grabbing the box of cigarettes before pulling one out and putting the box inside the wooden crate. "Apologize," Allen demands.

Alex narrows his eyes before dropping the cigarette on the bed. He turns around to face Allen. "For what?" he asks.

"Embarrassing me in front of your stupid ass friends." Alex frowns again.

"They're not stupid," he whispers.

"Sure," Erik snorts.

"Come on. Say it," Allen demands. "*Alex,*" he taunts. Alex turns around his back towards Allen as he closes his eyes. "Say it!" he yells.

Alex flinches, tears springing out of his eyes and rolling down his cheeks. "I'm sorry," he whispers.

"Turn around" Allen says. Alex can hear the laughter from Allen's friends. Allen looks at the tears that fall down Alex's cheeks, in disgust. "Of course you're crying, you fucking pussy," he says laughing with his friends. Alex's fist clenched at his sides. *First it was crybaby, then it was sissy, next it was wuss, and now it's pussy. At least they are coming up with new material,* Alex thinks to himself. "And clean this up before Dad gets home, you wouldn't want him finding about this, would you?"

"No," he says, a pleading look in his eyes. Allen smiles a cruel smile.

"That's what I thought." He turns to his friends. "Let's go," he says to them. They leave, but they don't forget to give Alex a nasty look as they walk out. Alex couldn't give any more of a shit. Allen stops at the doorway. "Just wait till I tell Austin about this." Alex can hear Allen's laughter as he travels down the hallway. He runs towards his white door, slamming it which makes the message board shake. "Slam that door one more time and it's coming off!" Allen screams from downstairs. Alex walks back over to the bed and grabs the wooden box and pushes it back under his bed, leaving the white lighter and the cigarette out. He lights the cigarette before throwing the lighter on the bed and flopping down on his back. He looks up at the white ceiling inhaling the bitter smoke, exhaling it, and repeating.

CHAPTER THIRTEEN

Mya looks down at her chipped Endless Blue painted nails. Just stares at them as if they'll fix themselves. There's nothing better for her to do now that she's basically on house arrest. Trapped in her own room without any form of electronics. No TV, laptop, not even her old d.s. that her mom ransacked her room for. Mya could die. Die unhappily but die none the less. The big red pimple that seems to grow every time she taps it lightly with her finger is what she blames for the pounding migraine. Not the fact that some girl, that she hardly knows, basically entered her mind a few hours prior. Mya shudders at the recent memory. She shudders again by the fact that it's about Shawn. *Shawn*. The name makes her stomach turn into notes as she looks at herself in the circle makeup mirror that sits right next to her bed, on the little school desk her mom insists she keeps. *No wonder Shawn doesn't like me.* Mya thinks to herself as she stretches the skin on her nose revealing the tiny black dots. There seems to be a million of them and Mya feels like they're everywhere. She cringes. *I'm disgusting. A freak.* The door barges open which makes Mya jump and take her hands off her face.

"What are you doing?" Jon asks, an obnoxious smile planted on his lips.

"None of your business," she says, not nearly as amused or cheerful like he is. Jon is always Mr. Happy. Her mom's angel, her pincey. And that is infuriating beyond belief. "And don't you ever knock?"

Jon stands incredibly still like a piece of stiff wood and makes a mock serious expression on his face. "It's dinner time!" he yells extra loud. Jon swipes the remote off her dresser before walking out the door.

"Shut the door!" Mya calls out. Jon walks back over, shutting it but not completely, he leaves the smallest bit open before turning back around and running back down the stairs. If only she could swear. If only. Mya sighs to herself and walks out of her door. The house is warm, and the TV is blaring loudly and switches channels every five seconds.

"Can you just stay on a channel?" Mya asks as she looks at her dad who continues to flip through channels.

"No," he says slurping on the sauce covered spaghetti. Mya rolls her eyes before going into the kitchen. She looks at the long noodles that remind her of slippery worms and the meatballs covered in sauce that make her want to vomit. The once frozen garlic sticks are the only thing that look slightly appetizing and the hot, garlicky smell fills her nose.

"Really, spaghetti again, Mom?" Mya whines, taking a garlic stick from the scraped and burnt up cookie sheet.

"You have no room to comment about anything in this house after the stunt you pulled today," her mom scolds.

"Yeah, Mya" Jon laughs from his spot beside them.

Mya turns to Jon. "Shouldn't you be sucking face with Sam or something?" Mya responds. Her mom turns her face, a tight frown on her lips. "I thought you and Sam were just friends?" she asks.

Jon's face flushes against his wishes a smile on his lips that he always has on when he lies. "We are." Mya snorts, resting her hand on the warm stove top. "Well, what about Mya and that A- Shawn?" Mya's face turns red. "I heard they make out in the hallway." Her mom turns to her, raising her light brown thin brows.

"That is not true and probably never will be." Mya says looking at her mom. She gives her a look. "Stop looking at me like that!" Mya yells.

Mrs. Cooper stands up from her chair with her sauce covered plate. "Don't give me that tone, Mya." Mya rolls her eyes as her mom walks past her going into the small pantry and flicking on the gray switch. Jon turns around a cocky smirk planted on his lips.

"Asshole," she mouths at him.

Jon puts a hand over his mouth. "*Mom!*" he yells. "Mya called me an a–hole," he says.

"Grounded for another week," her mom replies swiftly. Mya groans exiting the kitchen. She walks up to her room, and flops on to the bed, and hopes to get some sleep. She lays awake though, for god knows how long. Tossing and turning violently. Thoughts going a mile a minute.

Her light turns on suddenly, her glasses lay on her desk and she doesn't bother to put them on knowing who stands in the doorway. "You ok?" Mrs. Cooper asks.

"I'm just trying to sleep, Mom," Mya says dismissively.

"So you and this Shawn fellow?" she asks. "You know the rules, we have to meet him before you go anywhere together."

Mya slams her face in her pillow and groans. "He has a girlfriend. And he's definitely not interested" she says, voice muffled.

"You shouldn't like someone who's taken, Mya. You'll only get your heart broken."

Mya turns back on her back. "I know" she sighs, playing with the end of her blanket.

"And I thought you liked Noah," Mrs. Cooper says thoughtfully.

Mya bolts upright. "What? No. Not in a million years. That is just. '' Mya fake gags.

"Ok no need to be overdramatic."

Mya lays back down in her previous position. "You're the one who is spitting out nonsense, Catherine," she replies, using her mom's first name.

Her mother scowls and gives Mya a look. "You better shut up, Mya." She says, "Don't make me come over there." Mya rolls her eyes as she turns to the side, her back facing her bedroom door. She hears her mom sigh. "Goodnight Mya. I love you."

Mya can't help but smile, even though her mom can't see it. "Love you too, Mom."

She shuts off Mya's light and goes to close the door but stops herself. "And you're going to school tomorrow." Mya groans. Catherine slams the door shut and pulls on the doorknob one more time so Mya can't see the golden hallway light through her door. Mya turns on to her back and sighs to herself. Did she like Shawn?

But he's an asshole and some werewolf creature thing. So is Alex, however. Could she like Noah? But she's never had romantic feelings with him. She had a type and Noah didn't fit that criteria. Plus he harbors odd girls in his basement, well she wouldn't call Violet odd. Innocent? Naive? Yes definitely. But *odd* or *weird,* probably not. Thinking about how her and Lilac, and how they were separated or whatever the hell happened, makes her stomach turn. Mya couldn't imagine being separated from Jon or even her nineteen year old sister Madalaine, who's away at college in Pittsburgh. Jesus, this thinking is giving her a migraine. She turns on her right side. Her temple running some would say harshly into the pig pillow pet. As she closes her eyes, feeling a sudden wash of tiredness courses through her. Imagines of Shawn, Noah, Lilac, and Violet fill her mind as she finds herself in a sweet kind of darkness.

Thursday is probably the most normal day Mya had since the beginning of this strange odd week. It is ordinary to say the least. No talk about werewolves, or Violet, or what the hell Violet and Lilac are. The only thing that is said was that they are doing something important on Saturday at noon. Mya didn't even bother to ask Noah if they somehow found Bill and how they did so. By the glimmer of hope that shined in Noah's eyes, Mya had her answer. Shawn didn't try to talk to her, it wasn't like how he would ignore her halfway through class then talk to her nonstop for the rest of eighth period. Sometimes he would not talk to her at all but Mya would always catch him staring at her. But yesterday he didn't even spare a glance at her. Mya didn't know how to feel about it. It feels as if someone's pulling on each of her arms. A devil and an angel, pulling her in two different directions, but ripping her in half in the process. She slams her locker shut, but she can't even hear the sound because of all the kids around her. Slamming their own lockers and talking about things that won't matter in a week.

"Come on, Mya. You're killing me here," Evan says, his hands on his hips.

"I am. Calm your tits," she retorts, turning around to find Evan in a band she never heard of t-shirt. Her mom most likely would know what the band is but Mya doesn't care enough to ask. They begin to walk to the slowly deserted hallway.

"My tits are very calm. My dear, Mya." Evan nearly trips over his legs walking down the long staircase, that leads to the dreaded cafeteria.

Mya cackles at him. "I can't say the same about yours though," he finishes, running towards the cafeteria.

"You little dingus," Mya laughs running after Evans long strides nearly bumping into other kids in the dirty tan hallways. The disgusting heated phony meat smell that doesn't seem to faze Mya or Evan at all, Maybe they're used to it. The two walk over to their normal lunch table and Mya can't help but think that her own cafeteria reminds her too much about a cafeteria scene in one of the cheesy 80s movies Lilac forces her to watch. They have the book nerds, the emo weird kids, the in the middle kids, the boys table, the girls, and just right across from Mya's table are the 'popular' kids who make Mya roll her eyes every time she lays her blue eyes on them.

"You coming?" Evan asks, pointing over to the main line.

"No I'm good. Go ahead," Mya says her eyes falling on to Shawn who checks out of line with his friends or Mya would say toadies stand behind him.

"Ok see ya," he says before cutting line and standing behind Lilac, Jordan, and Noah, ignoring the protests and curses from his peers, Mya smiles to herself sitting across from Alex who's nibbling on his peanut butter sandwich that has the crust cut off while being in trance by the book that sits on the table.

"Um hello? Alex?" she says. He lifts his face, and Mya gets a good look at his right eye. Under his brown eye has a curved purple ring that looks slightly faded in some places. His eyelid has a tiny purple mark that extends up to his brow bone. She hasn't seen him all day, since they only have lunch and seventh period together. Since Alex has ninth grade math and English.

"What happened?" Mya winces, going to trace the bruise with her fingertip. Alex flicks her hand away from his face.

"I fell, Mya" he lies.

Mya stares at him. "On your face?" she asks, she realizes she shouldn't have commented by the look on Alex's face. She's only making it worse and he's just lying to her.

"I tripped on a wire and fell. That's it, Mya nothing else," he says after ten seconds of silence.

"Looking good, Miller," a mocking voice says. Mya looks to the side and sees Shawn and his friends standing at the end of the rectangular table. Their trays of processed food sit at the table across from them.

"Got into Mommy's makeup again," he taunts in a fake baby voice.

Alex rolls his eyes and stares straight ahead and continues to eat his sandwich. Even though he wants to chuck the sandwich at Shawn's stupid head.

"Shut the hell up, Shawn " Mya snaps. Alex drops the sandwich on the small plastic bag before looking at Mya with a questionable look.

"How did you have that bruise on your jaw?" Shawn's face flushes, as his friends look at him with a confused look on their faces.

"Or did *you* cover it up with *your* mommy's foundation."

Shawn's eyes darken when Mya finishes, and Alex sits there stifling his laughter. "You little-"

"What's going on here?" Evans' voice asks sitting on the right side Alex while Noah settles in at his left. "None of your business, Evan," Shawn spits out like poison. He looks Alex up and down, with a disgusted look. Noah stays shockingly silent.

"And definitely not anything important." Lilac rolls his eyes as he tells Mya to scooch over, while Jordan sits next to Lilac. "Then leave," Lilac retorts, picking at the squishy chicken nuggets that sit on his tray.

Shawn looks over at Mya whose eyes are fit into a tight glare. Shawn scowls as he looks away. "Whatever" he says, turning around and walking to his tables where his friends follow. Jordan looks at Mya from down the table.

"I seriously don't know what you see in that ass," he says, biting down on a baby carrot.

Mya cracks a small smile. "Well, what if I said I don't like him anymore?" she asks.

Jordan laughs. "I would say that you're full of shit." Noah claps his hands together before pushing his tray upwards. "Ok movie tonight?" he asks, looking at Mya, who stares at him in confusion.

"What movie?" she asks curiously. Lilac groans throwing a crusty and burnt potato fry at Evan.

"*Evan,*" he whines. "You were supposed to tell her."

Evan fondly smiles placing his chin on the palm of his hand, while he rests his elbow on the table. "Calm down, Little Li. It just slipped my mind" he says honestly.

Lilac throws another fry, this one hitting him straight in the forehead. "Don't fucking call me that, dimwit!" Lilac squeals. While Evan laughs at his reaction. Mya clears her throat, which makes Lilac stop glaring daggers at Evan and makes Evan stop laughing, but still has a goofy smile on his face.

"Well, *anyways,*" she says looking in between Lilac and Evan. "What about a movie?"

"We're all going to the movies tonight and we were wondering if you wanted to come," Noah says.

Mays stares at him. "Well maybe I'll have to ask my mom. But I'll probably be able to." Alex crunches up the plastic bag and gets up from his seat without saying another word. "What happened to him?" Mya asks, looking directly at Noah.

He shrugs. "How am I supposed to know? He obviously doesn't want me around." Lilac scoffs at him, looking at him increasingly. "You're really still pissed at him. Get over it, Noah," Lilac says.

"He let him do it, Lilac , how can I be over it?"

"It's not like it was his fault," Jordan says suddenly. "I mean he was scared. He's always been scared of them." The table falls silent after that and Mya doesn't want to ask what happened, knowing that it's bad. Noah's basically never mad at Alex and when he is there's usually a strong reasoning behind it.

"Hey?" Alex asks, a puzzled look on his face as he feels the tense atmosphere around the table. "What are you guys talking about?" He closes his dark blue lunchbox. "

Oh, just that… Um." Lilac pauses. Mya can see the wheels turning in his head. "Just that we were thinking of doing something before the movie," he rushes out. Thank God Lilac's quick on his feet, Mya thinks to herself.

"Like what?" Alex asks.

"Thrift Shopping," Lilac says. Everyone at the table looks at him.

"Thrift shopping?" Alex asks making sure he heard Lilac correctly."

Yeah, why can't we just go out to eat or something?" Jordan comments. Lilac turns his head to glare at him.

"Because *Jordan.*" Lilac says, turning his head to where it was before. "There's a thrift store like two stores down from the movies and we could take the str–Violet shopping." Lilac pauses again and all of a sudden smiles. "Also I want an 80s jean jacket."

Mya rolls her eyes before saying. "Fine, thrift store it is then." And the others nod in agreement.

CHAPTER FOURTEEN

Alex wonders why he puts himself in situations that he knows are going to be shitty. He definitely shouldn't have agreed to go to the movies, and he *most* definitely shouldn't have agreed to go when his parents are out visiting a neighboring pack. Oh, and also that Mya's brother Jon is the one who's picking him up. All these warning signs and yet he still stands outside Austin's bedroom door ready to ask if he can go. His knuckles grazing over the door just getting ready to knock, the loud music blaring loudly outside the door. He takes in a breath before lightly knocking two times. The music stops playing abruptly and the white door swings open. An invisible cloud of weed wafts at Alex, forcing him to smell the scent of skunk spray with a mixture of dirty laundry.

"What do you want?" Austin asks, looking down at Alex.

Alex struggles to hold eye contact. "I was wondering if we had a pack meeting today or anything," Alex says.

Austin scoffs turning around and sitting back in his bed. "Why don't you ask Noah?" he replies.

"What?" Alex asks, staring at him weirdly.

"Nothing. Nevermind," Austin says, shaking his head. "No, we don't."

Alex nods his head, turning around. "Ok, thanks" he says before beginning to walk away.

"Wait!" Austin calls.

Alex swears in his head, but he turns around. "Why? Plans for tonight?" he asks. Alex looks down at his sock covered feet. "Um, my friends and I were planning on going to the movies." Silence. That's a good thing. It means he's thinking about it and not out rightly saying no. Alex continues to stare at his feet.

"What movie?" Austin asks.

"The new horror movie that just came out today," Alex replies.

Austin hums. "Well, have fun" he says. Standing up from the bed and slamming the door in Alex's face. Alex stands outside the door for a minute, staring, confusion itching at him. He just shakes his head to himself before walking back into his room. Alex opens his closet door and pulls out a plain light gray hoodie that's stained on the end of the left sleeve. He puts it on over his light blue button down anyway. Tucking in the shirt into blue jeans to make it unseen to anybody. He moves to the mirror that stands largely on his dresser. He runs a hand messily through his hair but his eyes keep focusing on the bruise that covers his eye. He runs his fingertips over it wincing at the sudden pain that pops up even at the slightest touch. He looks up at the ceiling and sighs. *Goddamnit, Austin,* he thinks walking across the hall and into the bathroom. He shuts the door and turns the golden lock. The last thing he wants is one of his brothers walking in. He opens up his mom's makeup drawer and pulls out the liquid foundation that she uses daily. She must have forgot it, Alex decides. Turning the silver lid open and putting the small brush on his finger, making sure to get a generous amount of the product on his forefinger. He smears it under his eye repeatedly, successfully covering the bruise. He's mindful not to make it look blotchy, but winces at the pain, tears spring into his eyes which makes it harder to make it look natural. It wasn't the pain from the bruise that will be gone soon that made the tears well up. It was the fact that his own blood is the ones who caused it. When he finishes concealing his eye he takes a step back and looks directly into the mirror. He shrugs at himself staring for longer than was necessary.

Alex's phone suddenly vibrates in his back pocket. He fishes it out of his back pocket and his eyes widen at a text from Mya. '*Be there in about 5,*' the text reads. He darts out of the bathroom and grabs the light brown backpack that sits right by his door, which already has his wallet and a pack of Newport's inside. Alex swings the bag over his shoulders before walking out his bedroom and into the hallway. A chaotic mix of noises fill the once quiet and empty house. The TV blaring downstairs with the crunching of chips in the mix, and the loud overplayed music that vibrates Austin's bedroom door. Alex walks down the steps quietly, his eyes avoiding the fake plastic smiles in the framed photographs that litter the upstairs hallway and walls near the steps. They hang there like some stupid art gallery. Allen doesn't even spare him a glance as he walks past him. Far too fixated on the brainless reality TV show and crunching on the fat filled golden potato chips. Alex most definitely doesn't make an effort to talk to him either. He rather be ignored then yelled at.

His phone vibrates again, he repeats the motion he did previously in the bathroom and reads the text silently to himself. 'Here,' the text simply reads. Alex slips the phone into his front hoodie pocket and slips on his simple tennis shoes, before leaving his house without another word. The large cherry red Kia is squished tightly in the skinny alley. It honestly baffles Alex that a car that size can fit in such a tiny space. Jon sits in the driver's side, his bright blond hair sticking up wildly making him look like a porcupine. His best friend Nick sits in the passenger side, his smile wide as he laughs at something Jon says. His long dark hair falling in front of his eyes. Alex turns around and looks toward Austin's window. His cold dark eyes that peer through the grey velvet curtains, fixed into a glare. Alex shivers at an invisible wind as he turns around running to Mya's mom's car. He observes that Jordan's sitting on the right complaining about something that's more than likely pointless. Alex opens the car door and steps inside the car that smells of faded pink sand air freshener.

"Hola," Mya says, smiling, showing the small gap in her front two teeth. Her parents won't buy her braces like they did for her older sister. They say she'll just ruin her teeth anyways. Silver hoops dangle from her ears, her blonde hair in out of control curls, and the light blue sweater that matches her eyes that are lightly dusted in eye shadow and her blue and black tube socks that go over her jeans.

"Did Lilac make you dress like that?" he asks. She rolls her eyes at him, dramatically .

"No," she breathes out. "I'm trying out a new style."

Jordan snorts as the car begins to move. "A style's one thing to call it" Jordan says sarcastically.

Alex stifles his laugh when Mya hits him over the head. "So that's Austin's brother?" the three hear Nick ask, subtly giving Alex the side eye. Alex feels his heart start to beat faster and his stomach drops as he hears Jon and Nicks quiet whispers.

"Yep," Jon whispers back, equally as terrible as Nick. They both are idiots but Mya can't stay mad at either of them as much as she wants to. She's known Nick ever since she was three, when Jon started to wrestle with Nick. Then Nick's older brother, Brian started to date and Mya's sister the summer before their freshman year of college, and they've been going steady ever since. People thought she had a crush on Nick but truth be told she never has and probably never will look at him in that way. That's like her having a crush on Evan. Gross.

"I mean he doesn't look like a total jackass," Nick responds, giving Alex another look. "I mean he's kind of scrawny and sorta shy looking *and-*"

"Can you be any louder" Mya screeches.

Nick doesn't turn around, but Mya can hear the laughter in his voice as he says. "I mean yeah." He pauses. "Probably." Jon laughs at him like a lunatic.

As Mya desperately wants to exit the car by any means necessary, she murmurs, "Idiots." Leaning her head on the back of the tan car seat as she listens to Jon and Nick's obnoxious laughter. Alex spots Evan, Lilac, Violet, and Noah standing outside 'thrift and things'. Violet and Noah hold their handlebars as they watch Lilac and Evan argue. Well, Lilac yelling at Evan and Evan laughing at him. Jon parks right outside the small almost run down looking store. "Ok, this is our stop," Mya says, unbuckling her seatbelt, and ushering Jordan out the door.

"Thanks for the ride," Alex says softly, exiting the car after Mya's door slams shut.

Nick sighs dramatically, putting his hands on the top of his head. "You sure that's Austin and Allen's brother?" he asks looking over at Jon. Jon rolls his eyes, starting the car backup and pressing harder than necessary on the gas, strapping himself in for one of Nick's long rants. Alex knew that he shouldn't have even stepped a single foot in that car. He isn't even allowed at Mya's when Jon's there let alone having him chauffeur him around. God if Austin knew, Alex would be as good as dead.

"Can't you just shut up!" Lilac yells, his fierce glare focused on Evan who just laughs. Lilacs face contorts into rage, turning a bright shade of red. Evan laughs even harder while Jordan and Mya try to hide their smiles. Lilac storms into the small store ignoring Evans fake apologies as he follows after him. Alex is the last to enter and in instantly a pleasant smell of cheap perfume and old fabric tickles his nose. Lilac and Mya dart over to the old rusting racks of clothing, even though Alex knows neither of them have money. Jordan, Noah, and Evan run to the weird random section where clown sculptures, shattered mirrors, and old dirt crusted Christmas decorations lay. Evan insists that he collects all those things. Violet stands only a few feet away from Alex, her blue eyes running wildly around the store. Alex looks down at his shoes digging them into the ground. He looked up his eyes shouting directly to the book section where the walls are lined with shelves. The sound of soft pop music and his own friends laughter echoes in his ears.

"Do I look like Taylor Swift?" Alex hears Mya ask. A black velvet derby hat on the top of her head at an angle.

"You wish," Lilac laughs. Mya scoffs removing the hat from her head and slapping Lilac on the stomach with it. Her face set in a scowl but her eyes showing nothing but humor. Alex sighs quietly to himself, turning away from Lilac and Mya, who are both stacking hats on their heads. And who are also receiving vicious glares from the middle age employee who stands at the cash register, bored.

Alex coughs loudly attempting and successfully getting Violet's attention. She turns to him looking at him intently in the eyes. "I was about to head over to the books. Wanna come with?" he asks her.

Violet smiles. "Human books?" she asks hopefully. Alex can't help but look at her weirdly. Sure, he's a werewolf but he doesn't say 'human books,' but how can he blame her?

"Yeah, I guess you can call them that," he responds. Her smile widens as she follows Alex towards the books. The bookshelves are terribly unorganized which makes Alex cringe. Nonfiction thrown with fiction. Hardbacks lined up with paperbacks. The smaller books put ahead of the taller ones.

"I've never met a werewolf before," Violet says suddenly.

Alex coughs awkwardly. "Um ok," he says, focusing on the books in front of him.

"I've only read about them. They say they are really aggressive and scary," she says, eyeing Alex wearily.

Alex rolls his eyes as he turns to Violet. He crosses his arms. "Yeah well they say mutants are spoiled annoying brats. So I guess you shouldn't believe *everything* you hear," Alex replies.

Violet frowns at him. "I'm sorry," she says,

Alex sighs, turning back to the books. "It's ok. It's not like it's your fault." He pauses, picking up a random book and flipping through the pages. "So did Noah teach you how to ride a bike?"

Violet blushes. "Yeah. I'm not very good though. We usually go when it's dark, he says we're going to go tonight."

A small smile grows on his face. "That's great," he says.

"Hey," a voice says behind them. Alex turns around seeing Noah standing behind them. "We're about to go."

Alex nods his head in response. Before turning back to Violet. "You can borrow some of my books if you want," Alex says to her.

She smiles again. "Thank you." Alex smiles at her turning back around and walking hastily to catch up with Lilac, who just walked out of one of the aisles. "He seems really nice," Violet says to Noah.

"He is," Noah replies, watching Alex walk away. Violet walks to Noah's side, and begins to walk past him until she feels a hand intertwined with hers. Butterflies erupt in her stomach and her heart starts to race. "But we're not crossing a road," she says.

Noah smiles down at her. "I know," he says, his hands still grasping hers. The Jeffreyville Cinema was the only consistently crowded place in their slowly dying town. Bright purple and red lights shine in the darkening sky. The red brick pillars holding up the tan oddly shaped structure. Movie posters hung up on either side of the large movie sign. Noah and Violet walk in, hand in hand and the smell of buttered popcorn being the only scent around. A young teenager stands at a purple pillar, that sits in front of an average sized TV that shows a list of movies playing. The teenage girl chews on her gum loudly, her short light blonde hair falling in front of her eyes.

"Um, two tickets for *What Lurks Under The Bed,* please" Noah says, finally letting go of Violet's hand. The girl doesn't say anything just pulls out two red and white tickets and slides them across the pillar. "Eighteen. Right?" Noah asks, a wrinkled bill in his hand. The girl nods obviously annoyed with the question. Noah hands her the twenty, taking the tickets off the table, but not forgetting to grab the two dollars off of the girl. "Uh, thanks," he says before walking over to the Refreshments area where his friends stand. Violet feels her palms begin to sweat as she looks around at all the people who stand in the theater lobby. About a week ago she's never even seen a human before and now she's surrounded by them. Her mom would kill her if she knew. "You ok?" Noah asks, his eyes gentle and his voice concerned.

"Never seen this many people before," she says, looking around shyly.

"You'll be fine; you have super powers for god's sake." Violet looks at him weirdly.

"Super powers?" she asks.

Noah sighs. "It's nothing. Let's go get some popcorn." Violet doesn't even bother to ask what popcorn is, she just decides to follow Noah.

"Wasn't that lady a bitch? Didn't even say a word," Mya says when Violet and Noah get to them.

"Bitch?" Violet asks innocently.

Evan makes a fake sound of distaste. "You corrupted her, Mya!" Evan yells, which makes a few bystanders look over at him. "You've corrupted her!"

Mya rolls her eyes in response. "Three cokes, five popcorns, and a water," the middle-aged man says placing all the items in front of them. A chorus of thank you's shortly follows.

Noah frowns at them. "You ordered without us?" he asks.

Jordan looks at him. "Um yeah," he says as if it was the most obvious thing in the world. "You two were too busy smooching rather than walking." Noah's face flushes while Violet just blinks at him. Lilac inwardly gags.

"Oh shit," Mya says suddenly, the grip on her medium sized cup tightening, almost popping the plastic lid off.

"Ok, cut it with the language, Mya" Noah says softly glaring at her.

"No, look!" she defends pointing at the entrance.

"Oh shit" Noah echoes. Alex stomach drops as he watches Austin and his friends stroll in.

"That fucking asshole," Lilac says from beside him, but his voice is muffled in Alex's ears. Alex nearly drops his water as he and Austin make eye contact. Alex breathes in a shaky breath before he runs to the bathroom, ignoring his friends' protests for him to stop.

CHAPTER FIFTEEN

Lilac Smith is pissed. Not irritated. Not angry. Not even furious. But completely and utterly pissed. And all because of one asshole. The asshole? Austin Miller. Lilac shouldn't be surprised though it's not like this is something Austin wouldn't do. How did he know though? Did he sniff Alex out? Werewolves can do that, right? Austin strolls past the ticket booth, his hand in the back of a bleach blonde's back jean pocket. Lilac sighs and shakes his head. *Disgusting,* he thinks to himself. Lilac hears Alex let out a shaky breath from beside him, and the next thing he knows Alex is running away.

"Alex, wait!" Lilac yells after him. Alex just continues to run, not daring to turn around and meet Lilacs eyes. Austin laughs loudly, which makes Lilac clench his fist and his blood begin to run cold. Him and Austin lock eyes, Lilac scowls as Austin's smirk widens.

"Lilac," Evan says, tugging lightly on his arm. Lilac turns around peering into Evan's soft and warm dark brown eyes, spotting the little hint of green in them. "Don't let him get to you." Evan breaks eye contact, looking at Austin, his eyes glaring. "He's most definitely not worth it."

Lilac nods in reply and wiggles his arm out of Evans' hand. "I'm gonna find Alex," He says, looking directly at Noah whose eyes are fixated angrily on Austin. He shoves his way past them, his feet banging on the techno colored carpeted floor. He runs up the fat ramp that leads to the movie theaters main bathroom. His thoughts running rapidly inside of his mind, the rage still burning in his veins, his stomach that's twirling in big thick knots. The bathrooms in the theater go without doors, the woman's bathroom just one turn to the right while the men's is down a long thin brick red hallway. Lilac can hear Alex pacing halfway through the hallway. His hand probably tangled in his thick brown hair, knotting it.

"Alex," Lilac says, standing patiently in the open doorway. "I just don't know what to do anymore," Alex says, his voice full of defeat, like the smallest act has finally shattered him into a million little pieces.

"Alex, it's just the movies. We don't even have to go near them." Lilac cries softly. "It's not just today, Lilac!" Alex shouts, tugging on his hair one last time one last time before letting go of it completely. "It's yesterday and the day before and the day before and probably tomorrow. Cause they hate me so much that they have to freakin' hit me." Alex holds back his tears that he can physically feel building up. He can't cry. He absolutely positivity refuses to. Crying just makes him feel weaker. Makes him feel like more of a pussy.

"I don't know what you want me to say," Lilac says with a hopeless expression on his face.

Alex scoffs. "I don't want you to say *anything*," he says shoving his way past Lilac. "I'm fine." But Lilac knows he isn't fine, far from it. Every time the topic of Austin is brought up, it's like barbed wire is wrapped around Alex's throat. Not letting him say a word when he had so much to say and scream. Alex knows he can leave. Leave the pack. Leave the people who were practically ripping him apart from the seams. For some stupid reason something inside of him makes him stay, a feeling deeply imbedded in him, that it keeps him wrapped around their fingers. God, he's an idiot. The theater's lights are still on by the time Alex and Lilac arrive. Lilacs eyes scan the rows and rows of seats before spotting his friends who sit directly in the middle of the plaza. Mya on the end, Jordan next to her, Evan next to him, two empty seats, Noah, then finally Violet who sits on the other end.

Lilac then realizes that Alex's hands are empty. "Where's your popcorn?" he asks Alex.

He shrugs in response. "Threw it away," he says dismissively. Lilac decides not to push him into explaining further. The two walk up the oddly shaped steps, that are lined with neon pink lights making them stand out prominently in the darkening theater.

Lilac slides in next to Evan, who smiles at him when he sits down. "Took you long enough," he says.

Lilac side eyes him, giving him an annoyed look. "Shut up" he responds. When Alex sits down, he snatches a piece of popcorn from the top of Noah's light brown paper bag. Noah looks at him but Alex pretends not to see. Suddenly the door swings open and three sets of laughter follow suite, the sound echoing through the quiet theater. Nick, Jon, and Sam emerge from the shadows, instantly spotting Mya and her friends in the somewhat crowded the seats.

"It's like a fucking family reunion," Evan says with a laugh. Jordan shushes him, which results in Evan mockingly sticking his tongue at him. "Hello, Mya's chums," Jon says in his annoying voice.

Mya narrows her eyes at him. "What are you doing here, loser?" she asks.

Jon wraps an arm around Sam's shoulders, causing her cheeks to redden. "Thought I would take my lady out."

Sam removes the arm. "Don't call me your lady," she says, with a roll of her hazel eyes.

Mya turns to Nick. "What's your excuse?" she questions. Nick shrugs not giving any type of verbal answer.

Sam looks over at Noah, nodding her head a bit. "Noah" she addresses.

"Sam," he says back. He's still going to be furious at her. Acting like everything's okay when it's not. Practically refusing to say Bill's name. Pretending that he's not even missing. It makes Noah sick in the stomach.

"So who's this?" Sam asks, motioning over to Violet who looks at her with widened eyes.

"None of your business Sam," he says, the anger rising in his chest.

"Ok no need to get attitude" she snaps. "And it is my business. As much as you don't wanna be, you *are* my brother."

"Yeah well so is Bill." Sam falls silent, her jaw clenched as she walks one row behind them, not uttering another single word.

"Harsh, Noah" Evan whispers.

"Well, it's true," Noah responds.

The lights begin to dim, leaving only a strand that runs down the middle. *Maybe he's going to a different movie,* Alex thinks, but he still can't stop looking cautiously around the theater, just waiting for Austin to come in. A light tap on his shoulder makes him jump and quickly turn around.

"Oh sorry." Nick says. "Didn't mean to scare you."

Alex let out a laugh of relief. "No, it's ok" he responds.

"I just wanted to say sorry about what I was saying in Jon's car" Nick says. "It was really dickish."

Alex gives out another laugh. "It's fine I-"

"What's fine," a voice says down from them. Alex swings his head in that direction, staring into Austin's hard eyes. Nick slaps Jon on the shoulder, who's deep in conversation with Sam.

"What-" he asks before realizing who's standing across from him. Jon smirks, "oh Austin best friend."

Austin greets him with an eye roll. "Fuck off," he says.

Jon laughs along with Nick who snorts. "Aw how sweet," Jon says. Austin ignores him, his friends huddle behind him and the petite blond stands next to him with her arms crossed and her right hip pointed out. "What's fine," he repeats, staring at Alex who's avoiding eye contact like the plague.

"Why don't you just leave him alone?" Mya snaps.

"Why don't you just get out of his business?" the other blonde girl says. Mya looks her up and down, unimpressed.

"Trust me I wasn't asking *you,*" she says. "I don't associate people who hang out with assholes." Evan laughs from beside her.

Austin scowls at him. "And what are you laughing at, you act like I won't beat your ass again."

"What? can't take on someone your own size?" Sam scoffs. Austin goes to say something back but is thankfully interrupted by a loud outside voice.

"Take your seats!" The usher yells. "Silence any and all electronics and no talking during the movie." Right before the lights fully go out and the trailers start, Austin gives Alex a look. A look that says *you are not getting out of this.* A look that makes Alex shudder. A look that replays in his mind all through the uninteresting trailers. The movie was just as boring. The movie followed any other basic horror movie plot.

A basic brunette finds out there's something evil in their town, she almost dies but unrealistically survives, girl best friend dies, few jump scares, and add in some dirty sex jokes, and boom you have the movie. By the last fifteen minutes Alex has had enough. The obvious fake blood begins to make his stomach hurt. He gets up out of his chair.

"Where are you going?" Noah whispers.

"Need some air," he replies, catching Austin's attention. He wiggles his way through his friends' legs. He walks down the glowing steps trying to be as quiet as possible. He snatches his book bag off his back, opening it and pulling out a pack of new ports, looking left and right before heading out the back exit, the smell of artificial butter making him even more sick.

The air is cold, and it makes Alex immediately shiver. He lights the cigarette, his hand blocking the wind from disturbing the flame that ignites from the small lighter. He leans against the brick wall, blowing out the smoke and letting it dissolve in the air. The bitter taste filling his lungs. Alex watches the sky as he smokes, the mix of a soft pink , an even lighter shade of purple, and an enormous burst of bright yellow. He sighs to himself. He needs to leave the pack, but at the same time he can't. He can't leave his family, there's no way. He can't not talk to them for the rest of his life, he can't handle it. Even after everything, he couldn't. The heavy door swings open and Alex quickly throws his cigarette on the ground and crushes it under his shoe.

"I thought Allen was lying," Austin says as the door shuts behind him. "I thought there was no way Alex, Mr. Angel, would ever smoke cigarettes. They're far too dirty for him," he mocks in a fake posh accent.

Alex finds his blood boiling. "What are you doing here?" Alex asks. Austin's face hardens.

"What are you doing getting rides from Jon Cooper? Didn't I tell you to stay away from him?"

"Why do you care?" Alex finally snaps. Austin doesn't reply. Alex scoffs. "You know what I don't even care what you have to say." He pushes himself off the wall and goes to pull the door, but Austin grabs Alex's arm, stopping his movement. Alex panics as soon as Austin's hand is on his body his stomach begins to ache, and his heart beats fast. "Let go," he squeals attempting to get his arm out.

"No," Austin argues, pulling on him. Alex nearly falls if it wasn't for Austin holding on to him.

"Austin, stop!" Alex screams, getting his arm fully out and two hands shoving Austin away from him. Austin stumbles a bit but doesn't fall. The pit in Alex's stomach increases.

"Shoot." Alex whispers to himself, taking a cautious step backwards knowing what's going to come next. Suddenly, the door opens wildly, Noah, Violet, Jordan, Evan, and Mya run out with Nick, Jon, and Sam trailing closely behind them. Austin laughs steadily.

"Need your friends to protect you," Austin sneers. Noah pulls Alex behind him. Austin takes another step but blue hue from Violet's fingertips trips him up and drags him down. She flings him back into the plaza and closes the door tight before successfully locking it without using one finger on the door. Sam gasps, staring at her with wide eyes.

"What the-. You just-" Sam can't find the right words to say. Everyone's silent except for the light wind and everyone's ragged breathing.

"Ok. If no one else is going to ask," Jon finally says. "What the fuck is going on?"

CHAPTER SIXTEEN

The silence in the air is thick after Noah explained everything. No one interrupts him, they just listen to the unbelievable story he was telling. If it was any other day Jon wouldn't have believed it. It would just be some weird little thing that his odd little sister and her friends came up with.

"So let me get this correct," Nick says. "That guy over there," he points to Lilac who rolls his eyes.

"I have a name you know," he says. Nick ignores him. "And that girl." He points to Violet. "Are twins who are also mutants or whatever."

"We don't know exactly what they are," Noah specifies.

Nick nods slowly. "And you found her in the woods, while you were looking for some kid."

"Bill," Noah and Sam say at the same time.

"And Austin is a werewolf and so are you." Nick looks over at Alex, who nods.

"They're werewolves!" Jon exclaims. "Werewolves. Austin, Sheriff James, you! This is so ridiculous!" Jon takes a large step towards Alex.

"Jon, stop," Mya says sternly, her eyes flickering towards Alex then back to Jon. "Just calm down," she adds.

"No, I'm not just going to calm down, Mya," he nearly shouts. "He's the one who put you in danger because of his own problems!" He motions to Alex who stands there looking down at the floor then back up at Jon. The door swings open abruptly, Austin runs at Jon and slams him up against the brick wall just inches away from where Alex stands. Lilac stares at Austin with wide eyes. Austin gets close to Jon's face and Jon can feel his ragged breathing. His eyes were dark, and the veins bulging out in his neck. Even Austin's friends look at the situation with scared eyes.

"Let him go!" Nick yells, despite his fear making a move towards the two. One of Austin's friends grabs his, Nick smacks the arm away, but stays where he stands.

"No, he's not going to talk to him like," Austin growls lowly in his throat.

Alex wrings his shaking hands together. "Austin, it's fine I'm-"

"No, Alex, it's not fine!" Austin interrupts. "He's not going to talk to you like—"

"What you do is worse," Lilac snaps. Alex jabs his elbow into Lilacs side which makes him wince. "Stay away from him," he says to Jon, before he gets off of him completely. Austin turns to Alex and walks towards him. He grabs his forearm tightly, Alex winces at the pain, his skin reddening under his hoodie.

"Wait-" Alex begins but is quickly cut off.

"We're leaving," Austin demands, practically dragging him to his car. Alex turns back, looking through the bodies of Austin's friends to get a glimpse of his own. Lilac has a deep frown on his face and looks like he's about to run over and grab him away from Austin. The others all have similar expressions except Violet who looks around aimlessly. Alex makes eye contact with Nick who looks at the scene with fury and confusion in his eyes.

"Asshole," he mouths at Alex, who can't help but smile. Austin basically pushes Alex in the back seat of his car. Alex sighs to himself looking out the window and peering at the lilac colored sky as Austin's friends get in. And as Austin drives away, his large hand resting on the girl's thigh, Alex looks at the slowly darkening sky. Lilac runs away when the car is no longer in site. His fists clenched and his frown deepens. He's stupid. The stupidest person known to mankind. Tennis shoes slam on the ground behind, successfully following him to the thrift store where his bikes parked.

"Little Li!" Evan yells from behind him. "Little Li!" Evan grabs his shoulders to turn him around.

"Stop calling me that, you mouth breathing idiot," Lilac grits out.

"Mouth Breather and idiot mean the same thing, Li." Evan laughs in response. Lilac removes Evan's hands from his shoulders.

Evan is always irritating but right now he seems to be unbearable. "Fuck off Evan," he snaps, walking hastily towards his bike. He kicks up his kickstand, and hops on the leather seat. Evan follows his actions. Lilac grips his handlebars and begins to pedal.

"What's your deal?" Evan asks, riding up beside.

"I could've gone after him," Lilac states vaguely, looking at Evan in front of the side of his eye.

"Who? Alex" Evan questions in disbelief. It's not Lilacs fault, it's not Alex's either. And Evan realizes that they both need to stop blaming themselves. Austin and Allen are unbelievable assholes, simple as that.

"Yes Alex. Who else?" Lilac says in a 'duh' tone.

"Well excuse *me,*" Evan exaggerates. Lilac rolls his eyes at him. "But seriously Lilac you can't keep beating yourself up over this" Evan says. "For as long as I can remember Austin's always been a dick. Once a dick always a dick. You know." Lilac looks at him again and frowns.

"People can change," Lilac says.

Evan scoffs, "Not people like that." Lilac looks straight ahead, the darkening sky above him, creating a chill in the air. He doesn't want to talk about this, he'd rather talk about paint drying than this.

"You're riding home with me?"

Lilac asks. Evan snorts. "Not like I have anything better to do," he says.

Lilac turns to him. "What, Mom working again?" Lilac questions, his eyes remaining on Evan.

"When is she not?" Evan whispers so quietly that Lilac barely picks it up. "She's working the late shift tonight," he says normally this time.

Lilac frowns again; he hates it when Evan rides home alone in the dark, it's even worse now with the Bill situation. "I can ask my dad to give you a ride home." Evan shakes his head. It was stupid for Lilac to even say that. He and Evan both know what his answer would most likely be.

"It's fine. *I'll* be fine" Evan reassures.

Lilac's frown increases. "But Evan- wait maybe you can stay over. I can sneak you in my window or-shit!" Lilac screams almost running into a stupid tree that sits in the middle of the sidewalk. But luckily he turns hard on his handlebars, successfully dodging the tree.

"Better watch where you're going, little Li. Wouldn't want to break your *delicate* bones." Evan laughs.

Lilac looks straight ahead and rolls his eyes. "Ha, Ha, Ha. Evan, how funny, I nearly peed my pants," he says in a monotone voice.

Evan laughs again, peering at Lilac from the side of his eye. "Also I can't stay over. It would completely fuck up tomorrow's plan, and I'm not trying to have Noah on my ass." Evan pauses, taking in Lilacs narrowed and pinned together lips. "Speaking of which. You nervous for tomorrow?" Evan asks. Lilac shrugs, not wanting to talk. The past few weeks have felt like gun fire coming at him and there's nothing he can say or do to stop it, he just stands there defenseless. Lilacs oddly silent for the rest of the ride to his home. He knows he's being petty, acting like a brat all because he didn't get his way. He's being irrational, he knows that for certain. But it isn't about the fact that he didn't get his own way, it's the fact that he feels like he has zero control over anything. Austin and Allen, Bill going missing, his mystery "twin" showing up, and now he can't even get Evan to listen to him. God, what has his life come to?

The front porch light shines in the darkness, making Lilacs' house stand out in the field of dark houses. "Well, I'll see you tomorrow, little Li," Evan says; Lilac can see his soft smile in the night.

He copies it, but he can't help but wonder if Evan can see it. He peddles past him, the same smirk still on his lips. "Don't call me that," he sings songs, standing up on his pedals. Evan's laughter gets more and more distant as the seconds drag on and by the time Lilac has his bike parked right by the wooden stairs, Evan is gone. The wooden stairs creak with every step, and the bitter wind makes Lilac shiver. The frigid silver door knob makes Lilacs hands tingle when he turns out to the right. The warm and sweet smell of coffee hits his nose as soon as he walks into his house. He slips off his old white converse, without untying them. Being worn so many times made them easy to slip on and off. Lilacs has had the shoes, which now have begun to stink, for two years, and just didn't have the heart to throw them away. His dad is sitting on his lazy boy with the recliner out and his body leaned back, a large cup of piping hot coffee in hand. The pot sits on the kitchen table, half way full. Lilac runs to the cupboards and pulls out a light purple medium sized mug. Alex got it for him for his fourteenth birthday. He didn't even bother to wrap it, just handed the thing to him at school with a small smirk before walking to class. It was confusing for him at first, but after a few seconds of standing there like an idiot he put the mug in his locker and carried on with his day. Lilac smiles fondly at the memory, even looking at the mug makes memories flood back into his mind. He grabs the vanilla powdered creamer that sits next to the large array of coffee mugs. He goes back to the kitchen table, and pours the coffee into the mug, filling it more than half way. Steam shoots up from the cup, reminding Lilac of cigarette smoke. Lilac's eyes flicker over to the open living room doorway. His dad is too engulfed in the terrible comedy movie to even notice his presence. Lilac almost doesn't want to step one foot in there or say a word to him. He feels like a complete stranger, like this man that raised him is someone he can't recognize. Lilac sighs, dumping in the creamer, turning the dark brown hazelnut coffee into a lighter shade of tan. The steam that was once there disappears into nothing.

"You shouldn't be drinking coffee so late at night, Dad," Lilac says, waddling into the living room and catching his father's attention. He smiles at Lilac as he walks to the small couch, casually sniffing the coffee that is held right under his nose.

"You shouldn't even be having coffee past one," James says, ignoring Lilac's scoff. "It's not good for you."

"It's not good for you either" Lilac quickly responds, before sipping on his steaming hot coffee.

"I'm an adult," James defends, setting the empty cup on the small end table.

"You don't act like one." Lilac laughs, his mouth muffled by the cup that's still over his lips. James gives him a look, which causes Lilac to settle his laughter and remove the cup from over his mouth. James sighs, looking at the TV. Lilac stares in the same direction, finishing the rest of his coffee with the sound of the TV blaring.

James sits up from his chair, it swings as he removes his weight. "Goodnight, Lilac," he says before making his way up the rickety stairs, not waiting for Lilac's reply. Lilac gazes at the TV not moving or drinking from the mostly empty cup that lays in his lap. He wonders what his parents were like. Were they bold and brave or smart and hardworking? Before Violet, Lilac never thought much of his parents. Lilac tries not to think of them, assuming that they are both druggies who couldn't have given a shit about him, but now that doesn't seem like the case. His dad is obviously friends with them and one of them could've had a brother or another friend by the name of "Uncle Jax."

Did Alex's dad know his father? Where they friends? What about his mother? What if they dated? *Gross.* If they were anything like Lilac they would hate his guts. He doesn't even know his parents' names and he's assuming what they were like. Lilac rubs his face hard with his hands, the friction creating redness on both ends. He stands up walking over to the remote and shutting off the TV. Almost immediately after the sounds on the TV are silenced his dad's loud snores fill the house. His dad's a werewolf, a fucking werewolf. And he had no idea. He's known the man and lived with him for fourteen years and he had not even the slightest of ideas. Jeez he must be as blind as a bat. He walks up the stairs, maneuvering himself around in the dark halls. He stops outside his dad's bedroom door. What the hell is he doing? This is like a total invasion of father/son silent privacy agreement. *Screw it* he thinks to himself, turning the copper knob slowly and pushing lightly. The slow creaking of the door makes Lilac wince, his eyes going to his father who lays on his side in his warm bed. Lilac tip toes inside making sure to be as quiet as humanly possible he crouches down, eye level with his dad. Lilac lifts his right hand barely resting on James's left temple. He begins to shift, Lilac quickly retreats his hand. Imagining the scene that would lay before him if his dad would wake up. He would be disappointed, not angry. James is never really angry with Lilac. And Lilac finds that disappointment will always be worse than any anger in the world. When James shifts normally Lilac does his previous actions again, however this time James doesn't move. *Show me my parents!* He screams inside his head. *Any memory! anything! good or bad! anything!* Lilacs breath catches in his throat as he feels his wrist burn, his head has the same terrible pain as he closes his eyes and looks into his father's mind.

CHAPTER SEVENTEEN

Warm. The lights, the air, everything around Lilac is so undeniably warm. The type of warmth you feel on Christmas morning when your opening presents by the fire, a steaming cup of coffee in hand, the smell of pine needles and freshly baked cookies are the only smells arounds. That is the type of warm Lilac feels. His eyes wander the mystery room, seeing three rows of long tables on each side. Kids chattering in little groups. Andrew stands there with a group of boys that huddle around him. He looks scarily like Austin, but Alex has his eyes. The light, coffee brown eyes that looked to be lightly dusted with flakes of gold.

"Oh, come on, James, give us the dirty details," Andrew says, as if he was speaking to a small child. Lilacs father looks like he emerges from the shadows in Lilac's vision. His auburn hair burns brighter and is styled to look like dark flames. His face smooth and without wrinkles. The spark in his eyes burning brighter than Lilac himself has ever seen.

"There's no details to share," he says, looking at Andrew like there's a million other things he rather do. "We're just friends." Andrew scoffs.

"Oh friends," he mocks in a fake baby voice. "Friends don't watch other friends like it's their job. Friends don't hold each other's hands. Friends don't-"

"Ok, I get it!" James yells, as the ear piercing loud bell rings. He gets out of the crowd that huddled around him, Lilac runs hastily to follow him. He follows him out the door and into a long thin hallway. It doesn't look like a normal school. It is nicer and had plaques instead of trophies. No lockers either, and the floors and walls aren't dirty. Everything is cleaned and neatly polished. It is utterly beautiful.

"Oh, come on, James!" Andrew yells from behind James, Lilac looks in that direction seeing Andrew stand in front of his friends who follow behind him.

Lilac's reminded by Austin again. "It was a joke. Ok? Don't need to get all angry now." James rolls his eyes, before stopping in his tracks and turning around to face Andrew who quickens his pace to stand in front of him. "I like her. Everyone knows that."

That makes Lilac stop and stare. Mouth slightly gaped, eyes beginning to widen. "Who in the hell?" he thinks to himself.

"And I think she likes me. But she's so goddamn stubborn." Andrew laughs. "Her sister's hotter though, but she's not my type. I don't go for brunettes," he says.

James scowls. "I'm aware," he says with no emotion in his voice. "And I couldn't go for his sister. That's Nate's lane." James adds. "Maybe because they are half breeds. You know how they are," a boy behind Andrew says. Andrew turns around quickly, his eyes narrowed and his hands balled into fists. Lilac looks at the scene with squinted eyes.

"That's enough, Martin " Andrew spits his name like it's poison in his mouth. "Say that again and I'll kick your ass. Got it?" 'Martin' nods his head and keeps his shut. Andrew glares at the two others who watch the scene with fear and

112

confusion in their eyes, but once they see Andrew's eyes they immediately look away. Andrew smiles in satisfaction as he unclenches his fists and turns back to James who begins to walk forward. Lilac follows them.

"So where you headed?" Andrew asks casually.

"Library," James says, bored, taking a sharp right.

"Library? Ew why?" Andrew questions.

"Blair works there after school hours, and we all go and talk to her, keep her company." James sighs. 'Who's we?' Lilac thinks to himself. 'Could this Blair girl be my mom or is she just someone else'. Confusion itches at him.

"I see," Andrew says with a click of his tongue. "Maybe I'll tag along," he adds after pausing for a few seconds.

James laughs. "Really? Are you sure that's a good idea? Nate and Jax hate your guts."

Andrew side eyes him. "Which I don't understand why," he mutters. "Plus you really think I'm scared of some puny little mutants." He laughs. "You wish." James' side eyes him looking up at the sign that stands above a big glass door. 'SOSNC Library,' Lilac reads to himself. James pulls the door open as Andrew continues to follow him. He turns back to his assumed to be friends.

"You can go now," he says, waving them away with his hand. "Idiots," he murmurs when they leave. Lilac glares at his back even though he knows Andrew can't see him. Lilac walks into the library and stands side by side with James. He follows his father's eyes which are fixed on a tall fair skin girl who sits on the wooden main library desk. Her long legs dangle off the large desk that's covered in books. Alex would be in heaven, Lilac muses, with a smile. Her light blonde, almost white fluffy curls that fall down past her chest. Her face, covered by the plain blue book in her right hand, while a cigarette is held in her left.

"You shouldn't be smoking in a Library, Madam president!" Andrew yells. Blair puts her book down, showing her eyes bright green, with thin circle ringed glasses over them, and thick purple bags that hang under her eyes. "Oh Jesus, Blair!" Andrew exclaims. "Did you get any sleep last night!" Blair sighs, rolling her eyes and slamming the book closed on the desktop closed and hoping off of it.

"Nightmares. But what's new?" she says, looking at Andrew. "And you shouldn't be yelling in a library either, Andrew," Blair whisper-yells, pushing up her glasses.

"No need to get all crazo, B. Maybe you need to get some sleep" Andrew laughs. Blair shakes her head turning around, walking to the other side of the desk, and resumes her reading her book. "Oh the silent treatment. How rude," Andrew says and receives a hard punch in the shoulder from James. "Fuck, James. That hurt," he whines. Lilac sees that Blair smiles a little while her eyes scan the dirty brown pages.

"Where's your little gang, president Blackwell?" Andrew asks, walking over to the desk and placing his hands on either side of Blair's book.

"Out to get me coffee," Blair says, eyes still on the pages. "You should probably leave before they get back." Lilac's alarmed again. He's probably going to see his parents. And they aren't even going to know that he's there. That his eyes are on them for the first time Lilac can remember. He doesn't even know what they'll look like. Will he know it's them when he looks at them?

"Like I'm scared of them," Andrew puffs. James scoffs, looking over to the glass door and spotting four unfamiliar faces, or unfamiliar to Lilac.

"Speak of the devils, and they shall appear." James mutters.

"Got my coffee?" Blair yells, closing the book and leaning her head up. A man with long dark hair nods his head holding up a cup of steaming coffee. Blair Walks over to him and takes the cup out of his hand, she sips it, then moans at the taste. "Thanks, Jax. You're the best " she says, after a little.

The man, Jax, ruffles Blair's hair. "I always have been, B," he says, as his hand is swatted away. Blair rolls her eyes.

"Whatever," she responds, letting out a bored sigh before taking another sip of his coffee.

"Wow, the sass," an outside voice retorts.

"Oh shut up, Nate," a more high-pitched voice says, followed by a loud slapping sound. Lilac turns his head, nearly gasping at the two people where his eyes are placed. A man with dark green eyes and milky complexion stands with his arm around a girl's shoulders. Her tan skin and straight light brown hair, identical to Lilacs. Nate's nose and facial features looks like Lilacs though. The woman's eyes are a deep red and same with the girl who stands a few steps away from them, who James can't keep his eyes off of. 'Those are my parents,' Lilac thinks, blue eyes wide and glazed over. 'This is fucking insane.'

"That's rude, babe" he says, looking over at the smaller girl. She rolls her eyes, removing Nate's arm. "How many times do I have to tell you. To not fucking call me that," she snaps, beginning to walk to Louis.

Nate grabs the girl's arm. "Cynthia, I'm sorry" he says with a pout.

"That face isn't going to work."

Jax looks at Andrew, his eyes narrowed. "Can you leave?" he asks.

Andrew glares right back at him. "I mean I was here first, Vanrose." he sneers back.

"And," Nate chimes, crossing his arms. Andrew rolls his eyes looking at James and Blair. "I'll see you around, James" he says, his eyes shifting only on Blair . "Madam president."

He adds with a solute. As Andrew walks past, he purposefully bumps shoulders harshly with Jax.

When the glass library door fully closes Jax looks at Blair. "Such an asshole," he says. Blair Shrugs, not giving a verbal answer, instead sipping her coffee.

"Ok," Cynthia says, clapping her hands. "We have news."

James walks up to the other girl, who smiles up at him. "And that is?" he asks.

Nate puts a hand over one side of his mouth. "We can't discuss it here," he whispers. Blair slams her coffee down on the desk, causing some bystanders at the library tables to turn their heads.

"Classic halfbreed," someone whispers. Blair frowns, looking down at the white marble floor. Jax's green eyes begin to glow. With a quick swish of his left hand, bright green hue coming out of his fingertips, and a flash of a small snake birthmark on his wrist. Everyone's books at a certain table close with a loud bang, nearly closing on their fingers. The teens glare at him but don't say anything in response, just proceed in opening their books and attempt to find their page.

"Wait a second" Blair says. "Laura!" she Calls.

"Yeah!" A girl's voice calls back from one of the tall rows of books. The shelves look as if they touch the ceiling.

"Can you cover the rest of my shift?" she asks.

"Course boss," the girl responds.

"You're the best," she says. They all run out the library doors, as Lilac hastily follows them. They continue down the hallway and Lilac nearly slips on the slippery polished floors. They take a sharp left until they stop at a large black door. Cynthia pulls out a simple gold key, with two divots at the end out of her back jean pocket. She places the key into the small key hole and turns it to the right, while doing the same with the small silver door knob. The door opens and the five rush inside, with Lilac trails behind them, nearly getting the door slammed in his face.

"We're not even supposed to be here," Blair says, looking at Cynthia. "One, this is yours and Jade's room. And this is the reds dormitory. Unlike you idiots I actually care about getting detention." Jade. Must be the girl Andrew was talking about. They looked nearly the same. Cynthia and Jade, Cynthia was a bit smaller, but the two looked almost exactly the same, except for the small mole that was placed right on the left side of her nose.

"Here she goes," Cynthia laughs. Lilac out of the corner spots James slyly wraps his arm around Jade's shoulders. Lilacs never saw his dad with a girl in that way. He's usually single and never had any interest in anyone except for Lilac. That thought makes Lilac frown. Was this all his fault? That his dad couldn't move on from this girl? Was he holding him back? Lilac's hands begin to shake.

"Whatever," Blair says with an eye roll, before putting her hands on her hips. "So what exactly do you have to tell us?"

Cynthia and Nate exchange small smiles. Lilac furrows his brows as his mom extends her left arm. "No fucking way!" Blair Screeches grabbing her hand and looking at the small white diamond with a golden band closely . While James' face is pale and looks to be light headed.

"You're getting married," he questions in disbelief. Blair let's go of Cynthia's hand and turns to face James, eyes narrowed and mouth set in a thin line.

"James, stop worrying so much."

"What? How can't I? Nate didn't even know how to spell explainable till last week, and now you expect him to be able to take care of a family." Nate's face flushes, as Cynthia begins to smirk.

"Well, if James isn't happy for you, just know that I am," Blair says, her white teeth shining as he smiles. "

Well, thank you, B," Cynthia says, smiling graciously at her. James gives out an extra sigh.

"I never said I wasn't happy for you. But-but. " James sighs again. "Why now?" he asks. Cynthia and Nate look at each other again, with identical deep frowns on their faces. Lilac watches the scene with weighted breaths as his father grabs his mother's hand and squeezes it softly.

"With what's going on with my dad and the war." Cynthia pauses. "We-We don't know how much time we have left." Silence after that, Lilac wants to scream to say something, anything, to free him from the terrifying silence.

"So," Blair coughs. "Do you have names for your future kids yet?"The room breaks out into chuckles. Blair pouts. "I mean it's a valid question."

"They're seventeen, for Christ's sake!" Jax exclaims.

"I'm not talking about you now idiot!" Blair snaps.

"Ouch" Jax says, putting a hand over his heart. Lilac can't help but be reminded of Evan, and how every time they argue, Evan just laughs at him. Lilac would never admit it out loud but a part of him secretly loves it.

"Well, since twin girls run in my family" Cynthia says, smiling over at Jade whose face turns pink. "We were thinking about Lilac and Violet." Lilac's face begins to flush, his mouth and throat become painfully dry, and the urge to vomit becomes apparent.

Jade smiles. "They are really pretty names, Cindi," Jade says softly. James can't help but smile at the softness Jade's voice. It was always like that gentle, soft, but strong and powerful when it had to be.

"Thanks," Cynthia says in reply.

"Flower names I dig it," Jax says sitting himself on the black leather couch.

"Don't ever say that again," Blair laughs, sitting beside him.

"You really have everything planned out don't you?" James says, his skepticism shining through the tone of his voice. Cynthia and Nate look at each other, love with a mixture of lust in their eyes.

"Yeah." Nate smiles, eyes still on her. "We do."

"Lilac!" A voice echoes from a distance. "Lilac!" The voice screams again. He looks around trying to match the voice. Could his parents be the ones screaming? Lilac looks at them, their mouths closed and their hands still holding on to each other. "Lilac!" The voice is clearer now. Easier to hear. But he still can't place it. "Lilac!" The bodies of his birth parents and their friends begin to fade as pain explodes through his body and blood begins to drip down his wrist starting at the dark brown birthmark. "Lilac!" Pain in his head increases. The dark wooden walls begin to vanish along with the matching furniture. "Lilac!" James' voice yells, as Lilac's body goes completely numb.

Lilac can hardly breathe. His body feels as if it was dipped and coated with shards of ice. Tears stream down his face at the same time as the dark crimson liquid that slides down his hand and onto his dad's light carpet. James turns on the lamp that sits on the night stand that stands beside his bed. There sits a lamp, a picture of Lilac and him from Lilac's National Junior Honor Society formal, a small notebook that his thin reading glasses lay upon, a cheap lamp with a broken shade, and a small ink pen. James sits on his bed, pulling the thin white sheets off his body.

"I think it's time we talk," James says, his voice unfamiliarly stern. Lilac stares at him blankly. "Lilac come up here," he says calmly patting the spot next to him. Lilac does so, fiddling with his hands that sit restlessly in his lap. "You know you could've just asked me," James says, looking to the side at Lilac. Lilac gives him a look. "I tried but you wouldn't answer."

"I didn't think that you were ready to–"

"I have a right to know!" Lilac yells. "They're my parents!" Lilac doesn't know what he expects his father to do, after he just yelled. Yell at him back or send him to his room. Maybe even slap him in the mouth. Not too hard though. Lilac knows if someone yelled at him that way he would do a lot more than slap them.

"I'm sorry," James says.

"What do you want to know?" Lilac shakes his head. This is it, he can find out everything he's been wondering about in the past week. What he is. Who his parents are. What the deal is with his dad. But now that everything has fallen so perfectly by his feet, he feels nothing. Not curiosity itching at him, no excitement. Nothing. Just a small pain in the pit of his stomach that makes him frightened to know anything or ask anything at that.

"Nothing," Lilac says, standing up and beginning to walk out his dad's bedroom door.

"Wait what?" His father asks, eyes wide. He goes to stand up.

"No, Dad," Lilac continues to walk. "It's ok." He shuts the bedroom door, without another word and continues down the narrow hallway. He opens his own bedroom door, shutting it directly behind him. He slides down it in the darkness, his feet resting on top of colored pencils. Tears burn his cheeks, the frustration coming off of him in waves. He sits there alone. Wishing desperately for someone to be there with him. To comfort him. Someone other than his dad. Maybe Evan. With his dark always wide and cartoon like brown eyes, that are covered by his large glasses. His hair. God, his hair. Black ringlets that go in all different directions that Lilac says he hates, but he's also, somewhat of a compulsive liar. Not to others, to himself most of the time. The way Evans' body is always so warm. The way he smells of cigarettes and strong soap. The way he wraps his arms around Lilac, in a friendly manner of course. The way–Jesus Christ, what the hell is he doing. Has he lost his mind, finally? After everything this is his breaking point. Lilac wipes his stray tears away, before finally letting himself stand up. The bones in his legs and knees are cracking. Lilac doesn't even bother to change. He lays in his bed wrapping the thick and hot blankets around him like he's some kind of burrito. He closes his eyes, slowly drifting off to sleep. His dreams filled with the same familiar face.

CHAPTER EIGHTEEN

Jordan decides he needs to get some new friends. Friends who aren't werewolves or mutants or whatever the hell Lilac is. Friends who don't drag him into weird places to find their missing brother. That's what Jordan needs to be doing something normal. Like playing video games or taking his dog, Harry, on a calming and relaxing walk. That's how Jordan should be spending his Saturday. Instead he's standing on Mya's doorstep with his bike about to go on some mystery hunt. It's comical if you think about it. The ridiculousness of the whole entire situation. He knocks on the glass door softly, fear of damaging it washing over him. Who knows what Mya's mom would do if he did. Jordan remembers when Evan broke a vase in Mya's living room a few months back and she called him an "effing dumbass." Mya's told them stories about the fights her mom used to get in or how she once egged a boy who wouldn't get off her cousin's doorstep. Those stories were enough to scare the living shit out of Jordan. The front door swings open revealing Mya with Evan standing behind her. As soon as Jordan sees Evan he realizes there are two bikes parked outside Cooper's house instead of one. God, he really is stupid or just plain losing it.

"Took you long enough," Mya says, swinging the glass door open and pushing past Jordan, Evan follows her in silence. "Excuse me. Someone hit their head this morning."

Jordan looks at the small velvet box that is hooked onto Mya's jeans. What the hell. "What is that?" he asks, pointing to the small box. Mya stares at him for a second before a look of resolution crosses her face.

"Oh that," she says, unstrapping the small patch of Velcro and pulling out a medium sized jet black velvet box with two small silver bolts on top, and a shiny black button on the side. "Stun gun," she replies and for emphasis she holds the gun out and presses the black button causing volts of electricity to pop out, which makes a loud shocking sound occur. Jordan stares with wide eyes.

"Your mom's going to kill you," he says, hopping onto his bike.

"She has no clue, just told me to check in every half hour" she says, putting the stun gun back into the small pouch. "And to be home before dark."

"Before dark? That's your curfew?" Jordan questions.

"Yeah. It's always been that way. Guess you just don't pay attention all that well."

"Can we just go get Noah?" Evan suddenly interrupts . This is the first time Jordan's heard him speak all this morning, which seems to be a new record for Evan's silence . "I wanna get this over with." He pedals past them riding down the road and in the direction of Noah's.

"Is he ok?" Jordan asks, kicking up his kickstand.

"I don't know." Mya shrugs, using her black converse covered feet to start up on her bike. Mya's eyes never leave the road before her, her eyes never leave Evan's back. "He's been like this all morning. Something must have happened yesterday when he was talking with Lilac."

"What is going on with those two anyways?" Mya smirks to herself, she lowers her head looking at the rushing concrete below her.

She shrugs. The wind blows through her messy, dirty blond hair as she rides down Glendale street and turns up to where Noah lives. The air is cold as it pushes itself in Mya's face, but not the type of cold that if you stay out for five minutes, your hands begin to redden and your thighs begin to shiver. The three continue to ride their bikes in silence, the unanswered questions and theories hanging loosely in the air around them, but no one makes an effort to answer them. Mya can't help the glimmer of hope that she feels when she sees Violet's and Noah's bodies start to grow bigger and bigger with every pedal she takes. Violet's not in her usual outfit, she ditched the purple

124

pullover and traded it with one of Noah's green baseball hoodies from last year. The leggings and dirty tennis shoes are still on her body. Her chestnut hair pulled in a crooked ponytail, with stray hairs poking out in all different directions. Mya can't help but cringe when her eyes focus on it. Noah looks about the same. The only difference is the small black backpack that hangs on his shoulders, that is filled with unknown contents.

"Hey," Noah says, pedaling towards them and riding in the gap between Evan and Mya. Violet trails behind him, sometimes looking as if she's going to tip over.

"Hey," Jordan says, looking over Mya and Violet, his eyes squint. "What's in the bag?"

"Bill's things, maybe we can lure him out with them you know." Jordan didn't know, unlike Noah his sibling wasn't missing because of some weird people that may be just like Lilac. Someone he's known since kindergarten. Jordan doesn't even have a younger sibling, his older sister's been in college for two years in Pittsburgh and is engaged to the so-called love of her life. He can't believe it; soulmates don't exist and even if they did how likely is it to find them?

"You ok?" Mya asks, turning to look at them quickly. Jordan snaps out of his daze looking around and comes to the realization that they're close to the woods. So close that Jordan can spot the small chipmunk that crawls down a large and titled tree.

"So what's the game plan?" Noah asks. As the five of them enter the bone-chilling woods. He feels Deja vu eating at him. Images of Violet covered in mud, Alex running towards him like the flash, the small footsteps that were imprinted in the snow, Violet's footsteps. The memories flash through his head like projector slides. Noah adjusts his grip on his handlebars.

"We're getting Lilac." Evan speaks up. "He's gonna be with Alex and one of them is gonna have to ride on the back of one of our bikes."

"Why?" Mya asks.

"Because remember. Alex left his bike at Noah's." Evan halts his movement, on his bike. He swings his lanky, boney body off of it and begins to walk his bike on the dirt covered ground. Upon seeing this, the rest soon follow his actions. Violet however looks at him, a confused expression spread across her face.

"I didn't know you could do that," she says. "I thought you were supposed to sit on them." Mya can't suppress her pig like snort.

"Stop it, Mya," Noah snaps, sending her a threatening glare. Mya rolls her eyes but doesn't proceed to comment.

"What?" Violet questions as she practically runs her bike up to Noah's side.

"Nothing, Vi. Everything's fine"

"Vi," Evan snickers. Noah glares at the back of his head. The silence in the air is soft and mild, or at least to everyone except for Noah. He feels as if he is walking on eggshells around Violet, she doesn't even know what she is doing and that is the worst part. Every night with Violet wrapped in his old clothes sleeping in his bed while he would sleep on the floor. He would catch himself staring at her as she slept, how peaceful and innocent she looked. Or when they would go out late at night, and Noah would teach her how to ride a bike. Violet was already a natural Noah decided when after night two of practice she was already nailing it. Violet is smart and funny and way out of Noah's league.

"Are you ok, Noah?" Violet asks.

"What? Oh yeah. I'm fine. Just nervous is all."

"Do you think we will find him?"

"I'm hoping. I miss him, you know a lot." Violet looks down at the ground. "I miss my parents," she says quietly. "Even though I'm the one who left, I-I can't help but feel bad."

"Do you regret leaving?"

"No, definitely not." Violet shortly laughs. "I wouldn't have had a chance to meet Lilac." She looks and smiles at Noah. "Or you." Noah can't stop the heat and pink blush from filling out his cheeks. Many pairs of feet stomp on the hard ground, which makes Noah alert.

"Beep, Beep, Beep. Asshole alert," Evan says. Shawn and his posse of dickwads emerge from the trees. The beautiful blonde on his arm makes Mya's knuckles clutch the handles on her bike so hard that her hands turn a pale white. She is way prettier than Mya. Her perfect light blonde hair makes Mya's look like a rat's nest. Her tan skin lightly dusted with makeup, not a pimple in site, makes Mya quickly want to invest in more makeup to cover her problem spots. And her body, perfect from head to toe. Rounded hips, a flat stomach, and everything on her perfectly placed. She is wearing a light blue lace see thru crop top, with high waisted acid wash ripped jeans. Immediately seeing this makes Mya feel underdressed in her pancake stained black leggings, her stained hoodie, and knotted hair in a ponytail. Hey, she is about to go into an abandoned house to look for her friend's missing brother, what is she supposed to wear?

"So what are you people doing in *my* woods?" Shawn asks.

"They're not *your* woods" Evan says. Shawn exaggeratedly rolls his eyes and deliberately makes eye contact with Mya as he moves his hand lower on the beautiful girl's body.

Mya's jaw clenches. "What are you doing here, anyways?"

Shawn pauses, and looks around at them, counting them in his head. A devilish smirk makes its way on his face. "Oh, I see going to get your bitch, huh, Coleman."

"I would just stop if I were you," Noah pipes up, his knuckles turning the same pale white as Mya's. "I would just be careful though," Shawn mock whispers. "He's quite the crier and pretty whiny if you ask me and–"

"You're the bitch!" Violet yells, blue eyes glowing madly. A tree branch snaps off a nearby tree, only a few feet away. For a split second nobody moves, everything's silent except for the wind blowing the bare trees. Until the other petite blonde speaks up. "And you're a freak!" she yells, then giggles. Mya then looks at her again and all she can see is dark marks on the girl's soul. The words she speaks to ugly and dirty for a girl who looks like her to say. To Mya she was a perfect example of the basic saying of don't judge a book by its cover.

"Don't talk to her like that." Mya tosses her bike to the ground, carelessly.

"Mya, chill" Jordan whispers to her. The other girl takes Shawn's hand off of her hips and takes a step forward. If the look Mya receives could kill, then Mya would be deceased.

"And who are you?" she snaps at Mya.

"It doesn't matter; don't talk to her like that."

"What are you gonna do about it?" Another step. Mya knows what she is, and also knows what she's doing. She's seen how Austin and Shawn have done the same type things, to get a reaction out of people. They're all the same, bred with the same mind set. Thank god for Alex.

Mya knows that getting in a fight with a werewolf is not something she has on her itinerary.

"What you need to do is back the hell up."

"Why don't you make me?" The girl laughs. Mya goes to comment but a harsh slap on the right side of her face stops her. *She slapped me. She really fucking slapped me.* Mya can hear the oohs and woops from Shawn and his friends. And the proud and arrogant smirk the girl wears makes something dangerous flash in her eyes that burn like an open and untamable flame. Mya clutches her cheeks and feels the tiny drops of blood that drip down her chin. *Always punch, never slap.* Her mom's voice screams in her head. *Slapping's for wussies.* Mya punches her on the left side of her face with all the force she can muster. The girl stumbles backwards nearly falling from the sudden impact. Shawn and his friends' taunts are silent now. The blondes eyes are big with shock and are beginning to darken in rage. She rushes toward Mya at full force, tackling Mya to the ground. She straddles her, raising her hand and starts to try and strike Mya with a closed fist Mya grabs her arm, and struggles to turn her off of her. The girl grunts in protest and begins punching her. She hits Mya again on the same side of her face as before, Mya slams her back on the ground. She lands punches on both sides of the girls, causing her knuckles to tingle and blood to get on Mya's hands. Her vision clouds in her intense anger. She's never been in a fight before. Plenty of arguments and she punched a boy in the face when he groped her at a baseball game, but never anything like this. Her mind blocks out Shawn's calls yelling at her to stop. Her mind shields herself away from the fact that the girl under her is fading to unconsciousness. What feels like a set of hands throws her off the girl's body slamming her back into the ground. Her breaths heavy as if someone was pushing on her chest. Mya realizes who pushed her off of the mystery girl, because when she stands, her back towards Shawn, Violet's eyes glow.

"We need to go," Noah urgently states, and begins to stand on his bike and pedal past Shawn, who looks at Mya like she's a monster. As much as Mya wants to avoid his eyes she can't. She looks at him as she quickly rides past him, he's on the ground beside the girl cleaning her blood off her face with his dark purple jacket.

"I can't believe you did that," Evan says, looking over at Mya who's vigorously pedaling on her bike.

"We're close to Alex's right?" Mya questions.

"Yeah. About five minutes away," Jordan replies.

"Ahh, thank God. I just want to get this over with," she whispers. Evan can't agree more. That five minutes felt like hours to Jordan. No one decides to make conversation or even bring up the fact that Mya just kicked someone's ass. How can you just ignore something like that? They park their bikes right at the end of the woods. Jordan can hear the party music blasting from Alex's house. Lilac comes running out of his house, pulling a bike with him, and a red, short sleeve shirt on his body. He's alone though and without Alex.

"Where's Alex?" Noah asks him when he makes his way over. Lilac parks the bike right next to Evan. His breaths are uneven and harsh.

"In-In-side," he breathes.

"What did you say?"

Lilac finally catches his breath. "He's inside. Austin or Allen threw a party and I tried to get in but they won't let me in. They said no little eighth graders allowed" Lilac rolls his eyes.

"Did you try calling him?"

Evan asks. Lilac nods, then gets an idea in his head. "Give me your coat," he says to Evan.

"What; why?"

"Just give it to me!" Lilac yells, startling Violet.

Evan takes off his coat and hands it to Lilac who puts it on. "No need to yell, Little Li," he says.

Lilac glares at him, pulling up the hood that covers his eyes. "Shut up," he says. "I'll be back. But when I say go, trust me; go" Lilac says to his friends before running in the direction of Alex's house. "What do you think he's going to do "Violet asks Noah, tugging on his sleeve. "I don't know, but I hope he'll be ok." Evan watches Lilac run, never taking his eyes off him until he enters Alex's house. The smell of weed, alcohol, and sex invades Alex's once lavender smelling house. Party music vibrates the walls, beer bottles cover the floors, and people make out in fairly odd places. In the living room, Lilac spots Austin with the same girl from the movies. She's straddling his lap, his hands are gripping her hips, his tongue is down her throat, while her pale hands are knotted in his hair. Lilac wrinkles his nose. Austin pulls away from the blond, despite her obvious pout. He sniffs the air picking up Lilac's scent of coffee and fresh fire. *Shit*. Lilac bolts up the stairs and runs to Alex's room. He slams his hands on the bedroom pounding on it.

"This is a no sex zone!" Alex yells.

"Alex, it's me.."

"Lilac?" Alex opens the door, his classic button down and jeans on him, with his signature backpack over his shoulders. "I thought you forgot about me for a second."

"No. Of course not. Why didn't you call me back?"

"Austin took my phone right after I got off the phone with Evan. Sorry." Alex looks down.

"No, it's fine" Lilac says quickly. "We need to go. Everyone's waiting outside." Alex nods and exits his room. Lilac readjusts his hood making sure it won't fall off. As Lilac walks down the stairs and a tiny shard of hope emerges from him. They might actually get away with this. He might actually br-

"I don't think you two were invited," Austin voice booms throughout the house demanding everyone's attention.

"On the count of three, run," Lilac slyly whispers to Alex in a rush. Alex nods a terrified look on his face as Lilac grips his arm. One more step, just one and they will have made it.

"Austin-"

"I thought I told you to stay upstairs," He interrupts.

"One." Lilacs grip tightens.

"Can you really not obey a simple order?"

"Two."

"You really think you and your bitchy friend can embarrass me like this/"

"Three." Lilac punches Austin in the face, which causes a shock of pain to explode throughout his wrist. His knuckles immediately start to flush red. "Shit," he states, wiggling his hand up and down. Alex still stands next to him, frozen in his place. "We need to go," Alex cries. Lilac, his hand still on Alex's, pulls him along as he dashes through the crowd of teenagers. Lilac can hear Austin coming up behind them, but that only makes Lilac and Alex run faster. Alex pushes the front door open and Lilac lets go of his arm. "Take my bike," Lilac says, out of breath as he continues to run towards his friends who are seated in their bikes waiting to go.

"Then where are you-"

"We'll figure it out." Alex's front door opens with a bang as soon as Alex steps on Lilac's bike. "Go! Go! *GO!*" Lilac yells. They all pedal quickly, except Evan who's two feet are planted to the ground.

"Hurry get on." Evan looks back at him, a glint in his eyes.

"You sure?"

"Yes, shut up and get on." Lilac sees Evan move up on his seat, obviously making room for Lilac. Lilac hesitates for a second but looking back and seeing Austin and his posse all make their way outside, and that makes Lilac hop on to the bike quickly. He (as casually as humanly possible) wraps his arms around Evan's waist. Evan pedals on as if Lilac isn't even there, like he literally weighs nothing. Alex looks back at Austin's shadow slowly fading away. It's sort of comical Alex suddenly realizes. The fact that he constantly gets beat every time he sneaks out then proceeds to sneak out over and over again. Or the fact that he deliberately disobeys Austin and his dad's wishes even when he knows the outcome. Alex laughs. Laughs harder than he's ever done before. Bystanders and random hitchhikers would probably think of him as crazy if they would come across him. Maybe he is. The thought almost makes him stop laughing, but then he can hear his friends, and their own laughter mixed with trees blowing in the wind. Alex realizes something as he rides through the woods. He's crazy, maybe even a little insane. But at least if he is really crazy, he has six other people that are crazy with him. They're all crazy, but they're crazy together.

CHAPTER NINETEEN

"*This* is the house?" Mya asks, looking at the big abandoned house on Luna drive. It's giant, no doubt about that. With the large double doors and the three stories, but it's still falling apart. The large windows are boarded up with wood, dirt and vines grow across the house and up the sides, and the roof is broken and slanted. The sun shining through the grey clouds and on to the dirty wood.

"It appears so," Jordan says.

"What, you've never been here before?"

"No, but my sister has."

"Then how do we know it's the right house"

"It is," Lilac says, all eyes turn to him. Mya opens her mouth. "Don't ask me how I know I just do.." Mya closes it. "I don't know it's like a–like a"

"Like a connection," Violet says, her eyes gazing dully and blankly at the house. She never takes them off of it for a second. "I feel it too." Her voice is monotone to the point where it scares Lilac.

"Freaky" Evan mouths to Mya, who snickers quietly. "Who's going in with me?" Noah asks, standing on the broken looking porch, his bike parked beside Violet. Only Violet raises her hand. Noah's shocked face looks around at his friends. They came this far, why chicken out now. "Guys, come on" he says irritably.

"Noah, you can't *actually* think we're going in there," Jordan says, eyeing Noah.

"No, I don't Jordan, I just dragged you all out here for shits and giggles!" Noah snaps, digging his fingers into his hair and tugging hard on his locks. "Noah, stop" Violet says. Alex looks at her for a second longer than necessary, before looking at Noah who untangles his fingers from his hair.

Mya sighs loudly. "Fine, I'll go."

Lilac looks at her. "Really?" he asks, raising his eyebrows at her. Mya gives him a look, walking up the unstable stairs, and stops in front of the doorway.

"Wait, what happened to your hand?" Alex asks, seeing Mya's bruised and dried blood crusted hand.

"I'll tell you later." Mya waves him off.

"If everyone's going in I guess I'll go to," Lilac says walking up beside them, Violet begins to follow him.

"You guys stand guard." Noah says, turning the dusty door knob before pushing on the left door. Dust and grime fall into the air and dissolves. The door finally opens, a thick cloud of dust emerging which makes Mya cough.

"Not everyone's going, Lilac," Evan argues. Looks at him, thinking of the way his hands wrapped around his waist. A faint blush makes its way on his cheeks.

"Just make sure everything goes ok out here. Ok?" Lilac says.

Evan feels disappointment and fear bubble inside of his stomach. Terrifying images flashing through his mind. "Just be careful, Little Li. And don't die on me, capisce?"

Lilac smiles, "Capisce, Asshole." He walks into the house behind Mya and with Violet trailing behind him. The houses wood creaks without anyone moving, it's cold, freezing even. The temperature makes Lilac a chill run down Lilacs spine. The door slams loudly behind him.

"Did you do that?" he asks Violet. She shakes her head, without looking at Lilac, instead her eyes remain on the broken staircase with certain steps broken off and the others with missing pieces.

"I think we should split up" Noah says.

"You're joking" Mya laughs, looking at him incredulously. "We literally just saw a horror movie. And staying together is like rule one."

"Yeah but we're not in a horror movie, Mya"

"Might as well be."

"And what's that supposed to mean?"

"It *means*-"

"Will you guys please stop arguing? We have more important things to worry about at the moment. You should understand that," Lilac says. Mya and Noah silence their arguing. "Thank you" Lilac sighs in relief. "How about this? Me and Mya go on the top floor of the house, while you and V-Violet stay on this floor."

A small smile spreads its way on Violet's face, at the mention of her name slipping past Lilac's lips. "Be careful" she says to him. Lilac looks at her and clears her throat.

"Yeah. Um, thanks," he stutters.

"Can we find Bill now?" Noah asks abruptly. Lilac's a little shocked by how anxious he is. But then he understands that he shouldn't be, it is his brother after all. Lilac admits that he's been anxious himself. It isn't just about Bill, but Violet as well.

"Yeah. Let's go, Lilac." Mya shoots Lilac a look before disappearing up the steps.

"You ready?" Noah asks Violet. She nods, and looks around the dark, creepy house. The only light that comes in is from where the wooden boards don't cover the spaces of open windows. Noah takes his phone out of his front jean pocket and flicks on the flashlight and turns the brightness of it all the way up.

"I saw you on that *thing* before," Violet says, following Noah. "What is it?"

"Oh, it's a phone."

Violet's eyebrows furrow. "I don't think we don't have phones where I'm from. What does it do?"

"Well you can call people, text, play games, you know the basic stuff."

"What's texting?"

Noah opens his mouth to explain before a big, dirty brown door is right in front of him. He raises his hand and balls it into a fist and knocks firmly on the door. "Bill!" he yells loudly and continues to bang on the door. "Are you in there!" Noah suddenly feels as if he's in a daze. His mind feels blank, and his body feels like it's floating.

"Noah?" Violet asks, looking at him wryly as she puts her hand on his shoulder.

"Noah!" he hears Bill's voice cry in his head.

"Bill?" Noah asks, tears filling the corner in his eyes.

"It's your fault!" Bill's young voice screams.

"Noah!" Violet yells, in full panic mode. She takes her hand off his shoulder and walks so she's in front of him.

"T-That's not true" Noah cries. "I love you, Bill."

Bill laughs bitterly, Noah's never heard him laugh like that before. He is always full of so much joy and life. His smiles are always bright, never mischievous or conniving and his laughs are always so loud and meaningful. Never like the laugh that Noah just heard. "It *is* your fault, you insolent child." A mystery voice hisses. It's definitely not Bill's voice, it's a man's or boy's cold voice that Noah's ears have never heard before. "It's your fault Bill's dead." *Smack.* Noah blinks, giving his mind some time to register what in the world just happened. His mind replays the previous events, and the stinging pain on his cheek-.

"You-You slapped me!" Noah exclaims in utter disbelief.

"You weren't doing anything. And you wouldn't answer me when I called your name." Violet looks at Noah with her same blank look. "What happened?"

"I don't know. I heard Bill. He was yelling at me saying how it was my fault that he was missing." Noah pauses and runs his hand through his hair. "I know it sounds crazy, but then his voice changed and it wasn't Bill's voice anymore."

Violet looks at him, her blue eyes wide. "Oh no" she says.

"Wha-." Noah can't even get the whole word out before the door opens and him and Violet are tossed in the room. They both lay side by side on their backs on the dirty floor. The door slams once more. Noah bolts upward, while Violet stays on the ground, looking blankly at the chipped and flaking tan ceiling. Noah twists and turns the dirt infested door knob but it doesn't. Fear tickles at him as he turns around to look down at Violet.

"It's locked." His simplicity is bone chilling.

"You think they're ok down there" Mya asks Lilac, as they exit the third room they've been in. Their only source of light being their phone flashlights, considering that there were no windows on the second floor.

"I hope so," Lilac says in reply.

"Noah really likes your sister if you haven't realized it yet." Lilac sighs, not ready yet to have this conversation. It's already weird enough having a sister in general. But why does he have to be reminded of it constantly?

Mya smirks. "What, still don't claim her?"

Lilac scoffs. "It's not that I don't claim her, I don't even know her."

"Yeah but she's your sister."

"But I don't know her. It's like when you don't know a cousin, you have literally no connection with them." A loud bang makes itself noticeable from the end of the hallway.

"Did you hear that?" Mya asks, whipping her head to the side to look at Lilac. Lilac dismisses her comment and begins to walk closer to the door. "Lilac!" Mya seethes. "What are you doing." He still doesn't respond. Mya feels something pass behind her, she quickly turns around, gripping the stun gun that's strapped on her waist. Nothing. Just a plain scary hallway. Mya shakily signs to herself and turns back around and follows Lilac. "Lilac!" She yells.

"What?" He asks quietly without turning around.

"What the hell is going on!" she finally exclaims. "I don't know Mya, but I'm about to find out." Lilac reaches his hand out and before his fingers even touch the clean silver doorknob and door down stairs slams. Lilac retracts his hand and looks at Mya with a worried look. The two stare at each other with the same expression.

"You don't think-." Mya can't even finish her sentence before yells are heard from downstairs. Noah's yells. Mya and Lilac bolt to the staircase that feels like miles and miles away. However they both begin to slow their walking when they see a girl's dark silhouette. Lilac knows her from somewhere, as he runs closer and closer he sees her chopped blonde hair and forest green eyes. For a split second he thinks it's his father's friend Blair, but the girl in front of him can't be more than twenty four. The girl chuckles when Mya and he stop in their tracks. Mya's hand is sneakily on the stun gun, ready for anything, ready just in case.

"Finally!" The girl yells as she continues to chuckle. "I get to meet the mystery son of the great Nate Montgomery, what an honor."

Lilac tries not to act scared but on the inside he's shaking. "Who are you? Where's Bill" he demands. The woman laughs harder. Mya unhitches the stun gun carrier and pulls it out. The woman stops chuckling, a scowl replaces her evil smile. She flicks her wrist and bright Christmas green wraps around the stun gun and launches itself off the side of the staircase. The sound of the gun dropping makes Mya visibly shake.

"That won't work, sweetie." She sneers. "Perhaps, I think it's time for me and blue here to go."

"Actually, it's blue and I, you bitch." Mya runs at her, with no plan, just on pure emotion and instinct. It might be the instinct of protecting Lilac, or self-defense. One thing is sure, she's a total idiot. The short haired blonde flicks her hand again in Mya's direction. Mya falls backwards, hitting the ground hard, completely knocking the wind out of her. *The second time today. Great.* Lilac's numb, not moving from his spot. The woman looks at Mya's body which has no movement, just low painful groans. She kicks Mya's side. Lilac feels rage run through his veins. "It's just me and you, huh?" she asks menacingly as she steps out of the shadows. He can see the dark rings under her eyes, her teeth sharpened like fangs and tinted a light and dirty yellow. Lilac raises his hand and attempts to conjure the power that lives deep inside him, but just like the time Austin challenged him, nothing. He chokes. He slams his arms to his side and clenches his fists. Maybe Austin is right, he is pathetic. The girl smiles showing off her terrifying teeth. Lilac's heartbeat thumps in his ears, and his breathes heavy as if an elephant is putting all its weight on his chest.

"Oh this just keeps getting better and better," she laughs. Lilacs first thought is to run, but there's no way he's going to leave Mya behind. She's been with him for too long and she would do the same for him. It's just the kind of person she is. A hand grips the bottom of his leg.

"Go." Mya says in a harsh whisper. "Run. The second she's gone, I'm going to get Noah and Violet."

Lilac shakes his head. "No. Mya, I'm not just going to leave you."

"Dingus. I'm literally telling you to leave me." Without another protest Lilac bolts down the hallway, leaving Mya behind. Even if she told him to leave her, he still can't help but feel bad. He's still confused about the bruises on her hand though, he'll have to talk to her later about that. If there's even going to be a later for him. The mystery girl is on his trail. He can hear her catching up to him. He swings the door at the end of the hallway open, and he attempts to shut it, but she's faster than him. She's so much stronger than him. She slaps her hand to the left causing the door to break off the hinges, by the strong force. Lilac stares. Not being able to comprehend what the hell just happened. How can someone just do that? How can *he* do that? It doesn't make any sense. She then turns to Lilac, her eyes blazing with undeniable fury. As she takes a step closer, Lilac screams.

As soon as that disgusting door shut, Evan started pacing. For the past *five minutes* that's all he's done. No stopping. No pausing. Nothing. Just paced back and forth over a thousand times. And honestly it was driving Alex off the deep end.

"Do you think he'll stop?" Jordan asks from where he's seated beside Alex.

Alex sighs and rolls his eyes. He literally snuck out of his house and is probably going to be murdered for it when he gets home, and here he is sitting outside doing nothing. Is it worth it? Alex doesn't know. But he does know is that Evan's pacing is driving him bonkers. "Evan." His tone neutral. Evan continues to pace. "Evan." He says a little bit louder. Still the same outcome. Alex slams his open hand down on the black wooden step. "Evan!" Alex yells.

Evan stops his pacing and turns to Alex. "Good God, Alexander. You scared the fyjefus out of me" Evan says, placing a hand over his rapidly beating heart.

Alex rolls his eyes. "Well, if you weren't obsessively and obnoxiously pacing, I wouldn't have had to do that." Evan and Jordan stare at him wearily.

"Who peed in your Cheerios this morning?" Evan asks.

"Dude" Jordan says, looking at Evan like he's stupid. And to Jordan he might be. "Not the time."

"Yeah, yeah, yeah," Evan says, waving him off. "But seriously, Alex. You ok?" Alex searches his face for any sign of mockery, but surprisingly finds none. Alex sighs, resting his palms on the prickly wood, that will no doubt give him splinters. He recalls of a time when life was a lot simpler. When all that really mattered to Alex, was children's chapter books and who he would sit by when he finally did get to kindergarten.

It was before he met any of his friends, besides Lilac who he knew of. Everyone in the pack knew of the mystery kid their alpha suddenly appeared with. It was the pack gossip, that nowadays seems to be more toxic than it was before. Austin was out with his second grade friends and Allen was tagging along per usual. Alex remembered that he was bored. He finished all the child appropriate books in the house, his mom wouldn't let him read anything above seventh grade reading level, and his small action figures were not cutting it. He gazed out the basement window, before it was a workout room it was once a playroom. But as the three of them got older and their once strong bond slowly cracked and disappeared so did the toys that once sat in colorful bins. A tree branch hung into the view. Alex suddenly got an idea. He ran out of the basement door and outside. The humidity made him sweat and his skin feel sticky. Alex looks up at the ginormous tree that is in front of him. It's branches were thick and heavy, and if one of them would fall it would most likely crush Alex to death. The leaves on the tree were a bright green and some were even bigger than Alex's face.

"Alex?" A small and annoying, high-pitched voice called.

"What, Shawn?" Alex asked in response.

"What are you doing?" Shawn asked, running up to stand up next to Alex.

"I'm gonna climb that tree," Alex said proudly pointing up at it.

Shawn shook his head. "You can't," he argued. "You'll get in trouble." Shawn looked to the left and then to the right and said in a harsh whisper. "Your brothers are gonna be mad if they find out."

Alex rolled his eyes. He remembered a character doing that in a book he was reading in the same context, so why not try it out. "I'm not scared of them." If only that was true now.

"Then I'll tell your mom!" Shawn screeched, running to Alex's front door.

"Tattle tale!" Alex yelled from behind Shawn. Then Alex looked up at the tree, seeing one large thick branch hangs exceptionally low. He reached up, but it's too high. Alex jumped, hands out and feet off the ground. He gripped the branch, stray pieces of wood dig into his skin. Alex let out a small grunt as he pulls himself up. Alex climbed a few more branches up, till he's almost at the top of the tree.

"Alex!" He can hear Shawn's distance yell. Alex sighed, dropping five branches down till he's sitting on the second one down. "Alex!" An eight year old Austin said, coming out of the woods.

"What the hell?" Alex heard his parents use that word once or twice. Alex slipped off the branch, sliding his hand against the lost pieces of wood. A piece or two sticking into his fingers. He fell on the bright green, almost artificial looking grass. He hit his head hard causing him to wince. "Ouch" he whispered in a small voice.

"Alex." His mother gasped, running at him. "I told you you're too little to climb trees. You are in so much trouble right now," she scolded. Alex inwardly shook. What's it going to be? The touture chamber? A whipping? Maybe being cooked in the oven like a cake? Alex has never been in trouble before so who knows what's going to happen to him. His mother picked him up like a baby and he mentally rolled his eyes. "Let's get you cleaned up."

"Ow "Alex said with a wince. His mom got the first splinter out, but the second was lodged in there. In too deep. She stretched the skin around the tiny brown dot. She should be able to get it out, she was one of the pack doctors. It's halfway out; Avery grabbed the tweezers and clipped the top in between the metal and pulled upward. She threw it into the trash and rubbed her hands together.

"No tv for a week, Alex," she said, getting up from the wooden seat.

"Wha—"

"No arguing and stay right here till I get back." Alex frowned, before he heard the front door open, then closes.

"What's wrong with you?" Austin asked strolling into the kitchen.

"Mom says I can't have the tv. I think this is the worst thing that's ever happened to me."

Austin pressed his lips together. "Mhm, Alex. Sure." He ruffled Alex's hair, then walked to the silver fridge.

A scream breaks Alex away from his short flashback. The scream sounds too familiar. Evan breathes in a shallow and shaky breath. "Lilac," he breathes out, rushing into the house. "Evan, wait!" Alex yells after him feeling his legs tremble as he stands up and runs after Evan. He can hear Jordan following them.

"Lilac!" Evan yells. His voice echoing through the deserted house. Hands banging on a door makes Alex turn his head.

"Evan!" Noah yells from behind a closed door. "Is that you! Evan!" Jordan and Alex rush over to the door, while Evan's eyes dart all over the house.

"Noah! Me and Alex are going to get you out of there."

Jordan yells and looks at Alex then back at the door. "Alex, there's a lock," Jordan says. Alex's eyes look down at the rusty lock and then to the floor where a plain gray medium sized rock lays. He picks it up and feels adrenaline and power move through his body. It makes his bones tingle, and the veins in his arms pop out as he smashes the lock with the rock. The lock breaks into two falling to ground with a clatter.

"Holy shit," Jordan says, looking at Alex with eyes filled with awe and shock. Noah and Violet push open the door, eyes wide and alert.

"Where's Lilac?" Violet asks.

"He's up here!" Mya yells standing on top of the staircase. "And Jordan hand me my stun gun." Violet and Evan run up the stairs, following the sounds of soft whimpers. Violet and Evan go into the

142

room where the hinges on the door are broken. Their shoulders brush from standing so close to one another. Lilac's on the floor, his hands around his own neck as the girl stands in front of him cupping the air, as if she were holding an invisible drink.

"Lilac," Evan shakily says. The girl turns around so fast that Evan is surprised she didn't whip herself with her short hair. Violet pushes Evan to the side, staring into the girl's eyes. She flicks her wrist to the right, causing the girls back to slam into the wall. "Lilac." Evan rushes to Lilac's side crouching down to his level. Lilac's hands and arms tremble around his knees, tears streaming down his dirt dusted face. Noah, Jordan, Alex and Mya come running into the room. Mya gasps seeing the tall girl passed out on the floor.

"What happened?" Noah asks, looking at Violet. "

"She was attacking Lilac. So I made her sleep," she says blankly. Alex looks at Jordan, nudging his head in the girl's unmoving body. Jordan is the only one who's paying attention to the situation at hand, well besides him. Everyone else is preoccupied with Lilac and Violet.

"What?" Jordan whispers.

"Check her pulse."

Jordan nods. Getting down on the ground and putting two fingers under the girls defined jawline. The pulse beats slowly, about once every two seconds. "She's fine," Jordan says, looking at Alex. Alex breathes a sigh of relief. She isn't a good person, that is evident. What good person would steal a ten year old. But there's no sense in killing her. Killing is never the answer for Alex.

Hot tears run down Lilac's face. "S-She." He pauses out of breath, the memories come in too fast and too powerful. Evan grabs his face in both hands, making Lilac stare into his eyes. His rapid heartbeat slows down. "Taylor!" an unfamiliar voice yells, the voice gets closer and closer. "Taylor!" Lilac's head turns and he recognizes the boy who comes in almost instantly. The boy pushes his way past Alex and Jordan, he shoves them both so hard that they fall to the ground. He goes down to his knees and kneels to the side of 'Taylor's, unmoving body. Lilac gulps audibly. The young boy grips the girl's right wrist, his lanky and long fingers covering Taylor's snake shaped birthmark. His whispers are incoherent to everyone else in the room. "*You,*" he snarls at Violet. Red eyes blazing as he stares clearly into her eyes. Violet falls to the ground with a high pitched scream. She withers on the ground, feeling millions of needles and spikes piercing her skin. Lilac chokes out a sob, Evan turns his face away.

"Lilac!" he yells, over his friends' screams. Lilac's clear vulnerability makes Evan's stomach churn. For the first time in so long, Evan has to be the strong one. "Look at me! Lilac! Look at me!"

"Violet!" Noah screams clearly, stepping forward. The boy releases his gaze from Violet, and moves it to Noah. "Pain" he mutters.

"No!" Violet yells, shooting her hand out in one quick movement. He gets flung backwards, his body colliding with the ground. Lilac removes Evan's hands from his face and stands up.

"You shouldn't have-." Mya pulls out her stun gun in one swift movement, she places it on the side of his neck and presses the small rounded button. The shocks crackle against his skin, sending volts of pain through his body. "We need to go," Mya says after the boy falls to the ground, beside Taylor.

"No. Not without Bill," Noah says, shaking his head.

"Noah. She's right." Violet says.

"No-" Alex grabs his arm and drags him out the door. The seven of them stumble around the house without Bill by their side.

CHAPTER TWENTY

It is as if World War III has erupted when James finally arrived at Luna Drive. He is fuming. Absolutely and positively fuming. "Lilac Gerald Smith," he nearly growls, walking out of his sheriff's car. He grabs Lilacs arm, pulling him away from his spot next to Evan.

"Dad-"

"No I don't want to hear it, Lilac get your ass in the car. Or I swear to God I will drag you there. By your flipping hair."

Lilac knows that it isn't a threat, it is a promise. A promise that has Lilac rushing into his dad's car and slamming the door behind him. The sound echoing through the quiet street.

James watches his son, then turns to the other children. He narrows his eyes at them threateningly.

"Mr. Smith it wasn't Lilac's fault we swear." Jordan says sincerely.

"No, I swear. I swear if I hear about *my* son." He looks at Violet for a moment before shifting his eyes. "Running around on a wild goose chase, I will put all of you in handcuffs."

"We wouldn't have to look, if you would do your job." Noah mutters.

"We're doing the best we can, kid." James sighs.

"Well your best isn't good enough," Noah retorts.

James sighs again, rubbing his temples before looking directly at Noah. "Just from now on, keep Lilac out of it." He pauses looking around at Lilac's friends. His eyes finding Alex in the back of the small crowd. "And a piece of advice I would keep Alex out of it too."

Alex looks down and digs his shoes into the light colored dirt on the ground. James turns back on his heels, and walks to the driver's side of his car. Lilac turns away from James, not saying a word as they drive off. The remaining six follow James's car halfway down the street, bikes left behind them.

"So we know where Bill is, and we can come back tomorrow and get him."

"You *cannot* be serious. right now." Alex says, looking at Noah as if he's lost his mind.

"What?" Noah asks.

"What? Really. You are as thick as a rock, Noah my boy." Evan's words might have sounded like mockery but his tone was far from it. "Lilac could have died. And Alex probably will."

"I didn't make anyone come with me," Noah argues.

"Might as well have," Evan says.

"And what is that supposed to mean?"

"Exactly what I said."

"Guys!" Mya finally yells. They're arguing for no reason. What exactly is it solving? "This is what those psychos want! Us to fall apart and crumble. Do you really want to give them what they want? Because honestly that sounds pretty stupid to me."

Noah crosses his arms. "Tell him that," he says stubbornly.

Alex rolls his eyes. "You're being so ridiculous right now."

"How am I being ridiculous?" Noah asks.

Evan snorts. "How aren't you?" Noah turns his head to Evan quickly. "It's not my fault Lilac was that stupid in there." The silence that follows is thick, so thick that Alex doubts you would be able to cut it with a knife.

"Not your fault, you say?" Evan asks mockingly.

"Evan, stop," Mya says.

"Well it's not *my* fault that you made us drag that freak out of the woods."

Alex can see Noah's fists clench. "Evan. Mya's right you need to stop."

Evan ignores his plea. Too blinded by his own anger. "And it's also not *my* fault that Bill's most likely dead."

Noah makes a drastic move towards him getting dangerously close to Evan's face. "Take that back!" he yells at him. Evan shoves him back with two hands.

"Why should I? It's the truth, isn't it?"

Noah returns the shove. "Take it back!" he repeats.

"Fuck off, Noah." Evan says with another shove. Noah doesn't shove him back this time around. He clenches his fist again and delivers a blow to the side of Evan's cheek. Evan collapses to the ground because of the force. He makes an effort to get up, but Violet's invisible hand keeps him down.

"Violet, stop!" Mya cries, grabbing on the hand that keeps Evan frozen in his place.

The unseen force is removed from Evan's body, he jumps up and dives for Noah, he swears up a storm. Alex and Jordan hold both of his arms. "You know what? I'm leaving. Fuck you guys. If you wanna go get yourselves killed, so be it." Evan says getting himself loose from Jordan and Alex's grip before walking away. Alex watches him leave and takes a step after him.

"You're seriously leaving too?" Noah asks. Alex looks at him, seeing the disappointment in Noah's face almost makes him stay. However, Alex wants to get the loaming argument with Austin over with. He'll heal sooner if he just gets it over with. He could heal himself faster if he really wanted to, by shifting a little into his wolf. Alex has grown a deep hatred for shifting and much rather heal the natural way. Or as natural as a werewolf can heal. "I'm sorry, Noah, but I got to go."

"Um, yeah, me too," Jordan says, leaving with Alex by his side.

When the two are gone from Noah's vision, he slams himself on to the curb. "Fuck," he groans. Slamming his palms down with the rest of his body.

"I'm gonna take Violet back," Mya says. Violet's looking at him, trying to meet his eyes, and has no clue to what is going through his mind.

"Yeah go ahead, just use the basement door" he says dismissively.

Mya feels a pain in her chest. "Yeah ok." She says, "And Noah?"

"Yeah?" he asks.

"Make sure to call me later." Noah gives a slight nod. Mya huffs, before grabbing lightly at Violet wrist and dragging her out of Noah's sight. Noah sits on the curb, hands buried deep into his hair. All his friends are gone and without them, he sits completely alone.

"Well whadda you know a wolf without his pack, no pun intended," Shawn says, smelling Alex's lonely scent. He didn't even bother to turn his head to make sure it was Alex. Alex's scent is distinct and far too familiar. A scent that Shawn can't forget.

"I could say the same to you," Alex says while walking Lilac's bike through the woods. He sees Shawn sitting on a fallen down tree, staring lazily at his fingernails.

"Your friend beat the shit out of my girlfriend today, you might want to control her." Alex snorts.

"I couldn't control Mya even if I wanted to," Alex says. It's weird how easily he can talk to Shawn, even though he's an asshole. But he's an asshole that Alex has known since he was a baby.

"I'm gonna walk with you," Shawn decides aloud, getting up and walking beside Alex.

"Why?" Alex asks, looking at him strangely.

"Can't have the Beta's youngest son walking all alone in the woods now, can I?"

Alex rolls his eyes. "I know we haven't talked in a while, but you know how much I hate that label stuff."

Shawn looks at him from the side of his eye. "It's not my fault we haven't talked, maybe it's because you've been too busy punching people."

He's still bitter, Alex realizes in his head. "I actually feel really bad about that; I'm sorry. I just lost my cool. I never think violence is the answer."

Shawn chuckles. "Never thought I would meet a werewolf who's so anti-violence," Shawn mocks.

"Well, maybe if more werewolves had that mindset there would be less pack wars," Alex snaps.

"What would we do then, hold hands and sing Kumbaya all day long?"

Alex rolls his eyes again. God, is Shawn always this exhausting? "Maybe more about the real issues like the unfair ban of human

148

communication at eighteen and the withdraw of emancipation from packs, and—"

"Wait, hold on a sec. Emancipation, so you think people should be allowed to leave packs. Leave their birthright?" Shawn says, unable to fathom what nonsense Alex is speaking of.

"If they want to, it should be their decision," Alex says. "Everyone should have their own choice for their life. Even if it's their birthright."

Shawn stares at him for a solid thirty seconds before turning away completely. "You're gonna leave, aren't you?" Shawn accuses.

"Not that it's any of your business but not right now."

"But you will. If it came down to your stupid human friends or the pack, we all know who you would pick."

Alex can't confirm nor deny it, because honestly he doesn't know what he will choose until the situation happens. On one hand his friends have been on his side for as long as he can remember. On the other hand, the pack is his family, even if they don't treat him as such. "Why do you even care, Shawn?" Alex asks. "You hate me."

Shawn shakes his head. "You're not as much of a victim as you pretend to be, Alex. You can continue the pathetic act but just know that I see right through your bullshit."

Alex wants to punch him and that's when he realizes why he stopped talking to Shawn in a normal manner. "You know what, Shawn. Screw you. Because when Monday comes you're still gonna be you, and I'll be me. Nothing different. So why not do us both a favor and stop freakin' talking to me." Alex jumps onto Lilac's smaller bike and pedals away from Shawn. That's the thing about the pack, he feels as if that he can never walk away from them ever without feeling like trash. He can see his house through the trees, his stomach beginning to churn. *Please don't be home.* He prays in his head. *For whatever reason. Please don't be home.* But at the same time, he hopes that he is. It will get rid of the anticipation and the painful certainty. He'd rather be hit and beaten down, then lectured and ridiculed. The purple bruises on his body would fade, but the bruises on his heart would scar permanently. He can see Austin's and two of his friends' cars parked in the driveway. Alex hates Austin's car, how big and bright it is, and how it stands out in any old crowd of cars. He looks over at the house beside his own and doesn't see James' car parked in its usual spot. He walks Lilac's bike to the side of Lilac's house and just under the window that Alex used to sneak into, when they were much younger. He quickly runs back to his house and up the concrete steps. He opens the clean glass door, and rests it on the right side of his shoulder. He turns the doorknob. The thought of Austin locking him out passes through his mind. It wouldn't be the first time. But when he turns the knob all the way he sees that it's unlocked. Alex pushes the door open and then immediately turns towards the stairs right when he takes a step into his house. His back to his kitchen.

"Alex," he hears Austin say, voice unsettlingly calm and steady. "Turn around" he urges. Alex's heart thumps loudly in his chest, so loud that he can hear it in his ears. Alex does turn around despite his intuition. He sees Allen and three of Austin's friends seated at the kitchen table, Austin's standing at the head of the table, his hands resting on the wood, showing his purple and red knuckles. He takes his hands off the table when Alex turns around fully. He crosses his buff arms over his chest. "I'm going to ask you one time, where the fuck were you?"

Alex's hands start to clam up at his sides. "O-Out" Alex stutters.

"O-Out where, I know you're not *that* stupid, Alex." Austin takes a few steps forward.

"My friends and I were just hanging out at Noah's."

Austin's hands close into fists. He runs at Alex and slams his fist on the wall right above Alex's head. Alex jumps, fear consuming his body. Allen jumps out of his seat, the action making the wooden chair fall to the ground. "I know when you're lying, Alex!" he screams in Alex's face.

"Austin you need to stop," Allen says, an unfamiliar look of pity in his eyes.

"Stay out of it, Allen," Austin sneers at him.

"But Austin I think you're-"

"Allen, if you don't shut your fucking face, I'm gonna come over there and beat the *fucking* shit out of you." Allen doesn't say a word after that, he puts his hands on the top of his head and sighs. "You're gonna stay the hell away from them. And this time I mean it. If I see you talking to stupid ass Noah, I will break every bone in that kid's *fucking* body."

150

Alex shakes his head, tears running rapidly and freely down his face. "I hate you so much," he says, voice cracking. Austin removes his fist from above Alex's head and takes a shaky step back. In the sudden silence you could hear the dripping faucet from the pantry. And the furnace from down in the basement. Alex's lower lip trembles as he hiccups, tears falling and falling like his eyes were the beginning of a waterfall. He pushes past Austin, who stands there frozen in time. He bolts up the stairs and into his room. Alex slams the door behind him, so hard that a message bored slides down his wall, and for the first time nobody yells at him for the noise. The cold tears then begin to burn. They burn Alex's cheeks like acid. Every emotion comes back at him. The anger. The fear. The hurt. He blacks out,; he lets the cold hearted rage consume him, and the next thing he sees is his message boards down on the ground, thumb tacks and polaroid photos covering the floor. The thumb tacks getting lost in the thick carpet. He picks up one of the black and white photos. Alex closes his eyes, rubbing his thumb over the photo of Noah's back staring out Alex's window. Alex knows the day that picture was taken. His parents and his brothers were out and Noah was the only one who could come over. The snow was falling down from the sky and Alex was fiddling with his camera.

"Shoot me," Noah had said, kneeling down in front of his window, back towards Alex.

"What?" he asked.

"You're good at taking pictures so take a picture of me." And Alex did, and now he and Noah might not even be friends anymore. He throws the picture across the room and rubs his palms over his face.

"I can't do this anymore," Alex whispers to himself. He starts crying again, no sobbing; he starts uncontrollably sobbing. He collapses on to his bed, his sobs become muffled by the pillow. Alex can't breathe; he feels like he's dying when dark spots cloud his vision. But he doesn't fight it. He lets darkness cover him like a thin sheet of pure white snow.

CHAPTER TWENTY-ONE

Lilac knows that James is not going to take him straight home, but he is way too pissed off to ask where they were going. Hell, he is too pissed to even look at his dad well. It is either anger or embarrassment, either one could be considered true. Lilac still can't believe himself, crying like that in front of his friends, how humiliating. But that woman, Taylor, was terrifying. The things she says to him, still fresh in his mind. *You're so weak;* ***she'll*** *be happy to see this.* She had said, with a voice like ice. *After we take you and your sister, your friends will be next. Oh yes. Maybe we'll kill them in front of you. That would be fun, right?* Replaying those words makes Lilac shiver in his seat. She went on and on about some lady. Was she some crazy person who liked to kidnap kids in her spare time? Lilac can't even believe his own theories. Nothing's ever that simple. Not in this world.

"Lilac," James says, turning his head for a split second to look at him. Lilac continues to look out the window, silently. "Lilac," he repeats. Lilac still doesn't react, but he does clutch the side armrest hard. He'd rather sit in the back of the car, with thick, steel, cold bars separating him from his dad. That sounds much better than hearing his name repeated over and over again in the same damn tone. "Lilac." He grips harder. *One more time.* Lilac thinks. *Do it one more time.* "Lilac."

"What, Dad! What?" He yells, turning to sit facing front, and jumping in his seat. The seatbelt being the only thing holding him back from flying through the windshield.

"Mind your tone." Lilac bounces his leg up and down rapidly. "And it's time we talk about your parents."

Lilac cringes at the last word. "I already told you-"

"I know what you told me," James interrupts Lilac rather rudely. "But it's something that needs to be done and trust me this isn't an option." *How considerate.* He almost says out loud but thinks better of it. "Your parents are from a place called Roseville.'.

"Never heard of it," Lilac remarks.

James laughs. "That's the whole point."

"Well, why?" Lilac presses.

"Listen and you might find out." Lilac crosses his arms and leans back into his seat with a sigh.

"Fine," he says, looking to the side. "I'm listening."

"Ok great." James says, never taking his eyes off the road. "I met your parents when I was your age. We were all going to the same school, Blair, Jax, Jade, and your parents. They were all mutants like you, and I was the only werewolf in our group. Everything was normal for a while, until the war happened." James' breath takes a rapid turn.

" But Dad," Lilac says, every ounce of resentment evaporated.

"We're almost there." James says and pulls the car over to the side of the woods. They're miles away from Lilac's house, and that just adds to his confusion when James unbuckles his seatbelt, then tells Lilac to do the same.

"What? Why? Where are we going?" Lilac questions as he hesitantly unbuckles the seatbelt.

"You'll see, no need to get ahead of yourself, Lilac," he says, opening the car door and exiting the driver's seat.

"What the hell is that supposed to mean?" Lilac says aloud. Despite his fear of the unknown, curiosity beats him. He opens the car door, then slams it behind him, and follows his dad into the woods. "You were saying?" Lilac asks, stepping over the cold silver colored fence. The fence that is long and narrow and went on for miles.

"There was a war between supernatural creatures. For about a year." James looks straight ahead the whole time, gaze never faltering.

Lilac sighs dramatically and crosses his arms. "And what *exactly* does that have to do with me?" he asks.

"Getting there. Relax. You didn't even want to know all of this anyway."

"Well, now that you're offering, it would be kind of rude of me not to listen."

"Yeah, sure, Lilac," James says, fondly rolling his eyes. "Anyways when the war happened, it was originally supposed to be just between mutants, but both sides started recruiting other supernatural creatures. You know Vampires, Witches, Werewolves, those kinds of people. When the war was finally over and I guess you can say that my side won. We called ourselves the Good. But–"

"What caused the war?" Lilac asks before James could finish his sentence.

"Social class, bloodlust, blood status, the power hunger, all of them? I don't really know. I might have hung around mutants but I had no part in their political business." His eyes wander around the woods.

"What do you mean?" James sighs, rubbing his temples.

"Can't believe I have to be the one to explain all this," he mutters to himself.

Lilac squints his eyes close together. "Explain what?"

"There are different levels or classes for your type of mutant."

Lilac's head tilts to the side, eyes still squinted. "What does that mean? *My* type of mutant, I mean."

"Basically who are telekinetic."

Lilac's mouth opens, then closes again. "You're joking." Lilac says. James shakes his head. "I wish I was," he replies. "But basically It's like a color system, red, green, purple. It depends on your eye color."

"What about the people who have brown eyes?" Lilac comments. James sends him a sharp glare.

"Those people are the ones who can do shit with their minds. They're usually not mutants. Purples are at the bottom, mostly because all they can do is read minds." Reading minds didn't sound half bad to Lilac. Knowing if someone is mad at you or if they like you, without even asking them, which saves the embarrassment of painful rejection. "Reds can control people with their minds, make them feel what they want them to and do whatever they want." The guy. Lilac realizes. When that guy was looking at Violet she fell to the ground

155

and was screaming. Her loud wails that Lilac can still hear so clearly. He already knew that he was the one who did that to Violet, but it's good that he knows how. "Then there's the green. They can control objects and people's physical bodies. I'm sure you noticed that you're none of those," James says, sighing at the end. Lilac nods hesitantly, his stomach starts to hurt, and the feeling of it being tied into knots blooms. "You're blue, Lilac." Lilac stares at him, there still walking in the woods never stopping for even a second. "But you never mentioned anything about blues or whatever. What can we do?"

"Because it's not common."

"What do you mean not common?"

"Besides you and your sister." Lilac almost corrects him. "There's only one other blue that's been known to exist."

The wind starts to blow, tussling Lilac's hair and taking his breath away for a split second. "Well, who are they?" Lilac asks once he catches his breath.

"She's the one who started the war. And the reason why you're not with your birth parents." Lilac's jaw nearly drops.

"What's her name?" Lilac asks.

"Johanna Grey," James says. Lilac opens his mouth to ask another question, but James beats him to it. "Oh wait, we're here," he says, his tone completely different than the one before.

Lilac turns his head straight ahead, his eyes meeting a wide and short tunnel made of dark rock. "*This* is Roseville?" Lilac asks, unimpressed.

"No. Does this really look like a town, Lilac.?"

Lilac blushes, "Then why did you say we're here. Spreading misinformation, I see," Lilac says smartly.

"Don't play stupid, Lilac. This is just the way to get into the town," James replies. "Give me your wrist," he says shortly.

"Why?" he asks. James rolls his eyes. He grabs Lilac's right wrist and presses it against the side of the dark rock. His birthmark digging into the rock. "Woah, what are you doing?" Lilac asks, his birthmark begins to burn. "Ow. Ow. Holy shit. Ow."

"Language, Lilac," James says sternly.

"Well, it hurts," Lilac whines. His skin feeling as if it was burning, bubbling even. James let's go off his wrist. Lilac quickly removes it and sees the black imprint of the crescent moon. *What the hell.*

156

"Then you just step through and what do you know, you just arrived in Roseville." James says, his eyes looking longingly at the entrance.

"Do all mutants have birthmarks?" Lilac asks. He rubs his finger over the mark in the rock. Lilac doesn't know what exactly he is expecting it to feel when he touches the imprint. Burn his skin. Make him bleed. Or even hurt him in the slightest bit. But Lilac doesn't feel a thing. It feels just like normal rock. Cold and slightly damp, but Lilac's mark feels like it belongs there.

"It will fade away in about five minute," James says as he sees Lilac's fingers trace the mark. "So if you *really* want to go in, I would do it now, or else you'll have to mark the rock again. And from what I heard it is really painful to do."

Lilac scoffs. "Trust me it is." He looks one more time at the mark before looking at his dad. "And I don't want to go in there."

"Are you sure?"

"Yes, Dad, I'm sure."

James sighs. "Then are you ready to go?" James asks.

"Yeah we can go. And honestly I don't even know why you asked, you didn't give me much of an option before."

James snorts in amusement as if he was enjoying what's happening and the fact that Lilacs is angry. "You're being overdramatic," James says as he begins to walk back out of the tunnel. "And to answer your question, yes, all mutants have birthmarks. That is how they get in and out of town."

Lilac ignores the smartass tone that is threaded through James's voice. "Same as mine?" Lilac asks.

"No. Greens have a small snake. Reds have a star. Purples a small circle. All of them are on their wrists."

"What? Is that the only type of mutant?"

James lets out a laugh, which makes Lilac scowl. He shouldn't be laughed at all. All this stuff is new to him, so it should be expected that he's utterly clueless. "No, of course not. Some people can control plants, fire, and ice. There are over like twenty types of mutants; you're not alone, Lilac."

"Never said I was, Dad," he mutters. James frowns, his ears picking up the words Lilac whispered. Lilac isn't alone at all, ever. Even though sometimes he wants to be. He has his friends, his outside family that live two towns over in Viewport, and even though he gets on his nerves most of the time he still has his dad. At least for now. "How do you know so much about mutants anyways; you *are* a werewolf."

"Yeah I'm a werewolf, but I was around mutants my whole life." Hell, his best and only real friends were mutants.

"Did you love her?" Lilac asks. James looks down at Lilac, a puzzled look on his face. "Who?"

"My mother's sister, Jade?" James doesn't respond, the lump in his throat preventing him from doing so. "Dad did y-." Lilac pauses, noticing the tears that well up in his dad's eyes. But his dad looks as if he was fighting himself not to let them full down. James rapidly blinks, then rubs his eyes with his fingers, to make them return to their normal state and his face is neutral. "Was my dad a good person?" Lilac questions, changing the subject.

James looks at Lilac then looks away just as quickly. "It depends who you were," James says, his eyes fixed on the woods ahead. "If he liked you, he could be the nicest person ever, but if he didn't, he could make your life a living hell."

The moonlight shines through Noah's bedroom window and on to the bed where Violet and Noah both sit. Their legs crossed over the other, and their bodies positioned directly across from each other.

"Why do you have stars on your ceiling?" Violet asks, her head tilted upwards.

"Oh. Um." Noah lets out a short laugh. "My brother. He wanted stars in his room, but my mom says no. She thought his imagination would run even wilder. So I thought if he couldn't have them, then I would, and he could come in my room whenever he wanted." Most siblings would be annoyed that their younger siblings were constantly there. Noah himself couldn't even remember how many times Sam had slammed the door in his face and yelled at him to get out of her room. Noah remembered how it felt and he also remembered the way Alex's brothers treat him, and the day Alex came to school with a fat lip in first grade was the day that Noah promised to do better. To *be* better. And now look at him, he's sitting in his bed with some girl, while Bill could be getting tortured and murdered.

"That's nice." Violet's soft voice breaks Noah out of his thoughts. "You're very sweet Noah," she says it's so casually and without any regard with what she is saying, and without any notice of the way Noah's face flushes.

"Well um T-T-Than-. Are you hungry? Cause I-I'm gonna get something to eat," Noah stutters.

"Ok, can you get me some more of those pop tarts? The ones with the chocolate drizzle? Oh and the sprinkles!" She says. Violet's been going through pop tarts like a madwoman, ever since Noah gave her one on the night when him and his friends found her. Noah's not mad, however. They're easy to eat and easy to sneak through the kitchen and up to his room. The two are mostly always up there, with the exception of when they sleep. Then Violet retreats back to the basement. Noah's offered his bed multiple times, but Violet says it isn't polite for her to sleep in *his* bed. But for some odd reason Noah always wants to be near her.

"Yeah, of course," Noah replies, uncrossing his legs and getting up from his bed. He walks down the steps, not caring about the noises he makes as his feet hit the carpeted ground. He knows that his mother and father are dead asleep at the early time of nine-thirty and his sister is out with her friends. He walks slowly to the pantry and through shutters that swing in the doorway. The pantry, which is painted with a distasteful green, has the shelves stocked with containers filled with cookies and cakes. Noah takes his time scanning the shelves, where the paint has peeled over time. Noah knows he needs to stop, stop his feelings for Violet. From what he's gathered from endless conversations with her, she probably doesn't even know what a crush is. She's been cooped up in her house her whole life because of some lady, and her only friend is her cousin. Also she's Lilac's sister, and not even just that, their twins for Christ's sake. It would be like if Alex would date his sister. Disgusting. He stands tall and grabs the half empty box of hot fudge sundae pop tarts. Noah tried to give her other kinds, smores, strawberry, even cookies and cream, but Violet only liked the hot fudge. He grabs the silvery package and squeezes only the package with little pressure, mindful not to break the breakfast pastry. Noah walks out of the kitchens and up the stairs, not daring to make eye contact with Bill's plain and dull white door.

He opens his own door and walks inside, then closes it behind him. Violet's hands hold up her body as she sits in the bed and looks out his window that sits directly beside Noah's bed. She looks like she's in her own world as the moonlight shines in her eyes. Noah shakily breathes and walks over to his bed. He sits on the end corner which makes the bed dip slightly. Noah sees Violet in his hoodie and as her weight is shifted the right side of the oversized hoodie slides down, showing her soft tan shoulder. She turns her head to look at him and her eyes crinkle as she smiles at him.

"Do you have them?" she asks.

Noah forgot that he was even holding a pop tart. He runs a hand through his hair. "Oh, um, yeah. Do you want me to open it for you?" Noah asks, holding the pop tart out to her.

Violet considers it for a second, before snatching the pop tart out of his hand. "No it's fine" she says, pulling the wrapper open. She takes a small bite on the side of the chocolate crust, her mind never comprehending or noticing the way Noah avoids looking at her.

"Noah," she says as she finishes the last bite of her first pop tart. For some weird reason Violet can hear her heart beating rapidly in her own ears.

"Yeah, Vi," Noah responds.

"I like you," she says looking at him with a serious look in her eyes. Noah's heart stops beating and for a second he feels like he's paralyzed.

"What?" he asks. "I like you Noah. Like."

Violet pauses; her face turns scarlet. "Like the way Mya likes Shawn. I *like* you, Noah," Violet admits. *No.* Noah thinks to himself. *No this can't be real. No. This can't be happening.* It is way too good to be true and not a good idea at all and Noah knows that. Someday, someday soon, Violet will leave and it'll leave Noah in shambles.

"We should get some sleep," Noah says, switching the light switch by his wall off. Violet huffs and throws the pop tart across the room. She slams her body down on the bed and lays on her side, her back towards Noah who picks up a blanket and covers her body with it. "Goodnight, Violet," she hears Noah whisper to her. Violet clutches her eyes shut, and hears Noah lay beside her. She opens her eyes back up, hearing Noah's normally heavy breaths calm. Violet's eyes dart across the room as she lay awake. Her only source of light being the glowing stars above her and the pale moonlight in the darkness.

CHAPTER TWENTY-TWO

Monday morning comes around and Evan knows that he's being ridiculously over dramatic, but frankly he can't give less of a shit. Ok, but in the sake of being honest with himself, Lilac's texts saying how he should forgive Noah did make him feel bad. And he is planning on talking about it with Lilac today, only Lilac doesn't show up to school. It shouldn't make him nervous or anxious, but it does. He doesn't talk to Noah or Mya throughout their classes together, the only person he does talk to is Jordan. And in his current situation he sits across from him at lunch at his groups normal table.

"You're really not going to talk to him?" Jordan asks, picking up a French fry and then throwing it back down on the tan tray.

"No. That asshole is fucking annoying at the moment."

"How mature of you to say," Jordan says.

"Please don't harass me about this, I didn't see you talking to him either," Evan shoots back.

"Well, that was only because-"

"Hey, guys," Noah's voice interjects. Mya's standing beside him, but still Alex is nowhere to be seen.

"Well, this has been a lovely lunch time chat, Jord, but I have to get going," Evan says as he begins to stand.

"Evan. Wait," Mya pleads, putting a hand on his shoulder.

"No, trust me I'm perfectly alright with exiting this cafeteria." Evan peels Mya's hand off of him.

Noah groans. He came over here for a reason; he keeps reminding himself. Over and Over again in his foggy mind. "It's about Lilac, Evan," Noah says finally.

Evan stops all of his movement. "What about Lilac?" he asks as he slides back down into his seat. The anticipation makes his hands shake.

"Lilac — he's missing," Noah says looking straight into Evan's eyes.

"What the hell do you mean by missing?" Evan nearly shouts.

"He means that he's gone, and he took Violet with him," Mya says, sitting in Alex's usual seat beside Jordan.

Evan turns to look at Noah, his gaze as sharp as a knife. "I'm always one for jokery but this shit isn't fucking funny, Noah," Evan says, his voice unnaturally dark.

"I'm not joking, Evan. I swear to God." Noah says.

"Any ideas where they might have gone?" Jordan asks, fully engaged.

"Not a clue," Noah says, looking down at the dirty school table. Evan can hear defeat in his voice and even if he's supposed to be mad at him, he still feels bad. But Evan can feel the same defeat that Noah's feeling. He keeps seeing Lilac's face in there. How his tan cheeks were tear and dirt stained. His blue eyes glazed with vulnerability and clear liquid. And in that moment he finally saw Lilac break.

"Wait," Evan says, like an imaginary light bulb went off in his head. "He- I mean they're going after Bill it's obvious." A look of realization crosses their faces. Jordan's pride hurts a tiny bit knowing that Evan is the first one to figure this out. "We should go now. Come on, guys," Evan ushers and begins to stand. His arm gets pulled down by Mya.

"No," she says, her voice stern. "We can't go into this without a plan again, we saw what happened last time." Mya quickly glances at Noah then turns her face in the other direction. "He could be dead, and it seems like I'm the only one who cares. *Please* Jordan back me up."

Jordan looks down at his tray, then roughly pushes it forward. "She's right, Evan and you know it. Don't let your.-" Jordan pauses and looks back up at him. "Emotions cloud your already shitty vision." Evan's face flushes for some reason that's unknown to him. He crosses his arms over his chest irritation eating at him from his feet and upwards.

"Ok, whatever, professor. So what do we do?" Evan asks.

"We're telling Sam and Jon," Mya says without looking towards Noah.

"What?" Noah gasps, looking at Mya in disbelief. He would've thought she would have talked to him about something like this, but he guesses that he thought wrong. "You didn't think to talk to me about this?"

"Hold on. Maybe Mya's right. We know we can't do this alone or without some kind of help, so maybe if they tell us what to do we can finally get Bill back. Or they can at least drive us to the house" Jordan says, inserting himself into the conversation.

"She obviously doesn't give a shit about Bill. And right now I feel like I'm the only one who even cares." Noah replies sharply.

"Bullshit," Evan says. "We all care; we wouldn't be doing all this if we didn't care, Noah." Jordan, Evan, and Noah continue arguing, Mya blocks their vicious chatter. Her head turns to the side, and her eyes land on Shawn. Lord Jesus help her even after the fight she still can't get him out of her head. The way his hand made its way down that girl's body makes her wish he would do that to her. Shawn's brown hair falls in front of his eyes, he isn't talking to his friends, he doesn't even look like he's listening to them. Like he's off in his own little world. It's now that Mya realizes how boys are more so followers than girls. Despite the stereotypes. They have their leader (Shawn). Then they have their right hand man (Josh, Shawn's best friend). Then everyone else follows them as if they were the second coming. It's excruciating to watch. The boy's throw looks towards Shawn and when he doesn't speak the conversations are dry. Shawn turns his head to the gallery of doors on the side end of the cafeteria, his dark eyes focusing on a figure that stands outside. Mya nearly gasps as she follows his gaze, she would know the figure anywhere. She sees Alex crush a cigarette under his shoe before pushing open the cafeteria door. His earbuds tightly in his ears, slow music blasting through them. Mya sees no bruises on his face or his bare arms, but thick bags are ringed under his eyes and his normal high, perfect posture is slumped.

"Noah," she says, hitting him on the shoulder.

"What?" he asks, stopping his heated argument with Evan and Jordan.

"Look," Mya says, pointing towards Alex. Noah turns around, his eyes grow bigger.

"Alex?" he says, standing up from his seat. The bell rings making everyone stand up and crowd the exit. Alex quickly follows the crowd. "Alex!" Noah shouts, following him like a lost puppy. "Alex!" He knows Alex can hear him, but Alex keeps the silent treatment up and continues through the hallway. "Ale-"

"Dude, just stop," Evan says, catching up with Noah's fast pace. "He hasn't been talking to anyone all day." Noah runs a hand through his hair, sighing. Is he mad about Saturday still? Alex isn't one to hold a grudge, especially a grudge against Noah, so that wasn't it. Or does it have something to do with the two assholes that Alex calls his brothers. Now, that makes more sense.

"Really?" Noah asks. It does make him feel a little better knowing the fact that he isn't the only one that Alex is ignoring.

"Yeah," Evan responds walking up the stairs. "Maybe you should talk to him after school?" he suggests. Noah and Evan make it to the top of the stairs and have a clear few of the lockers that line both sides of the walls.

Noah watches Alex unlock his locker, the earbuds still in his ears. "Yeah that's what I'm gonna do," he says, as he begins to walk past Alex without saying one word.

Alex runs like the flash when he finally gets his brown book bag over his shoulders. He successfully gets through the whole entire day without saying one word to his friends. It is harder than he thought it would be, and it makes him feel worse than he ever imagined. Shawn didn't talk to him which wasn't all that shocking. Everyone in eighth grade saw Shawn as a leader, but in reality he was as much as a follower as everyone else. Alex is guessing that everyone thinks he's totally oblivious to the weird looks he's been getting, he's not though. He's completely aware about what's happening, and he's completely aware that he looks like death. Not getting sleep for almost two full nights will do that to you. He's gotten about two hours the past two nights, his own thoughts keeping him tossing and turning in his sheets. Austin and Allen barely looked at him at him for the remaining weekend, Alex might even swear that they're avoiding him, but Alex didn't or doesn't mind. He walks out the exit and immediately spots his brother in the school's parking lot. He's leaning against the hood, pitch black sunglasses covering his eyes even though there's no sun to be seen.

"Alex!" a voice calls from behind him. Noah. Of fricking course it's Noah at this time. Alex quickens his pace. "Alex!" Noah calls again, getting closer and closer and closer to Alex. "Ale-"

"What Noah! For God's sake, what do you want!" Alex screams, turning around.

"Why haven't you been talking to anyone all day? What's going on?" Noah asks, the questions coming out rapidly.

"Nothing's going on, Noah. Can you just stop creating problems that don't exist?" Alex says, rolling his eyes.

"I'm not. Just" Noah lets out a frustrated sigh. "If this has anything to do with your brothers-"

"Just stop, Noah," Alex says as he begins to turn around and walk away. Austin pulls his sunglasses to the bridge of his nose and glares hard. But for once his glare didn't feel directed at Alex, it is to something or someone else. Nevertheless, Alex's hands still clam up, and with every step they get stiffer and stiffer.

"Lilac's missing," Noah rushes out quickly. Alex stops dead in his tracks. Austin gives him a look. A look that is yelling at him to keep walking and to *not* turn around. Despite the deadly look, Alex turns around and swiftly walks to Noah.

"What?" he asks, blinking a few more times than normal. "What do you mean?" Noah runs a hand through his brown locks. Noah can't think right, with Alex's brown eyes boring into his soul, making his brain run rapid. Sometimes it's hard to talk to Alex, even harder than it is to talk to Violet. Alex just has something about him, something that makes him feel superior then whoever he's talking to. It's not like he means to do it or anything. It just sort of happens.

"We all think he's going after Bill. He took Violet with him. And-And we gotta find them," Noah says, his eyes silently pleading with Alex. Alex looks over his shoulder and shudders at Austin's glare. He turns back to Noah, a scared look in his eyes.

"Call me as soon as you're on the way," Alex says in a hushed voice. He glances back again, his mind racing. "Walk away and look like you're mad."

Noah's face contorts in confusion. "What?" he asks.

"Just do it." Alex replies in a harsh whisper. *Please get what I'm trying to say!* Alex screams at Noah in his head. *Please don't be stupid, Noah. And get it. Please!*

"That's bullshit, Alex!" Noah screams, flailing his arms like lunatic. Alex inwardly face palms and holds in his laugh. Noah turns around, his arms falling down at his sides with a slap. He stomps away, holding in his own smile as he walks away from Alex and towards the school. Alex rolls his eyes to himself before twirling on the balls of his feet and heading straight to Austin's car. Austin looks at him one last time before pushing himself off the hood of the car and stomping to the driver's seat.

"I thought I told you to stay the fuck away from him?" Austin asks, opening the car door then slamming it so hard that it makes the lavender air freshener bounce up and down on the rearview mirror.

"He was talking to me about a school project," Alex says quietly. He gently opens the passenger and with the same gentleness he closes it.

"Then why was he yelling at you?" Austin asks sharply. Alex doesn't respond. Just sits there and waits for Austin to start driving, so he can get home quicker.

"Alex," he says, voice laced with mockery.

"He wasn't yelling at me. Alright?" Alex whispers.

Austin laughs. "Bullshit," he says through his sadistic laughs. A shiver runs down Alex's spine. Breath, he reminds himself. He can't give him the reaction he's looking for, he refuses to sink down to his level. "This is your absolute *final* warning, Alex. That kid is bad news and will only just get you into trouble."

Alex can't hold his scoff. "Yeah, aren't you my freaking hero?" Suddenly, pain makes its way on the side of Alex's face. It only takes a few seconds for Alex to eliminate his shock and realize that Austin had slapped him.

"Hey," Austin says. "Cut the fucking attitude, acting like I won't beat your ass in the back seat.." Alex stares at him, the right side of his face burns. and he's assuming that a large hand print has already imprinted itself. Alex still feels like he should be a tad bit thankful that he didn't get punched this time. But the day is still young, it's only two-thirty. Without another word, Austin jams his keys into the ignition and turns, which nearly makes the dashboard vibrate. Alex retreats his gaze from Austin, whose eyes are solely focused on the road. He leans his head on the window, closing his eyes and drifting off in the silent car. He wakes up to the car coming to a sudden stop. His eyes slowly open and they focus on his father rushing out the front door. Alex tries to blink away the tiredness in his system.

"Is he in there with you!" Andrew yells at Austin. Alex sees Austin jump in his seat a little. He unbuckles his seat belt and motions for Alex to do the same. "Austin!" he yells again, Alex, even though he's so far away, can see the fury in his eyes.

"Yeah, he's right-" Austin can't even finish his sentence before his father stomps down the perfectly smoothed out walkway and grabs Alex's arm harshly. He pulls him up the walkway without uttering one word, his tight grip never loosing. He swings open the front door, Alex gets a quick glance at his mom before he's harshly thrown to the ground. He can hear the delicate phone in his back pocket shatter when he lands. He hears his mom and Austin share a gasp.

"You wanna act grown now?" Andrew says, his teeth grinding together.

"What are you talking about?" he asks through his tight pants and gasps.

"This," he says, holding up a full box of cigarettes. *Shit*. He launches the box at Alex and just barely misses his right arm. The almost full box of cigarettes spill and roll out all over the kitchen floor. "Is what I'm talking about, Alex. Care to explain?" Alex hears a choked back sob and he looks over at his mother. Her left tan and skinny hand over her mouth, while the right clutches the wooden kitchen chair. Tears run down her cheeks and Alex can feel himself slowly breaking.

"I-I" Alex stutters, his eyes still on his mom. Alex is yanked up to his feet and his body thrown to the wooden door that stands in the middle of the kitchen. Alex winces, looking at Andrew with eyes wide and glazed over.

"Why, Alex?" he asks him; his face red and his hand shaking as he holds Alex down. Alex thinks at this specific time it's better not to say a word, then say the wrong thing. His hands quiver at his sides. A fist collides with the side of Alex's face, and a heated pain erupts right by Alex's lip. Crimson blood rushes down Alex's chin and his slanted head makes a drop drip onto the tiled floor. Austin makes a stride to his father, but Avery grabs Austin's arm. Her usually gentle and loose grips are tight and unbreakable.

"Don't" she whispers, making sure her husband doesn't hear.

"You wanna act grown. Then I'm going to treat you like you are," Andrew says, voice steady as he grabs Alex's arm and pulls him to the wooden cupboards that are attached to the cream colored walls. He opens up an empty drawer, his hand still holding on to Alex's arm. He forces Alex's pointer and middle finger into the drawer. For a split second Alex has no clue what his father's doing, but then it hits him like a semi-truck.

"Dad, please don't. Please don't, Dad." Alex pleads, tears pooling at the sides of Alex's eyes. In one aggressive movement, Andrew slams the drawer shut. Alex screams out in agony, feeling the small bones in his fingers to shatter. Big tears slide down his cheeks as his fingers begin to swell and turn a harsh shade of purple. Andrew, as if he is just snapped out of his hateful daze, opens the drawer back up. Alex quickly retreats his fingers and clutches them to his chest, tears continue to slide down. Andrew turns to look at Avery, who has her hand on her heart. A terrified look spiraling in her dark brown eyes.

"Can you fix him up, Avery?" he asks, stillness in his voice despite the situation. She nods, unable to speak a single word. Avery walks over to Alex and wraps an arm around his shoulders as she walks him up the steps and into the bathroom.

"Sit on the counter," she lightly demands. "I'll be back." With another look towards Alex, she walks out of the bathroom. Alex lifts his left hand and places it on his lips, he then removes it and sees not a drop of blood on his fingertips. It's a good sign that the bleeding has ceased, it would be an even better sign if the throbbing of his fingers would stop as well. But right now he cannot dwell on it, the blood and tears have stopped, but the anger and pain are still present, clear as day. Alex takes his shattered phone out of his back jean pocket. A heavy cut splits the screen down the middle, and the bottom right hand corner is chipping glass. He puts in his password and sends a quick text to Noah telling him to pick him up as soon as possible. He can hear his mother's footsteps coming down the hallway. He shoves his phone back into his back pocket and puts both his hands in his lap.

Avery walks back into the bathroom, her hair up loosely in a pony tail and a first aid kit in both of her hands. "Ok, honey, let's get you taken care of," she says, voice sweet as honey. Alex cringes and looks away when Avery tries to make eye contact. She sighs. "I'm sorry, Alex," she says, reaching for his injured hand.

Alex snatches his hand from her. "Then why?" He asks.

"Why what, baby?"

"If you're sorry, then why don't you do anything to make them stop?" Alex can't help his bitter tone, or how tears of frustration burn his eyes.

Avery sets the first aid kit onto the bathroom counter. "It's not that simple," she says soothingly. She places a gentle hand on Alex's shoulder. Alex shrugs her off. The tears run down his face in streaks.

"No! You can't say that anymore!" he yells, jumping off the counter. "Why can't you put me first? For one time in your life, care about me enough to stop them from hurting me."

Tears well up in her eyes, which makes them shine in the fluorescent vanity lights. "Alex-" she begins but is quickly cut off.

"If you really loved me, you would put me first. Not him. Or all of them." Alex pushes past her and walks out of the bathroom. He closes his eyes as he walks straight. The thought of turning back and apologizing for being selfish crosses his mind. But the images of his fingers being broken, and every punch, kick, and slap conceal the previous thoughts. When Alex does open his eyes, he's faced with another photo. A photo of his family. Smiling, perfect clothes , not a black and blue bruise in sight. Alex's blood starts to burn through his skin. His eyes flashing a quick shade of dark red. He yanks the metal and glass frame off the wall and sends it flying down the steps with all the power he can muster. It lands on the ground with a loud crash, which makes Austin and Andrew turn their heads in that direction. The glass over the cursed picture shatters and the outer frame cracks down the center. Alex rushes down the steps ignoring the shouts from his father and Austin. They can say whatever they want to him at this moment, but it won't stop him from leaving that damn house. He runs out the front door and into the woods, forcing himself not to look back and to keep on running.

CHAPTER TWENTY-THREE

"You fucking asshole, dickwads, let us the out," Lilac screams, pounding vigorously on the old wooden door. It wasn't the brightest idea to go back to Luna drive, without a plan and just him and Violet. But it needed to be done and Lilac was tired of not having Bill safe at home again. He was tired of constantly wondering if he was alive. So he snuck out at about twelve am on Sunday night. His first thought was to go at it alone and face the two of those assholes alone, but after another thought, Lilac eliminated the thought. He might be reckless and sometimes stupid, but he isn't *that* reckless or stupid. Violet, he decided, would be his best companion for the particular situation. Even though he doesn't really like her, he will admit that she has control over her power, which Lilac does not. "Damnit," Lilac whispers to himself as he pushes the door with his hands. Violet's casually sitting on the floor, knees to herself, looking calm as ever. Lilac sighs and forces himself to face Violet. "Aren't you going to at least *try* and get us out of here?" Lilac asks her. Violet shakes her head. "Great," Lilac mumbles. He walks across the dingy and moldy small room, the whole house smelled like dirt and garbage. He sits down in front of Violet. "So now that we're stuck here, we might as well make good conversation," Lilac says.

Violet stares at him then casts her eyes downward. "What do you do if you like like someone who doesn't like you back?" she asks quietly.

Lilac takes a few seconds to process the question. "Well, you would usually move on," Lilac replies, he pauses and thinks about who she might be referring to. Then it hits him. "Are you talking about Noah? Because he likes you, you know. I can tell."

Violet looks up, a smile making its way on her face as her cheeks begin to flush to a light shade of pink. "Really?" she asks, looking up at Lilac, her eyebrows raised. Lilac snorts.

"Trust me; I know when Noah likes someone. He isn't the best at hiding things." Lilac laughs.

"Then why did he reject me?" she asks. Lilac can see the hurt in her eyes. She likes him, a lot. Whatever doubt that was in Lilac's mind is completely gone now. It's confirmed. He feels sorry for her, and Noah. He's sure that Noah likes her back, almost positive. But why would he reject her? Is it because he has too much on his plate? Or does it have something to do with her?

"I honestly don't know, Violet." Lilac says. "I'm sorry."

Violet shakes her head. "It's ok. It's not your fault." She pauses and looks around the bland room, that has nothing but some broken and torn up furniture.

"I mean you could kiss him, break the ice. Show that you really like him," Lilac suggests, not thinking that she might actually do it. Does the girl even know what kissing is?

"Do you think that'll actually work?" She's seen her mom and dad kiss, but she thought that was only for married couples.

"Maybe," Lilac shrugs. Silence consumes the two until Violet speaks. "So do you like anybody?" Lilac can feel warmth spread across his cheeks. Suddenly Violet's eyes go wide. Her hand goes straight to Lilac's cheeks. "Are you ok? You feel hot? Are you getting sick?" Her questions shoot out of her mouth rapidly.

"No, I'm ok," Lilac replies. Lilac can't believe that she can see his face in the dimly lit room. He can see from the tiny spaces in the boarded up windows that the sun has begun to set. Which makes the skies painted with shades of yellow, blue and pink and the sun to burn anyone who looks at the skies, eyes. Violet takes her hands off of Lilac's face. "But yeah, I have a crush on someone. Doesn't everybody?" Lilac says. Violet leans in close to Lilac and puts her hand on the side of her face.

"Do you like, Mya?" Violet whispers as if Mya was somewhere listening to their conversation.

"Ew no, not like that." Lilac says, shaking his head. He sighs as Violet pulls her head away from Lilac and puts her hand back down. "I don't even know if I like anyone like he," Lilac says.

Violet squints her eyes together. "What do you mean?"

"I mean that-." Keys begin to jingle from the outside of the door, which makes Lilac and Violet jump to their feet. Lilac can hear the old lock unlock and fall down to the ground.

The man with the red eyes opens the door and stands in the doorway, his arms at his sides. The cut on his wrist looks to be healed, but his eyes are bloodshot and the whites of them have red lines scattered atop of them. "Let's go," he demands. Lilac looks at Violet, who nods at him. He rolls his eyes but walks forward, nonetheless. "And don't even think about trying anything." he sneers. Lilac inwardly scoffs. *Yeah right.*

"Where the fuck is Bill?" Lilac asks.

The man laughs, goosebumps cover Lilac's bare arms and it wasn't because of the cold air in the abandoned house. "You're not in the position to ask questions." he responds, taking a few steps ahead. Lilac laughs, harder than the other.

"And you are?" Violet gives him a confused look as the two twins walk out of the slowly darkening room.

"Just go with it," he mouths. She nods still not getting what Lilac means. The man stops and turns around.

"What?" he asks, eyes starting to glow.

"Well, I'm just saying, since you are a useless red," Lilac says, Violet looks at him again still confused. The man's fist clench at his sides, eyes burning like fire. Lilac knows it's working.

"You don't know what you're talking about." A crazed smile makes its way on the nameless guy's face. "You're human bred. A goddamn *traitor.* You don't know a thing, you wretched useless brat," he snaps.

Lilac laughs again despite his rage. "I may be a traitor as you put it, but at least I'm not a lap dog like you. Following a green like a lap dog, *you're* the one that's useless."

The other man shakes his head. "Shut up" he says almost in a whisper.

Lilac puts his hand on his heart and leans back. "Oh, did I hit a nerve," Lilac mocks.

"Shut up." The young adult says louder this time. Putting his hands over his ears and begins to pace.

"Be ready" he says to Violet, quietly.

"Ready for what?" Violet asks, still clueless.

"You'll see," he replies. Lilac takes a step forward when the man stops pacing and stands normally. His breathing erratic and hot tears sliding down his face. "Don't try to act powerful, red," Lilac says, his tone taunting. "You're nothing more than Taylor's bitch."

"*SHUT UP!*" he yells, finally losing his cool. The tears burn hotter till they feel like lava. "Pain," he says through his clenched teeth. Lilac collapses to the ground, feeling millions of knives pierce through his entire body.

"N-Now" Lilac stutters through his pain. It continues to hurt, with each passing second the pain just increases. It hurts to move and it hurts worse to breathe. Violet looks into Lilac's eyes which are looking into hers intently and she knows what to do. She looks at the man, whose eyes are on Lilac. Whose eyes are hurting him. She flicks her wrist. Feeling the adrenaline run through her veins. The man goes flying across the room. His head colliding with the wall, knocking him out, but not killing him. The pain is lifted from Lilac's body, causing his skin to tingle. He lays there, trying to catch his breath.

"Are you alright?" she asks, crouching down to be at his side.

"Yeah" he says, his voice scratchy. "I'm fine, let's find Bill." Violet stands up and helps Lilac to his feet. The front door opens and pairs of feet come rushing into the creepy house.

"Lilac," Evan says in relief. Alex, Jordan, Mya, and Noah, follow in.

"What the hell are you guys doing here? It isn't safe for you guys" Lilac says. His eyes sweep across his friends until they land on Alex. "What the fuck happened to your fingers.?" Alex looks down.

"It isn't safe for you either, Lilac," Noah says; he avoids meeting Violet's ocean eyes. "And especially bringing Violet into this. Seriously what were you thinking!"

Lilac opens his mouth to defend himself but is interrupted by an outside voice. "Noah?" A small voice asks from the top of the stairs. Lilac turns his head to the staircase, eyes immediately filling with tears. Not tears of sadness, but tears of happiness and relief.

"Bill," Noah says; Lilac can practically see his smile. The seven of them run up the stairs., Noah getting ahead of everyone else he picks Bill up into his arms and holds on to him tightly. Scared that even if he let' go of him for a second something might take him away from Noah again. "I love you so much, Bill." Noah cries, pulling away from Bill and holding his small face in his hands. His face has patches of dirt and a healing bruise on his forehead but other than that he looks ok.

"Well, Well, Well. The gangs all here, ah," the girl's voice says in a singsong voice. Lilac turns to face her, when the two make eye contact, Lilac feels the fear gripping at his chest.

"Just leave us alone." Lilac says, going to step in front of his friends. "We have what we came here for. We can just- uh forget that this ever happened."

The girl, Taylor, laughs. "Oh no Lilac you and your sister aren't going anywhere. She'll be very pleased to know that Violet isn't her only young blue." Her gaze follows Evan. "Maybe you just need some motivation and since the brat wasn't enough." She doesn't finish her sentence before her hand closes half way. Evan starts to gag. Invisible pressure is applied to Evan's neck. His hands go up to them attempting to peel off the force. His eyes start to get heavy and his breaths fall short.

"Evan!" Lilac screeches. His friends crowd around Evan, full on panic mode. Eyes wide, screaming at each other violently. Violet just stands there confused like always, looking at Evan curiously. Lilac turns to Taylor, seeing the insane smirk on her face. Lilac focuses on her with eyes like blue flames. His rage builds up in him and consumes him like waves. The smirk goes off of her face as blue wraps around her neck, her hand falling down because of the sudden painful weight. Evan begins to cough at the sudden release. As Lilac's fingers move back and forth, the weight on the girl's neck gets heavier. And then suddenly Lilac's fist closes. He doesn't know what he's doing, his mind goes on autopilot as his body takes control. When his fists closes it makes Taylor's neck snap instantly. Her breathless and lifeless body falls to the ground, banging on the old floor.

"Lilac," Jordan says. "I think- I think you- Oh God, you killed her." Lilac shakes his head, swallowing the lump in his throat. *Oh my god, I just killed someone.* Maybe he's a sociopath. He feels nothing, no guilt, no remorse. Just numbness. A part of him is screaming at him that he should feel bad. Feel sorry. That he should be on the floor balling his eyes out in remorse for what he did. An even stronger part of him is telling him that it's not his fault. She was going to kill Evan, he was just defending his friend. Defending some he cares for greatly. Lilac doesn't know what to believe.

"Like he had a choice." Mya scoffs.

"A girl is fucking dead, Mya," Jordan argues.

"Language, guys!" Alex interjects, as he goes to stand beside Bill.

"What would you rather Evan be dead?" Mya asks.

"Well, no but–"

"See. And frankly I'm glad that fucking bitch is dead. Better her than us," Mya says.

"Ruthless, Mya," Evan whispers to her.

"It's the truth," she says back to him. Sirens wail in the distance, getting closer and closer to the house on Luna Drive.

"Shit. We need to get Violet out of here," Lilac says to Noah. Noah's eyes snap to him. "What? Why?" Noah's eyes are buggy as he looks at Lilac. "They can't know she's here. We need to get her out of town. They might kill her if they find her." Lilac thinks about the woods just outside the back of the house, only about three miles to the entrance of Roseville.

"We'll go out the back." Noah sighs, grabbing Violet's hand and grasping it tightly. He looks at Alex. "Can you watch Bill for me?" Noah asks. Alex nods. Noah lightly pushes Bill's back, directing him to Alex. Lilac, Noah, and Violet walk down the creaking steps. And out the back door which is halfway off the hinges. The three of them miss the missing red who was once unconscious on the floor. The rains raging outside and Lilac is stupid enough to be wearing a plain light blue t-shirt. Violet and Noah pull up their hoods, covering their hair from the downpour, Lilac's hair immediately gets soaked, turning two shades darker. It's freezing too, and Lilac's shivering as he walks to the beginning of the dark woods. They're even more freaky at night. The trees look like big monsters with obnoxiously long limbs. Violet stops first, turning around to face Lilac and Noah, who stand side by side.

"You know the way. Right?" Lilac asks, silently wishing that she would say no so Lilac could go with her. For some reason it hurts to let her go. His sister that he was so mean to is leaving, right after he just started to get to know her.

"Yeah I do," she says, looking at Lilac. "Goodbye, Lilac," she says. Lilac doesn't think he pulls her into a hug, tears coming out of his eyes.

"I'm sorry" he says softly.

"For what?" she questions, hugging him back.

"For being an ass to you."

"An ass?" she questions.

If it was different circumstances Lilac would have laughed. "It's nothing. It's just-I- I love you, Violet. You're the sister I never had." He pulls away from Violet.

Violet smiles, tears and raindrops running down her face. "I love you too," she says.

Lilac rubs his eyes and coughs. "Yeah, well, I'll leave you two alone." he says looking in between Noah and Violet. "Bye, Violet," he says, before running through the freezing rain to get back to the just as cold house.

"So" Noah says, taking off his hood and running a hand through his already damping hair. "I guess this is it, huh." God he sounds like an awkward turtle. Suddenly his face is lightly grabbed and he's looking at Violet's blue eyes in the darkness.

"Can I kiss you?" she asks quietly. Noah can't bring himself to say anything; he wants this, but he just can't say it in words. So he nods. Her lips collide with his, and Noah immediately returns it. Violet's lips are cold, but not in the way that most find uncomfortable. They feel like a cold glass of ice water on a hot summer day and Noah is the sun slowly making the water warmer and warmer. Noah hands wrap around Violet's waist lightly and Violet's other hand makes its way on the other side of Noah's face, deepening the kiss. Their hearts beat loudly in their chests, blocking out the blaring sirens and the flashing red and blue lights. They pull away, catching their breaths.

"You should get going before the rain gets too bad." Noah says. Violet nods, turning around and taking a step forward. "Wait, Violet!" Noah calls. She looks over her shoulder. "I like you too," Noah says. Violet closes her eyes and turns around completely. She runs into Noah's arms in one last tight embrace. Her skinny arms wrap around his neck, while his wrap around her lower back.

177

"I'm going to miss you so much" She cries into his shoulder. The tears don't stop as they fall down from Noah's eyes.

"I'm gonna miss you too, Vi," he says, reluctantly unwrapping his arms from Violet. "You need to go," he says. Violet nods, looking into Noah's soft eyes one more time before running into the woods. Noah chokes out a sob, the sirens stop the only sounds outside the dreadful house being the rain, the wind, and Noah's cries. He puts his hand over his mouth, his knees buckling under him, but he resists to fall to the ground. His feet sink into the wet mud, but Noah doesn't care. Footsteps run out the back door and Noah doesn't have to turn around to know who it is. "Go away, Lilac," he says dismissively. "I don't want to talk to anyone right now." Lilac grabs him by the shoulders. He can see that he's been crying and that he's weirdly pale. "No-No-No Noah, you don't understand." Lilac babbles.

"What, Lilac; what's wrong!" He finally lashes out.

"It's Alex. He's hurt," Lilac says. "He's hurt really bad, Noah."

CHAPTER TWENTY-FOUR

The whole thing's slow motion in Austin's eyes. Alex falling to the ground, from the staircase and banging his head against the disgusting floor. That fucking red pushing him. Austin would have killed him if James didn't get to him first. Austin runs to Alex's side, his eyes are closed and his breathing is steady. He can hear Lilac running out the back door. His brother's annoying ass friends screams and cries. But Austin doesn't give a shit. His focus is on the up and down motion of his brother's chest and the fingers that are still broken and bruised. Police officers surround the area and the Colemans stand there too, Bill being held tightly in Mrs. Coleman's arms.

"Alex," he says, grabbing him by the shoulders and shaking him. "Alex!" he yells, shaking him harder, panic consuming him, goddamnit. Footsteps get louder and louder in his direction, till Noah is sitting there at Alex's other side.

"Is he ok?" Noah asks him.

"Does he look ok?" Austin snaps. Noah rolls his eyes, as the paramedics get there. They drag a stretcher through the busted down door. They wheel it in, two paramedics grab Alex gently and lift's him onto the gurney.

"Is he going to be ok?" Noah asks the female paramedic.

"From the looks of it, he'll be ok, kid," she responds, looking at him with a look of pity. Noah nods his head, as he watches Alex get wheeled away. As Alex goes through the door and into the flashing ambulance, James comes into the house. Rain drops all over his shirt and his hair soaking wet. His eyes wander the crowded run down house, attempting to find his son.

Lilac pushes his way through Evan and Jordan, and runs into his dad's arms, crying hard. The guilt and the realness finally settling in and hitting him like a soccer ball in the chest. "I-I killed someone," he whispers to him, tears streaming down his face like the unstoppable rain outside.

"I know Lilac. It's ok; everything's going to be fine," he says softly. Lilac nods, still not sure he can believe him.

"She's gone," he cries.

"I know," James replies holding him even tighter.

"You can't stop us from seeing our kids," a woman's voice says. "This is bullshit!"

"Mom?" Lilac hears Evan ask, walking up to the doorway. Lilac unwraps his arms from his father's upper body.

"Can you stop swearing, Jennifer?" Avery says, giving Evan's mom a harsh glare.

"Oh, shut up" Catherine says. She pushes her way past the police officers and walks over to Mya who mentally curses herself out. "You are so grounded!" she yells at her. "Oh and Jordan," she says nicely, "Your mom wants me to take you home." Mya stops herself from rolling her eyes. She would rather not be grounded for the rest of her teenage years.

"Evan Lee Peterson! What the fuck were you thinking! Sneaking out of the house! Sneaking into another house! You could have died you dumbass!" Jennifer yells.

"Um. Ms. Peterson? Lilac asks hesitantly from behind her. She turns around her dark eyes softening from her previous glare.

"Lilac," she says, pulling him into a hug. *Jesus, I'm going to be suffocated before this night is over.* "I haven't seen you in a while. How've you been" Ms. Peterson asks.

"Oh, I've been alright." he replies.

"Mom," Mya says. "I know you're mad at me right now but Alex-he's." Mya feels her throat start to tighten. She blinks a few times to regain her composure. "He's in the hospital and we *have* to go see him."

Evan looks at his own mom and points to Mya. "What she says."

Jennifer and Catherine look at each other, communicating with each other through their eyes till a particular annoying voice interrupts the silent conversation. "Exactly. *My* son is in the hospital, not your children who should honestly be the ones-." Avery can't finish her sentence before Jennifer is lunging at her, directing cuss words at her. James holds her back. It takes every rational thought in her mind to stop her from punching Avery in the face. And if Catherine was twenty years younger she would have, but back then she didn't have a family and a job to lose. But that doesn't mean she can't say whatever she wants.

"Listen, you bitch," she says. Lilac holds in his laugh at the look on Avery's face. "Say whatever you want to me. Honestly, I don't really care. But don't think for one second that I'm going to let you drag the kids into anything." Avery opens her mouth to respond. Her eyes are a darker shade of brown and her face is flushed in true miller fashion.

"Mom, just stop," Austin whispers, pulling gently on her arm. She glares at Catherine, before pushing her way through the crowd of officers, and walks out the broken door.

"Come on, kids; we need to get you to the hospital," Catherine says, with a nod towards Jennifer.

"Wait," Mya says, looking around the packed room. "Where's Noah? We can't just leave without him."

"He already left with his family. They're taking Bill to check him out at the hospital. Don't worry; he'll be there," James answers. Mya nods and walks past him without another sound. Jordan follows her out.

Jennifer looks at Evan and Lilac, who stand next to each other. "I'll go start the car," she says, pulling up her hood and bracing herself for the storm that rages outside. Lilac's eyes focus on the ground, hands shaking vigorously at his sides, the urge to throw up weighs heavy in the pit of his stomach. He killed someone, his only real sibling is gone, and his best friend got carried off to the hospital, unconscious. One of those things would cause a person to go nuts. Lilac's shocked that he's staying together now. But the intensity makes him want to fall to his knees and sob hysterically is shining in his mind like Christmas lights. A pale hand rests on his shoulder and makes him jump. Lilac goes on high alert, his hand flexing on impulse. That's one thing that feels good about everything that's happened, the power in his body feels at ease and easier to control. The second that he snapped Taylor's neck his power felt calm, like waves before a bad storm. Lilac knows that sounds terrible. He looks into Evan's eyes that are swirling with sympathy. It should make him sick and angry but some of the fear that flows through his body disappears.

"I'll see you at the hospital," Evan says, a small smile forming its way on his face. Lilac nods and looks back down. He hears Evan sigh before walking away, until Lilac can't hear his footsteps anymore.

"Come on, Lilac. Let's get going," James says, soothingly. He places his hand on Lilac's back pushing him gently ahead. Lilac sees the looks from the officers that are sent his dad's way. The looks of respect and fear. He gets respect for doing nothing at all and is feared for nothing that's fearful. It doesn't make any sense. Were they werewolves too? Lilac doesn't know. As Lilac gets closer and closer to the door he can hear the howling wind and the water that falls like a waterfall from the gutter. The blue and red sirens still blink in the darkness, Lilacs eyes hurt from staring at them for too long. The door handles cold and wet when he pulls the car door open.

"Is this gonna be another talk?" Lilac asks, when James comes into his car and buckles himself in.

"Depends if you have any questions to asks," he responds, putting the keys into the ignition and turning , successfully starting the car. James glances to his right side where Lilac sits in the passenger seat with that glare through the windshield.

"Who were those people, Dad? What did they want?" Lilac asks, his face turning to look at the right side of his dad's face.

"They're eradicators," James says, gripping the steering wheel, hard.

"Exterminators?" Lilac questions, weirdly. He thought exterminators were the things that killed bugs or something. Why would anyone name their cult after something like that?

James tries to hide his smile and suppress his laugh. "No, Lilac. Eradicators," James enunciates.

Lilac's face flushes red. *Idiot.* He calls himself in his head. "Ok, Eradicators or whatever. What the hel- heck does it even mean."

James sighs, eye moving from the dark, and slippery road. "There Johanna's Grey's followers." A chill runs down Lilac's spine. "They see her like she's their god. The mark on their wrists is their symbol."

Suddenly everything clicks into place. It all makes sense, why they came to Jeffreyville, why he and Violet were kept alive instead of being killed on site. It all makes sense, well except one thing. Why Bill? "Why him? Why not me?" he questions. If they could get Bill, why couldn't they get him. But how could James know the answer. He's not in those weirdos' heads.

"My guess," James says, pulling into the hospital. Lilac sees Evan standing on the curb, next to the back entrance, cigarette hanging from his two fingers, and the dirty grey smoke coming out from his lips. "Is that they used him to get to you. They knew you would come for him and they used that to their advantage." It is scary that a stranger could know that about him. They were watching him and no one noticed. They could have taken anyone. Lilac doesn't know what he would've taken one of his friends. He doesn't know how he would have survived if they did. Especially if they took Evan. The thought alone makes his stomach churn.

"Dad?" he asks, looking at James.

"Yeah" He responds, looking back at him. "Were you in love with her?" James stares at him, not sure what he means. "Jade. I mean."

His face goes stone cold. His eyes look stormy and angry in the dark. *Touchy subject.* Lilac makes a mental note in his head. "Yes" he responds, sharply.

"I'm not like you, Dad," Lilac says. James' eyes squint in confusion.

"What do you mean, Lilac," James asks. Lilac swallows the growing lump in his throat.

"I–" he chokes out. Tears fall down his cheeks, his hands begin to shake violently in his lap. *What if he hates me?* Lilac questions anxiously in his head. *What if he thinks I'm a freak.*

"Woah, Lilac!" James exclaims. "What's wrong?"

"I don't like girls." Silence. Oh god Lilac fucking hates silence.

"Are you trying to tell me you're gay?" James made sure to make sure it didn't sound rude. Because frankly he didn't really care if Lilac is. Lilac nods. He closes his eyes tightly expecting a yell or a punch in the face. But what comes is a laugh. Lilac's eyes spring open and he looks at James with bug eyes. "What?" James asks through another laugh. "You thought I was gonna be angry?"

183

Lilac can't help rolling his eyes. "Well it's not the kind of thing some parents wanna hear." Lilac says somewhat annoyed. "And we haven't really talked about this kind of stuff before."

James sighs and rubs his creased forehead. "I don't care, Lilac. I'll love you no matter what you do." Lilac smiles and turns to look out the window to find a pair of coffee brown eyes staring back at him. He blushes as his and Evan's eyes stare into each other's. James' eyes squint. "Well, go on and get out there," he says. Lilacs head whirls back to face James.

"Dad, I thought you hated Evan?" Lilac asks.

"Not because he's a boy, Lilac. Because he's a smartass who smokes," James replies. Lilac chuckles and unbuckles his seatbelt, face still flushed bright red. "But I swear to God if you smell like cigarettes I will-"

"Good bye, Dad," Lilac says opening the door and running out of the car, running to Evan. James watches him go. Jesus, he's getting old. Both of them. He remembers when Nate asked him to take Lilac. Johanna found out about him and Violet, and Cynthia and Nate thought it would be safer for the twins to be separated. They knew James wasn't going to have kids of his own, he would never find someone like Jade. Jax had a family of his own and Blair was gone. So they asked him and right when James saw Lilac he agreed. If only life was that simple. He didn't regret taking Lilac in, ever. But who knew raising a kid could be this difficult? He glances back at Evan and sees that the two are gone. He sighs restarting the car and pulling out of the parking lot. One recurring thought in his mind. *I need to talk to Nate.*

CHAPTER TWENTY-FIVE

Tonight is the night that Noah realizes how much hospital waiting rooms suck. But why wouldn't they. They're designed for the friends and family of people who are hurt or dying and are just waiting to see if they're ok. To see if they're even alive. Alex's waiting room was more awful then Noah could imagine. On one side is Alex's family, there is only one person who Noah could even tolerate, Alex's Aunt Abby who seemed just as mad as Noah. On the other is Noah's friends. Everyone is there, well, except Austin, which Noah isn't even a little upset about. Shockingly, Allen is completely silent. His forehead is resting in his hands and his right knee is bobbing up and down. The urge to pace around is strong ever since Noah walked through the open door. And the urge to punch Allen in his stupid face feels even stronger. Noah doesn't think it is the time or the place and Noah can only imagine what Alex would say. Bill is thankfully ok, and Noah already explained to him not to tell their parents what he saw. Bill reluctantly agreed. But now Noah's alone in the waiting room, where the wobbly wooden shelves are filled with bored games with missing pieces and old dirty children's books. A coffee table divides the two couches on both sides of the room and the smell to be smelt is the pungent scent of bleach. Everyone has left to go down to the food court, they invited him, but eating felt like the last thing he would want to do. Noah drags his cut finger nails down his covered thighs, the jeans are thick, so Noah can't feel a thing. But the action is successfully distracting him. The thought of Alex dying has been on his mind and so has the anger of Alex's broken fingers. Seriously how can someone do that to another person, it is disgusting. Especially your own family. Noah couldn't even imagine pushing his brother too hard let alone all the things he's seen Austin do to Alex. The nurse came by what feels like hours ago. She says the force of the fall left him unconscious and that he most likely has a concussion. There was probably more but Noah stopped listening after that. He tried to stop thinking of Alex and Violet but the memories of her still hunt his mind. The feeling of her lips on top of his almost makes him scream. He wants to push the memories away at least for now, but he can't. Noah stops the movement of his fingers and stares at the white wall ahead, never breaking eye contact once. Suddenly, footsteps are heard in the quiet atmosphere. They bang against the white floor and echo in the quiet hallway.

Noah sits up completely straight and his eyes watch the door frantically. *The nurse!* He yells in his head. *Did he wake up? Is he ok?* The question bangs against the walls of his brain. But it's not the nurse and Noah is up on his feet in a flash. Austin walks in a beat up copy of *Catcher in the Rye* in his hand. He's gripping the book so tightly that Noah's surprised the spine doesn't crack even more. Noah and Austin make eye contact. Noah's glaring fiercely while Austin rolls his eyes.

"Great you're in here," Austin says, his voice rough from lack of water. He throws the old book on to the coffee table. Noah would recognize that book as Alex's anywhere.

"What the fuck is that?" Noah asks, his fists tighten.

"A book," he says, looking at Noah like he's a boring old ant.

"Why do you have it?" he demands.

"Why are you on my dick? Some don't need to be answered, Coleman," Austin responds, his signature smirk on his lips. Noah really hates him. He's the one person he really truly hates. Over Noah's dead body is Alex going back to that house. That house and the people in it are ripping Alex apart. Never again. He'll do anything to stop him. "Get the hell out," Noah says, slightly above a whisper. He knows he didn't have the power to kick anyone out of a public waiting room but Noah doesn't care. He also knows if it ever came down to an actual physical fight between him and Austin, Noah would get his ass kicked. But he will never admit it aloud. His pride is way too big.

"What did you say?" Austin asks, smirk wiped completely off his face.

"Get the *hell* out." Noah says louder this time. Austin takes two long strides till Austin and Noah are only about a foot apart. "You have no right to say that to me,"

"Really?" Noah asks in mock shock.

"Because I don't think you do either." Austin laughs darkly.

"Bullshit" he says. "As much as you wanna act like you are, you're not his brother. Blood's thicker than water, Noah. And last I checked you were just another annoying ass friend who he's gonna have to leave at eighteen. So don't act entitled." Noah can hear the spite in his voice and that only makes him angry. But it isn't just spite in Austin's voice, it is envy. Envy that is hidden, like a treasure map. But Noah can hear it form a mile away. "You're jealous." Noah says to both Austin and himself. The smirk leaves Austin's face, he glares. "Yeah right. You're nothing to be jealous of." Austin turns around and begins walking to the doorway. That just confirmed Noah's suspension.

"If you're not jealous then why? Why do you do that to him?" Noah asks. He's sick of not having answers, and he knows there's a reason as to why Austin does what he does. Allen's motive is clear. He's just following what Austin's doing. Which doesn't make what he does any less horrible. Noah remembers one day when Alex climbed through his bedroom window with tears in his eye and a giant bruise on his cheek. Noah also remembers vividly what it looked like. Swollen, black and blue, with a deep dark red line surrounding it. He didn't say what happened nor did he mention any time Noah asked about it later. Alex simply asked if he could spend the night, which Noah obviously says yes. Alex took the floor, even though Noah offered multiple times for him to sleep on the bed, Alex continued to refuse. Noah couldn't sleep that night. His mind wandered from Alex to himself. What kind of best friend was he? Letting someone do this to him. The realization as to what was going on finally settling in and never fading away after that. Noah just wants it to end. After tonight, Noah's so done with people he cares about getting hurt. He won't let Alex disappear like Violet, he can't go on without him. Right now he needs him more than he ever has.

"It's none of your fucking business," Austin says, what looks like flames swirling in his eyes. Causing them to shine like gold in the hospital light. He shoves Noah. Hard. Making him fall to the ground. Noah's body shoots up from the floor. He shoves Austin back, but Austin barely stumbles a step. Noah notices the height difference between him and Austin. Noah's head barely touches Austin's nose, he beats Noah by at least three inches.

But Noah refuses to back down. "Are you gonna hit me? Shows your character." Noah laughs, with no humor. "You're going to hit your brother's *best friend* while he's in the hospital." Austin growls lowly in his throat and shoves Noah again, even harder this time. Noah expects it this time so he manages to stay on his feet. A small cough causes both of them to turn their heads to the door. Lilac stands there his arms crossed and a look of boredom in his eyes.

"Are you two *babies* done now?" Lilac asks, irritation dripping from his voice. Austin scoffs at the word babies, he is most definitely not a baby. And if Lilac thinks that, then he's wrong. "I need to talk to you," Lilac says, eyes on Austin. Austin raises his eyebrows, while Noah stands there just as shocked.

"Him?" Noah asks. Lilac nods. He wants to talk to Noah but right now he can't. He's a bit wary to be talking with Austin alone, especially because of last time. He nearly peed his pants. Austin smirks as he walks to the doorway and past Lilac. Lilac rolls his eyes at Austin's cocky smirk. He tries to meet Noah's eyes, but Noah turns his head, and walks over to the coach, ignoring Lilac's presence. He runs his hands through his hair as Lilac sighs and turns around, walking down the hallway. Austin leans against the wall lazily, his back to the empty receptionist desk. The glass window is slid open showing countless files that are organized in alphabetical order. A small silver bell is the only thing sat at the outside of the desk. When Lilac was younger he remembers a jar full of lollipops. He always tried to get the cotton candy ones. But they must not put it out anymore. Which Lilac finds somewhat depressing.

"So?" He hears Austin ask. Lilac turns his head from the desk, and sees Austin, a bored look on his face. "What do you want?" He doesn't sound any different, just bored. You would think that he would be at least a little upset, but no, nothing. But Lilac is barely surprised.

"Alex."

Austin scoffs and rolls his eyes. "Wow, this is a new conversation" he says sarcastically. Lilac crosses his arms and takes a few steps toward Austin.

"Can I finish my fucking sentence?" Lilac asks, with a roll of his eyes. Austin looks at him expectantly, a plain look of entitlement in his eyes that makes Lilac want to punch him. Lilac sighs. "I heard your aunt talking to your parents. She-She wants Alex to live with her." The emotion drains its way from Austin's face. But then they come in flashes. First hurt, then panic, then realization, and finally fury. He charges at Lilac, slamming his small body up against the wall, successfully knocking the air out of Lilac. Lilac attempts to breathe but he can't for a second. The wall shakes at the collision and Austin's strong arm holds Lilac down. Lilac struggles, wiggling around, trying to get Austin's arm to falter. But it doesn't.

"What the fuck did you say? You act like you care, but where were you when he got hurt?" he seethes, too close to Lilac's face. Lilac lets out a shaky breath, he bangs his fists on Austin's chest, but he doesn't move an inch. *Godamnit!* "You're hurting me," he says quietly. Lilac can't help it, he's scared shitless. The way Austin's eyes are dark, the way his sharp claws are growing longer by the second, digging into Lilac's arm. He's surprised he isn't bleeding. "Austin, please," he reluctantly cries.

"What the fuck are you talking about?" Austin hisses again, some spit gets on to Lilac's face, and it nearly makes him gag.

"It's exactly what I said!" Lilac snaps, gaining some of his courage back. Austin knows that he's being dramatic. Aunt Abby just lives across town, near Evan's. On the "poorer" side of town. But the thought of Alex leaving the pack, the house, the *family,* secretly terrifies him. "Now let me go!" Austin doesn't, so Lilac has no other choice. Austin feels himself being pulled back then he falls to the ground. His back rests against the opposite wall, his breathing weighing heavy in his chest. He thinks Lilac somehow pushed him, but Lilac didn't touch him. Then Austin realizes.

"Finally got your freakiness in check, huh?" He laughs. Lilac glares at him, coldly. *Shut up!* He yells at him in his head. His glare falters as a thought pops into his head.

"You knew," Lilac accuses. "You knew before the woods." Austin laughs again and stands back up. He wipes the invisible dirt off of his loose sweatpants. "Yeah I knew, my dad told me when I was thirteen. About your fucking privileged snotty mutant parents." Austin scoffs at the end as Lilac's fists clench. "Maybe that's why you bitch so much, maybe it's hereditary." He feels pressure on his neck, tightening with every second. Cutting off his breathing.

He looks at Lilac, his hand looks like he's holding an invisible glass and his blue eyes glow under the harsh hospital light. "Don't you *dare* talk about my parents." Austin chuckles as best as he can, until the pressure gets even tighter. "You wanna call me weak again." Lilac says, and the lights start to flicker. Lilac can see the rare terror in Austin's eyes. "Go ahead try." Austin's eyes go wide and he attempts to shake his head. The kid has lost his mind, gone deranged. Lilac realizes what he's doing and looks up at the flashing lights. He calms himself down and reminds himself that he's ok and he needs to relax. His hand falls down to his side and the weight on his throat is gone. He coughs uncontrollably, his face flushed. He looks at Lilac with disgust in his eyes. Lilac doesn't want to look at him but he can't stop himself. He doesn't feel bad though and there's no sense of remorse in his body. How much shit has he put Alex through, a ton. And he can barely deal with the slightest bit of pain. *That's* pathetic. Lilac can hear the elevator ding from down the hallway. Shoes tap the tiled floor and a nurse in lavender scrubs strolls down quickly. The scrubs also have tiny yellow ducks planted in them. Scrubs always looked like kid pajamas to Lilac. With the bright colors and cartoonish designs. She walks past Austin and Lilac without sparing either one glance. Her short brown hair lays just below her ears. Austin sees her heading towards the waiting room that Austin was previously in. He runs up to her as Lilac stares at him.

"Excuse me!" he yells, jogging closer and closer to the nurse. Lilac follows him. The nurse turns around and crosses her arms.

"Yes?" Lilac can hear the somewhat annoyed tone in her voice.

"Is Alex Miller awake?" Lilac asks before Austin gets the chance. Lilacs ready to run to that hospital room as if his pants busted into flames.

She raises her dark brown brows. "Well, yes he is," she replies, uncrossing her arms. "Why do you know him?"

"I'm his brother," Austin interrupts. She looks him up and down, studying him. Her eyes go to Lilac, looking at him the same way.

"Can I see your I.D.?" she questions. Austin sighs and rolls his eyes. Talk about paranoia. He reaches into his sweat pants pocket and takes out his leather wallet. His student id is right behind his driver's license which is scrunched behind two fifty dollar bills. He pulls it out wanting to cover the awful school photo. Most people say it looks ok, but Austin seriously doubts that. With the terrible outfit his mom made him wear and the awful lightning. All around it's just bad. His name *Austin Anthony Miller* is planted in bold at the bottom light blue line. The nurse snatches it out of his hands, her eyes looking over the sturdy plastic card.

"Ok, room 325." Her voice raises an octave higher. Austin doesn't realize it, but Lilac does. She looks over at him. "Are you family?" *Lie.*

He thinks quickly. "I–"

"He's not," Austin interjects, his upper lip rising at the look on Lilac's face. If the nurse wasn't there, Lilac wouldn't think twice to flip him off or cuss him out. Either one would be fine.

"Ok, then back in the waiting room you go," the lady says, grabbing lightly at his arm. Lilac let's himself get dragged away as Austin's footsteps disappear from his ears. Austin presses harder than necessary on the up button attached to the pillar in between the two metal elevators. The metal is shiny and Austin can see his reflection. But he avoids it. He probably could have taken the stairs. It's only one floor up, but he doesn't feel like it. What is he going to say? After the way Alex walked out and how he gets blamed for it. Total bullshit. As much as Austin wants to he can't control Alex. He's tried and nothing worked. His dad went too far though. Way too far. Austin's never seen his father that angry before. Even on the nights he caught Alex sneaking out. The elevator dings and the light above the two metal doors comes to life. He looks up from his clean red shoes and at the elevator. They open slowly, revealing an empty elevator. It was plain with tan walls and a simple silver railing. He's relieved to be alone, not in the mood for any useless small talk. He presses on the third floor button and the close door button as well. Austin knows his way around the hospital fairly well. During football season, when he doesn't pick Alex up from school, he walks to the hospital with his teammates to get mozzarella sticks. They're actually pretty good and it's basically the only food in the cafeteria that isn't ass. Also, the hospital is only a few streets up from the high school, and with a car, it's an easy three or five minute drive. The elevator dips, then moves upward slightly, and then stops completely. The elevator dings again and the doors open in the same slow way. Austin's stomach tightens. *What the fuck!* He screams at himself. He has no reason to be nervous or scared.

Especially because it's Alex. He could probably crush the kid with one hand. Austin exits the elevator and sharply turns to the left. He walks in a straight line, eyes scanning the embedded thin black numbers. 323. 324. 325. The light wooden door is shut tight. Austin doesn't bother to knock, just turns on the silver handle and pushes. Alex is looking at the pitch black sky through the window. The headlights of the cars that pass and large bulbs attached to edges of surrounding buildings, glow in the night. The short hospital bridge that divides the two sides of the building is dark though, making everything completely dark. The lights are off in the room. Usually he hates it when it's dark but after the head thumping concussion, which makes his head feel like a hammer being pounded into a wall, he can't stand the light. Alex can hear footsteps coming down the hall. He's hoping it's Noah or Lilac or even the fucking janitor, anyone besides his parents. He looks down at his healed fingers. Alex wonders why the doctors or nurses didn't think anything of it. How his fingers were black and blue and now perfectly tan. Or if they healed before he even entered the cold and bleach smelling hospital. He knows his clothes are going to smell like hospital for at least a week, even though he's going to wash them so many times until the color fades and they fall apart. Alex will still be able to smell it or still be able to imagine it clearly. The handle turns and Alex's doesn't turn around. He can see Austin's face in the window.

"Hey Alex," he says, calmly. Alex doesn't turn away nor does he answer. His fists clench the grey hospital sheets tightly. "Alex!" he calls louder this time, taking a few steps into the small room.

"Get out," Alex says, shutting his eyes tight. Alex can't see his reflection in the window.

"What?" Austin asks, feeling himself get worked up. Alex shivers and suddenly it's like he's somewhere else. In a different time and place.

192

Alex was in fourth grade, getting off the bright yellow school bus alone. He looks around at the empty driveway and goes down the grey side walk. His brothers were at football practice which Alex was thankful for. He opens the screen door and feels the front door unlocked. Alex slowly pushes it open. "Mommy?" he asks hesitantly. He drops his bag at the door and walks slowly through the kitchen. Alex's small key tucked in between his two fingers. "D-Daddy?" he stutters, walking up the steps. "Did" Alex swallows the giant lump in his throat. "Did you get home early?" A gloved hand places itself over his mouth. Alex gasps and his big eyes widen as his small form is lifted from the ground. Alex screams loudly when he sees three more figures emerge from the shadows. Oh my god. Alex yells in his head. This is it, this is how I'm going to die. At the hands of a murderer.

"Don't scream again." The voice whispers harshly in his ear. Alex feels tears run down his face. The man drags Alex to his room and throws him roughly to the carpeted ground. The three others follow. Alex scrambles to his bed leaning against it and catching his lost breath. His eyes widen fearfully seeing the four hooded men.

"Please, I-I won't s-say anything. Just please let me go." Alex pleads. Chuckles fill the room and Alex knows who the people are. "A-Austin?" he asks, still stuttering. The laughter increases as they take off their hoods. Showing Austin, Allen, Erik, and one of Austin's main lackeys.

"You shoulda seen your face" Allen laughs. Austin walks closer to Alex and grabs his hair in an iron grip.

"Next time don't talk shit to your friends, you little mutt." Alex knows what he's talking about and who narced him out. Fucking Shawn. He is just so sick of him. The constant nagging and hits, and all he wanted to do was rant. But of course Alex couldn't even do that. Alex decides to play dumb, it's the best bet.

"I-I didn't." They begin to laugh again and watch the scene like some kind of bad movie.

"Y-You d-d-did," Allen mocks. Austin tugs harder on Alex's hair which causes him to wince.

"Don't do it again. Ok?" Austin says. He tugs on Alex's hair again when Alex doesn't answer right away.

"Ok," he whispers so quietly that Austin can barely hear him.

"Good," Austin says, giving out one last tug before releasing it. "Let's go," he says to the boys behind him. He walks out the door without another look towards Alex. The rest follow looking at Alex while laughing. The humiliation grips at Alex as he's left alone. Alone in the cold room, staring at the open door.

Alex whips his head around, as he's awakened from his daydream, to stare at Austin, who notes the unfamiliar fire in his eyes.

"I said get the hell out." Austin stares at him, taken aback for a second. He then looks to the side and scoffs.

"Why, so Noah can-"

"You know what. I didn't choose for you to be my brother, Austin. But I choose Noah to be my friend." Austin's chest begins to burn. "I can't do this anymore, Austin."

"What do you mean?" Austin asks, his voice cracking.

"I'm leaving. Even if I have nowhere to go I'm still going." Austin shakes his head, glaring. "No." He says. "I won't let you."

He reaches out to grip Alex's arm, but Alex shoves him away. Head throbbing painfully. "Fuck off, Austin." He says, turning away and looking at the window again. Austin stumbles back, looking at Alex one more time before turning out the door. He runs down the hallway, his mind feeling as if it's been caught in the waves and ripped apart by the vicious waves in midday. He presses the button on the elevator and grips his hair as he waits for it to open. Lilac hears the elevator ding as he stands out in the hallway. Then footsteps running straight down the hallway. Lilac turns walking around the corner. He sees Austin stomp into the bathroom and Lilac slyly peers into the bathroom. Austin's hands are gripping the sink so hard that his knuckles almost blend into the white marble. Lilac can't believe his eyes, as he sees Austin in the mirror. The tears running down his face and his eyes downcast and focused on the faucet. His tears run down the sink, pilling up near the drain. Lilac can't remember a time where he saw Austin cry. When Lilac was six he went to one of the elementary school football game with Alex. And when Austin got hit so hard that he became unconscious, he still didn't cry. It's scary. It's like seeing a butterfly with one wing. Or a four leaf clover. He's always angry but now he has a broken look in his eyes. And Lilac sees Austin finally crumbling to the ground and into millions of pieces.

CHAPTER TWENTY-SIX
MAY

As the leaves on the oak turn green and the petals on roses bloom, so did the sense of relief and relaxation. It is warm in the crowded gym and smelled of teenagers sweat. The DJ. playing generic pop music, and blue and black balloons hanging in the corners. It is sad to Lilac though, this is the last time they would go to the National Junior Honor Society banquet. Lilac is frankly shocked that they all made it through. Specifically, Noah who missed like a week of school and had make-up work piled up like mountains. Luckily he had Alex who practically spoon fed him every lesson after school. He practically did the work for him. You needed a 3.0 GPA to be in the Society, which is led by a lady who was the biggest witch Evan has ever come across. Her cracked stained brown teeth, hair that looks like burnt noodles, and a body that reminds him of an egg . She hates Evan says he has a smart mouth and is a class clown. Evan wouldn't disagree, but his mom doesn't take too kindly to the comments. Only a few people are on the dance floor while the others are leaning on the closed bleachers or at the snack table talking. However, Noah and his friends sit at the small circle table and watch the people around them, not talking much. It isn't tense, just boring. Alex sits next to Lilac and Noah, while he tears the end of the thin light blue plastic tablecloth. It is weird after he left everything, the second he got to his aunt's house across town he immediately locked himself in the bathroom and cried like a baby. The worst part about everything wasn't packing up the items in his medium-sized room. It was walking out that front door. Alex envisioned that moment in his head so many times that it felt like a memory. It never felt like how it actually happened. It didn't feel like a weight being lifted off his shoulders, it felt like more being added on. The memories didn't disappear, they just kept repeating themselves, and Alex has to live through everything again. And all he wants to do is forget.

Forget the good, the bad, everything. Everything to just fade away into the shadows of the house. He hasn't seen his parents or Austin and Allen since he left, which he's thankful for. He's also spent most of his days and nights at Noah's. Avoiding the clubhouse and Lilac's as if his life depends on it. It's just too close to them, to the pack, his family, everyone he doesn't want to see. Aunt Abby goes to Roseville a lot, she works as a werewolf lawyer, if that makes any sense. She helps people who want to leave the pack and defends them against the court. Alex knows someday he'll have to stand in front of them and frankly he's terrified. But Aunt Abby tells him not to worry. Alex looks over at Noah who has his chin resting in his hand, thick bags are ringed under his eyes and he stares at the other side of the gym blankly. Alex knows where he goes at night when the rest of his family's asleep, and Bill is safe in his bed. He takes his bike and rides through the night until he gets to the woods. He wanders around and finds the spot where he first saw Violet, shivering and covered in dark mud. He sits on a nearby log, waiting for the slim chance that Violet may come back someday. Noah feels someone tap him on the shoulder. He stares at Alex, who has the same look in his eyes that Noah has.

"Do you want to get some punch?" Alex asks him, as he begins to stand up.

Noah does the same thing. "Yeah," he says, taking a step forward so that he's standing shoulder to shoulder with Alex. "Let's go."

Mya watches them leave with a sigh from her lips. She runs her hands over the short, fluffy, dark red dress. She stands up making sure the bottom of her skirt isn't flying up. Her mom told her to wear shorts under it, but Mya refused; she hates the way it feels.

"Wait?" Evan asks, before Mya can barely take a step. "What?" Mya questions dully.

"Where are you going?"

Mya rolls her eyes. "Bathroom; where else?" she replies, walking away. Her matte black hills tap on the school floors and for once the hallways are completely empty. The bathrooms are directly downwards and most of the time disgusting. Things have been strange ever since the night at the house. The police officers and some parents were looking at her constantly and sometimes coming by the house to check up on her. Mya thinks it's to keep her quiet about everything. She doesn't think they know about Jon, Sam, and Nick knowing about everything. Jon and Nick ask about Alex and Violet sometimes, and Mya is bullied into telling them about everything. It only makes their hatred for Allen and Austin stronger.

Footsteps follow Mya down the hallway; she stops dead in her tracks. She whips around expecting the worst, but when she turns around she sees Shawn coming towards her. She looks at him then plants herself against the wall, her hands resting against her back. Her and Shawn haven't talked since everything. She moved to sit closer to Lilac and Evan, who bicker their way through class. Mya avoided eye contact at all costs as well. But sometimes she wished for them to talk again and for him to look at her the way he did before.

Shawn stands in front of her looking down at her and Mya realizes how much she hates being short. "Hey," he says, smirking down at her. His eyes remind her of a predator stalking its prey. They're scary even to her.

"Hi," she says, holding eye contact even though she wants to look away. "So what do you want?"

Shawn licks his lips and rests one hand on her waist, while the other places itself on the wall above Mya's head. Mya can hear her heart thump in her ears. "I like you Mya, I always have."

She can't help but smile. "Ok. What are you going to do about it?" The anticipation builds as he leans in, his eyes closed and smirk on his lips. Mya closes her eyes as his hand falls from the wall and down at her waist with the other one. Then they begin to slide lower. One part of Mya wants to slap him in the face for even daring to touch her in such a way. And never speak to him again.

But the other part of her wants him to keep touching her. She feels shameful but shameless at the same time.

Mya shuts her eyes, but she can't see his face, at least not in a healthy way. Her mind flashes to every rude thing he's ever said to her, everything he's done to Alex, the night by the raging fire. *What he is.* The time he beat the living shit out of Noah in grade six when he wouldn't let him into the clubhouse. She remembers Alex's screams through the window begging him to stop, she remembers her own. And she realizes she can't do this. When his pink lips are practically on hers, she whispers a soft, "No."

Shawn pulls away and takes his hands off of her as if she was on fire. "What?" he asks in disbelief.

Mya rolls her eyes and steps away from Shawn. She looks at him, the feelings she had for him disappearing in seconds. Like the rain on the ground when the sun rises. "I'm sorry, Shawn. I can't be with you. Not after everything."

He shakes his head and scowls at her. "That's bullshit, and you know it, Mya."

"No, what's bullshit is the way you treat my friends. I may like you Shawn, but I'll always like them more."

He laughs again taking a step towards her; he's practically in her face. "You're such a fucking bitch, M-" Mya punches him in the face, making it swing to the left. His hand is brought up and he clutches his cheek, eyes bright and wide with anger. "You're so lucky you're a girl." Mya punches him again, this time drawing blood from his full and sinful lips.

"Mya, stop!" A voice yells from behind her. Jordan comes running down the hall, his grey suit jacket running behind him. Shawn shoves his way past Mya giving her one last glare before, stomping down the once empty hallway. "What's his problem?" Mya backs herself to the light blue tiled wall and slides down. She brings her knees to her chest, closing them tightly as she wraps her arms around them. Jordan sits on the ground next to her. "Well," he says, "he tried to kiss me," Mya says, staring down at the floor.

"Ok" Jordan says with a nod.

"Then I pushed him away and he called me a bitch." Mya pauses and looks up to see his reaction.

"Continue," Jordan replies, still nodding.

"So I punched him in the face?" Mya says it like it's a question. She's expecting Jordan to scold her for punching someone. For being overdramatic, he yells at practically everyone about everything but instead he smiles.

"The asshole deserved it." Mya looks at him and laughs and Jordan does the same.

Lilac and Evan sit alone at the table; it feels like they haven't talked at all since that night. Maybe it's just too awkward or maybe Evan thinks Lilac's a monster. But it's not all Evan's fault; Lilac's been staying at his house more and more often since everything. Mostly painting outside, since the weathers been getting warmer and warmer and his dad hates the smell of paint. He mostly paints flowers or plants, with colors ranging from purple and blue to yellow and green. Painting's basically the only thing that's kept him sane through these past few months. Especially with the recent news of him coming out. He guesses word gets around and werewolves are super nosy. His friends didn't care though and that is basically the only thing that matters to Lilac. Alex and Mya said that they already knew. Alex says it's because he always caught him staring at *someone,* and Mya because she says she has excellent gaydar. The rest barely says anything at all and just continue to talk about nonsense. Sure, there are a few snide remarks, but Lilac just simply flipped those people off and moved on with his day. Lilac isn't shocked though it was a small town with people with even smaller minds. Sometimes while he's painting, and Austin is outside with his friends he'll scream stuff about Lilac having some boyfriend. But Lilac usually has headphones in and pretends he can't hear him. Karma's going to run him over like a truck one day. Lilac just hopes he's there to see it happen. It's weird though how no one questions anything that happened with Bill. James just covered it up really well. He says that two psychos from out of state wanted to kidnap some kid and that the boy killed the girl in front of a group of teens. It was an easy answer and it satisfied the Colemans which was the only thing that mattered.

"Hey, Little Li." Evan says, in the dark gym with the bright techno lights being the only source of light.

"Don't call me that, *Even*. And what?" Lilac asks, turning his head to look at Evan. Lilac still can't believe his mom let him out of the house in a lime green suit jacket and pants. Lilac is somewhat embarrassed to even be around him, and when Evan walked across the small stage in the even smaller auditorium, he saw his father's disappointed head shake. He nearly laughed however. "Do you think I should try out for football next year?" Evan questions. Lilac laughs. "Where did this come from?"

"Well, you know how I played in elementary school?" Lilac nods. "Well I was talking to my uncle, and he says I should get back into it my freshman year. *So.*" Lilac looks at him one more time before looking down at his hands that rest on black napkin.

"Yeah, I'd say go for it." Lilac looks up and lightly smiles. His eyebrows suddenly furrow together. "But don't you have to, like, I don't know, train first? I mean you haven't been in the game or whatever in three years."

Evan smiles. "That's what this summer's for." Lilac suddenly frowns. "Hey, what's wrong? I'm still going to be around." Evan asks.

Lilac doesn't want to tell him right now, maybe the day before he leaves but definitely not now. Not when things feel the slightest bit normal again. "No, I'm going away for the summer." Evan sucks in his lips and nods; they always spent summers together all of them. Jordan's family has a pool so they usually swam till dawn. Either that or they hung out in Noah's hot and stuffy basement. "To my uncle's. My dad says it'll be good for me to get out of town for a little." Lilac leaves out the part about him yelling at his dad and saying that he ruined his life. Which he ended up apologizing for the next day.

"Well, that's great, Lilac," Evan says; Lilac still frowns. "Maybe it's a good thing you'll be able to see my glow up when you come back." Lilac smiles and rolls his eyes. Evan places his hand on top of Lilac's. And Lilac looks down at it, his face feeling hot. Evan's pale hand is rough against Lilac's own and is warmer than Lilac's skin. "And if you ever need anything, call me, Lilac, please."

Lilac sucks in a breath as he looks at Evan and smiles. "Yeah," he says, licking his suddenly dry lips. "Of course."

He looks down at their hands and at the moment, Lilac doesn't think about the events in the previous months that haunt his dreams in the night. No. Because with the party music in his ears and Evan's warm hand on top of his, everything is alright.